The New Empire of Malplaquet

Andrew Dalton

Illustrated by
Jonny Boatfield

Ⓛ

The Lutterworth Press

For Susanne

First Published in 2009 by
The Lutterworth Press
P.O. Box 60
Cambridge
CB1 2NT

www.Lutterworth.com
Publishing@Lutterworth.com

ISBN: 978 0 7188 3096 0 hardback
ISBN: 978 0 7188 3093 9 paperback

British Library Cataloguing in Publication Data:
A Catalogue Record is available from the British Library

The Malplaquet Trilogy takes much of its initial inspiration
from *Mistress Masham's Repose*, one of the less known work
of the great English writer, T.H. White

Contents

The Prophecy

A Child no more, the Man appears,
He comes of Age, the Hope of Years.
Our Fount of Wisdom, whose Way is Delight,
True Source of all Pure Knowledge and Insight,
Our Guide, for whom the Bells do Ring,
Thy Presence much Warmth in Friendship Bring.
Thou makest the Sea-people great Appear,
This Blessed Island shalt have no Fear.
In every Quarter defend our Shores,
Unite our People, grow strong in Wars.
The Capital gained, our Frontiers Sealed,
Temples Restored, the Nation Healed.
Through thee the Great Empire newly Starts,
The Garden Kingdom, true Home of our Hearts.

— after Alexander Pope

1. Opening Plans

The enormous mansion of Malplaquet dominated its thousand acres of parkland that were full of woods, vast lawns, lakes and weird garden buildings – its 'temples'. And on this April evening, on the leaded expanse of the mansion's flat roof, some extraordinary creatures were gathering.

Their colour was wondrous – a soft golden-yellow warmth, a fresh and vibrant liquid honey. These creatures were glowing.

Some of them were people, but not in the normal sense. There were a few baby-faced cherubs, barefoot and dressed in flowing linen, yet walking around and conversing like adults. In a corner of the balustrade stood a woman, no taller than half a metre, who was dressed in a toga and carrying a water-jar. Towering above her and staring out across the South Front to the Octagon Lake, was the armour-clad figure of a stern Roman general, the height of a street-lamp. Stomping amongst the gaggle of guests were what looked like small Vikings, faces full of wild hair and scowls. Elsewhere were figures of a more usual size and proportion; proud men and women in Tudor ruffs and doublets; a Queen in full regalia, carrying an orb and sceptre; and a weather-beaten old man with a full beard and straggly hair, stretched out in light robes, a trident by his side.

Then there were the animals. A horse, sniffing the air and pawing the ground, with its reins held by its owner, George I. Two monkeys scampering about, one holding a mirror under an arm. A large turtle, two metres in length, carefully stepping over the roof joins. A camel. An alligator. Two lions, male and female, nuzzling their heads together in intimate conversation.

A medieval king suddenly interrupted their peaceful murmurings. He'd noticed some movement in one of the two reclining female statues, named 'Liberty' and 'Religion', on the front of the west wing. The former was rippling slightly, the folds of her dress quivering, an arm slowly rising, her head turning to one side. 'She is coming,' he announced to the others on the roof.

The creatures immediately stood in respectful silence, attending to Liberty's swift arrival, as she stepped over the balustrade as if from a doorway in the air itself. She composed herself, smoothing down her garments, softly brushing her hair back, surveying her audience. Her words came with the richness and worth of gold itself.

'It is good,' she said, 'to be alive.' With a warm smile, she acknowledged the murmurs of agreement. 'To be alive,' she repeated, 'after so many years. Years of waiting, and of watching. And, as we had hoped, or even known, the young man, Jamie, was the key.' Many confirmed that opinion with their neighbour. 'But,' she continued, and all fell silent, 'our new-found life has been noticed. We must be careful to use our freedom wisely.'

A hand went up from a small troll-like Viking. She nodded at him. 'I didn't say nothing,' he urged. 'I was stuck on that big vase like always, when the Thompsons' car went over my bridge. I winked, can't deny it, but I never said. . . .'

Liberty held up her hand; his defence ceased. 'But your friend did,' she stated, looking at the hairy figure by his side. 'When a log fell off the tractor that Jamie's friend Vicky was driving. She heard you.'

The first troll glared at the other and clipped him across the head.

'But it matters little now,' added Liberty, grinning as the second troll returned the playful gesture, but with more force.

'Some friends from Lilliput also know that we are alive. Bleynet, I hear, on guard-duty alone at night, was joined by two monkeys, a hawk, a horse. . . . Then something breathed down the poor man's neck.' The guilty male lion lowered his majestic mane in quiet apology.

'And there have been snorting horses. Lengthy conversations amongst the British Worthies,' she continued, looking at the Tudor figures. 'Even sneezing – yes, George II, in the Golf War. Then there's the singing; opera, to be precise.'

'Sorry, but it's what I do,' admitted a Classical woman, usually stood atop the Grenville Column. 'Look, it's on my banner – non nisi grandia canto – 'of great deeds I sing.' I can't help it.' She showed her sash, printed with the Latin words.

Liberty accepted the excuse. She herself, more than anybody else present, knew the value of such freedom and expression. 'Timing, my dear,' she said. 'Timing is everything. Try pure solos, when no-one else is around. We must be careful.'

'I think we . . . er . . . got it wrong,' confessed a voice at the back. The seven Saxon Deities, who lived in a yew-lined grove to the east, shuffled forward, wearing a bizarre variety of clothes that included breastplates, togas, crowns and tunics, and carrying weapons such as swords, bows, and spears. One, with a sunburst of a halo, was half the size of the others.

'No,' responded Liberty firmly. 'You were right to help the Lilliputians against Biddle's henchmen at Hawkwell Field; they deserved their rough handling.' She paused. 'But we must be careful not to intervene – not to change the necessary course of events.'

'With the greatest respect, Ma'am, are you suggesting we now just sit back and watch?' It was Britannia from the pediment of the Grecian Temple. 'I've been doing that for far too long – and to be honest, if I see anything wrong. . . .'

Liberty shook her head. 'Of course not,' she agreed. 'We all know where we stand – if you see what I mean – so we can certainly help. Support. But we cannot gain *their* victory. It is the Lilliputians, with their human helpers, who must be victorious. It is their prize to win – and theirs to lose.'

'You speak with much-valued wisdom,' offered Socrates from the Temple of Ancient Virtue, standing by his three companions.

He cleared his throat, which they knew preceded a speech. 'However, we dare not forget that *our* destiny is also at stake. Jedekiah Biddle, as the Property Manager, has admittedly restored our physical bodies; replacing fingers, rebuilding faces, even tanning some of us. However, he is also the descendant of the sea-captain who kidnapped that Lilliputian band – but then lost them here. That freedom brought our freedom.' Socrates looked sombrely around. 'If they are recaptured by Biddle, we will forever remain entombed within our cold stone prisons. Not being personal, Madam, but Liberty will be lost. For good.'

The noble woman and all those present considered this prospect.

A sweet voice interrupted their thoughts. 'I must say something.' It was the small woman with the water-jar. She normally stood amongst the flower tubs in the yard of Jamie's great friend, the dear old lady known as 'Granny' who had for years looked after the Lilliputians. 'Before I left,' she said, 'I heard Granny talking to Nigriff in her kitchen. She'd just been on the phone to Jamie; his younger brother may know about the little people.'

This was significant news. The existence of the Lilliputians at Malplaquet had been a great secret, known only by Jamie and his close friends (and sadly one or two of their enemies). If such knowledge were to spread, especially to his annoying younger brother Charlie, it could jeopardise the tiny people's chances of victory.

'We are aware of the calibre of Jamie, but we are also fortunate that Nigriff is the brightest of the Lilliputians,' replied Liberty thoughtfully. 'He comes from the finest Elysian stock. We have seen Nigriff and Jamie find solutions before. They will think of something.' She looked around at the apprehensive faces. 'I am sure of it.'

She tried to sound confident. She just wished she also felt it.

Early next morning two teenage boys were pedalling hard down the track to the Bell Gate entrance to Malplaquet gardens. The smaller one was shouting at his older brother just ahead of him. 'Why are we coming all the way here?' yelled Charlie. 'And why couldn't you tell me the answer last night?'

'We need to be in the gardens,' replied Jamie, over his shoulder.

'Why?' came the response, barely audible above the bouncing tyres and the pinging of stones. Jamie ignored him, freewheeling down the final approach, then braking hard by the old lodge. Granny ambled across the yard with a small rucksack.

'Morning, boys!' was her cheery greeting. 'Just a few refreshments.' She passed the bag over her gate to Jamie, who had a quick peek inside.

'You knew we were coming?' Charlie asked, with some suspicion.

She nodded. 'Jamie phoned late yesterday.'

Jamie wanted this conversation to end immediately. 'Come on,' he said, 'we'll go round the corner – thanks, Granny.' He pushed his bike through the double gates, and Charlie meekly followed. Granny watched them go, happy that Nigriff had been safely transferred, then she bustled inside to rejoin Vicky and Ralph in her sitting room.

The boys leant their bikes against the temple's steps, sat down on the slatted bench against its back wall, and looked across the Octagon Lake to Malplaquet House. The air was remarkably still, a marked contrast to yesterday's wind and rain. Jamie eased the rucksack off his shoulders, placed it by him on the flagstones, and loosened the top drawstrings. Winking at Nigriff hunched up inside, he pulled out two bottles of juice and some Brownies, and gave one of each to Charlie.

'So,' said the younger boy, not prepared to wait any longer, 'what's going on?'

Jamie stood up, walked slowly to the steps, and peered both ways down the path. Then he returned to his seat, took a deep breath, and in hushed tones announced, 'Very few people know about this, so you can't tell anybody else.'

'Not even John Biddle? He's my best friend.'

Jamie paused. He should have expected that. He made a swift decision, hoping it would mislead Jedekiah's son as well. 'Just him,' said Jamie bluntly, 'but he must swear to keep it secret.'

'That's fine,' replied Charlie. 'He hardly knows anybody. So what is it?'

Jamie spoke slowly. 'I've discovered that there are fairies at Malplaquet.'

Charlie gave a loud snort, a burst of laughter, then a series of giggles. His merriment stopped when he saw how serious Jamie was. 'This is a joke, right?'

Jamie shook his head. 'Good guess about the battle – they were there.'

Charlie, however, knew what his brother was now up to. When Charlie was six, Jamie had told him about the 'Toe-nail Fairy,' who collected and paid for any clippings left in sugar-bowls. Jamie had blamed Charlie for leaving a really big curly one.

'This is such a wind-up,' Charlie retorted. 'You're always taking the mickey. I'm telling Mum and Dad.' He got up.

'You can't say anything to them!' blurted out Jamie.

'Why? Will a fairy drop dead?' Charlie sneered, walking over to his bike.

'Don't be stupid,' replied Jamie, following. 'It's just that Mum and Dad won't believe you.'

'So there's no problem,' said Charlie, swinging a leg over his crossbar.

Jamie grabbed the handlebars. 'Listen,' he urged. 'I've seen them.'

The younger boy stared at his older brother. 'Okay, describe them,' he demanded. 'Wings, dressed like ballet-dancers?'

'No,' said Jamie, 'normal stuff . . . trousers, jackets . . . skirts.'

'So they're like the Borrowers?' said Charlie, who had seen the television series. Before Jamie could reply, the rucksack suddenly toppled over. He knew from experience that the professional Librarian inside hated being labelled as a 'Borrower.'

'No, definitely not Borrowers,' insisted Jamie.

'And they live here?' Jamie nodded. Charlie thought briefly. 'The temples?'

Jamie agreed, and then faced a barrage of questions. 'Has anybody else seen them? Has Vicky? You fancy her, don't you?'

That irritated Jamie. 'Course not, but yes, she's seen them. So has Granny. She's even made clothes for them.'

Charlie paused. 'So when can I see one?'

This was a fair question. 'It's not that easy,' said Jamie.

'Really?' said Charlie, pulling his bike from Jamie's grasp. 'Well, if they're in the temples, I'll start with those. . . .' Pressing hard on his pedals, he set off towards the ruined building called the Temple of Friendship. There was no stopping him.

But that didn't bother Jamie. He stared after him then clambered back up the steps to retrieve the rucksack containing its small, insulted occupant. He peered inside. Nigriff was looking up and applauding.

'Master Jamie, allow me to congratulate you. Even I was convinced that within Malplaquet there exists a colony of fairy-dwellers.'

'Thanks, Nigriff. Sorry about the Borrowers bit,' muttered Jamie. 'Come on, let's go back.' He carefully picked up the bag and placed it over one shoulder.

'Well, that was a stroke of genius,' said Granny approvingly. Ralph and Vicky murmured their agreement, and Nigriff again offered his praise. 'The finest Elysian minds could not have found a more clever solution.'

'Shouldn't it be *Lilliputian* minds nowadays, Nigriff?' chided Granny gently.

'I do apologise, Madam,' he accepted. 'You are correct. Now that the qualities of the four provinces are being shared, it is unlikely that Elysium will retain its monopoly of intelligence. All peoples may well enjoy our gifts and talents.'

'But what if,' said Ralph, 'Charlie actually sees a Lilliputian?'

'It's not if but more like when, I reckon,' said Vicky.

'That's years away,' said Jamie. 'Remember, they're only visible to people who really appreciate the place. He's never been that interested in Malplaquet.'

'But the restoration programme is making it look amazing,' corrected Vicky.

'Then again, if he does see anything, he'll think it's a fairy,' mused Ralph. 'Clever. Very clever.'

'He won't talk to any friends about that,' said Jamie. 'And John

Biddle doesn't matter. His Father's the real problem.'

'Which reminds me,' said Granny, 'what were you saying on the phone about your Father – about freedom?' asked Granny suddenly. 'Is he thinking of giving up teaching?'

Jamie grinned. 'Often,' he said. 'But he'd been telling me that lots of the buildings and inscriptions here are about freedom. Which is odd.'

'Odd?' queried Ralph.

'Well, freedom is what the Lilliputians want.'

'And they have it,' said Granny. 'Once they escaped from Captain Biddle's clutches to the island on the lake here. They've been free ever since.'

'Madam, there is some truth in your judgement,' said Nigriff, 'but my people are in exile, and they can never be truly free until they live in their own homeland.' He paused. 'Our enemy here has great cunning and power. It may be possible to defeat him – and I believe that we can do so – but we may still be forever separated from our true country.'

His poignant words changed the atmosphere. Under Jamie's leadership, the new Empire of Lilliput was certainly becoming stronger, for the people were more united, and links between Malplaquet and their island-home had been found; the two lands even had similar outlines. Yet such connections also emphasised their separation; Lilliput was so near in some ways – and yet also so far.

Nigriff sensed the sadness that had settled on the group and, feeling partly responsible, changed the subject. 'On a – please excuse the pun – *relative* matter, I can inform you,' he began breezily, 'that I am currently doing research on my genealogy.'

'On your what?' asked Ralph.

'My family tree,' said Nigriff. 'I am trying discover the name of my actual ancestor who was kidnapped from Lilliput. I know his son was Lebojel. I believe the original victim himself may have been one Gothep.'

'Go-what?' asked Jamie.

'Gothep,' repeated Nigriff.

'What makes you think that's his name?' asked Vicky.

'As a young boy, I once heard a mention of the Illustrious

Gothep. I'm sure it was in a conversation about my background. I would like to confirm this.'

Nobody doubted he would do so. Not only was Nigriff a fine Archivist, but he also spoke often of his distinguished family line, which apparently somehow included twelve of the sixteen notables in the Temple of British Worthies – even William Shakespeare. Another celebrated ancestor would be no surprise.

These thoughts were interrupted by a sudden burst of distant clapping and cheering outside. They all leapt up from their seats, and hurried round to the path by the Octagon Lake. Vicky had the good sense to pick up Nigriff, dropping him into her sleeve for the usual 'mobile-phone walk' (holding her arm up to one ear).

Initially all they could see at the far end of the vast lawn below the mansion was a swarm of people, waving and pointing. Other visitors were streaming in from all sides, but the cause of this commotion was not yet clear.

Then came a deep and throaty roar, a long and rumbling resonance beyond the trees. A short pause, then the same blast, swamping the garden with its noise.

The head appeared first, an enormous human head, faded yellow in colour, with staring eyes and cropped hair. As the huge shape rose up, its shoulders and upper body became visible, clothed in an ancient breastplate, powerful muscles rippling. Soaring above the mansion, it gradually revealed its full Roman armour.

'It's the big statue from the Cobham Monument!' gasped Granny.

Jamie was stunned. Recently he and his friends had – to their amazement – actually seen some statues in the gardens moving. Especially in the battle of Hawkwell Field. But nobody else had seen them. Not until now. . . .

'*Everybody* can see it,' he said. 'Every single person. Something's changed.'

Vicky stared at the massive person dominating the far skyline. Then she announced her verdict. 'Nothing has changed,' she declared. 'Nothing at all.' She looked at Jamie. 'It's not a statue; it's a hot-air balloon.' She was right, and everybody felt reassured – until Ralph spoke.

'It's Biddle,' he said, screwing up his eyes. 'In the basket.
Might have known.'

The balloon was gently drifting above the treetops, and inside
its wicker-box stood Biddle and two others, one of whom was
firing an occasional roaring jet of flame into the billowing canvas.
The other was waving at the public below.

'You've got to admit,' said Vicky, 'Biddle as the Property
Manager knows how to pull a crowd. . . . And what's he up to
now?'

The balloon was floating above the South Front lawn, pursued
by people who were chasing after the swirling leaflets being hurled
from the basket. Children were scampering around, gathering up
the pages, some of which had flapped onto the lake, attracting the
attention of inquisitive ducks. Litter was soon everywhere.

'Look at it,' moaned Jamie. 'What a stupid idea.'

Granny picked up a nearby sheet with its large lettering.

MALPLAQUET – FULL OF SURPRISES!

*As the temple restoration programme reaches its climax,
enjoy the beauty and mystery of this enchanting place.*

*For your entertainment and enlightenment, we have
arranged a wonderful range of activities for all ages. . . .*

There was a huge list of events; Watercolour Workshops, an
Archaeology Study Day, a live Antiques Roadshow, a Country-
House Murder Mystery Weekend . . . plus all the usual picnics,
woodland walks, floodlit evenings etc.

One event caught Granny's eye. 'This isn't good,' she
murmured. '*A Mistress Masham's Repose Day, about the famous
story of Lilliputians at Malplaquet.*'

'The Trust will stop him,' said Jamie. 'After this mess.'

'You spoke too soon, Master Jamie,' said Nigriff. 'The clear-up
has begun.'

As the balloon sailed away, its job done, people were scurrying
around the lawns, gathering up the sheets and, remarkably, tearing
off strips and stuffing them into their mouths. Granny nibbled
at a corner of hers. 'Mmm,' she mumbled, 'that's really nice
– Strawberries and Cream.'

'Not this one,' said Vicky, chewing another. 'Rum and Raisin.

Try some, Nigriff. Ralph, grab that one – what's it taste like?'

'Who cares?' said Jamie in some irritation. 'It's not food!'

'Actually, Jamie, it is,' said Granny, who in spite of her opinion of Biddle was enjoying her Elevenses. 'It's a high-quality rice paper.'

'Bio-degradeable as well,' added Ralph. 'Be gone by tomorrow.'

'That is a generous estimate,' said Nigriff. 'I would suggest that within four minutes is more likely.'

He was right. The lawn had already been virtually swept – or eaten – clean, and even leaflets lodged in inaccessible places in bushes and trees had almost gone. Birds and squirrels with sophisticated tastes may have been responsible, but, as the five of them realised, it was probably the work of tiny people.

'Well, at least they'll read about the chaos Biddle's planned,' said Jamie. 'They'll realise at long last what a villain he is.'

'To the contrary, sir,' said Nigriff, 'my poor countrymen may regard this as a helpful warning about the likelihood of increased crowds. He has also provided them with a tasty feast, as if he was concerned about their welfare. Our analysis of his character may yet again fall on deaf ears. And on full stomachs.'

A thoughtful Jamie set off home on his bike through the woods later that morning. Their lengthy discussions had revealed many anxieties and few plans. They could only carry on warning the Lilliputians about Biddle, talking about the new Empire, and hoping that the statues might still help at times. He felt very low.

However, behind him something remarkable was happening.

A large yellow disc, the size of a table-top, was hurtling and spinning above the trees from the north. It was drawing in its wake swathes and ribbons of a light mist, which gently settled on the waters and wooded walks of Malplaquet.

When Jamie finally reached the Corinthian Arch on the crest of the hill and turned back round to admire the view, he was stunned to see the gardens totally enveloped in this low cloud. Only the tops of the tallest trees and the high points of the mansion roof were peeking through the soft covering. This grey-white blanket halted at the encircling ditch of the ha-ha, and misty waterfalls cascaded in drifts over its edge.

It made Jamie realise that this place, with its tiny inhabitants, was probably *far* more magical than anybody had so far discovered. And without knowing exactly why, he suddenly felt much more hopeful.

It wasn't just up to him and his friends to defeat Biddle. Thank goodness, they weren't on their own.

2. Plans are Laid

Taking the steps two at a time, Jedekiah Biddle bounded up the front entrance of Chackmore Manor, proud of his morning's work. The Roman Soldier Balloon, visible for miles around, had entertained the masses, and he himself had spotted the likely homes of the rubbish-collectors as the edible leaflets had been dragged down burrows or into crevices in old walls.

Indeed, Biddle wondered if his inability to spot Lilliputians was changing, for once or twice he thought he'd seen a vague outline of a tiny person. However, he wouldn't become too excited yet; his mind might be playing tricks. The minds of his assistants were certainly messed up; Hawkins, in the basket with him, had pointed out with his walking-stick some small people cunningly disguised as squirrels. Biddle had explained to him that they were, in actual fact, squirrels.

Nevertheless, the event had gone perfectly – apart from that incredibly dense fog that had appeared out of nowhere, forcing them to land sooner than planned.

The owner of the Manor punched in the numbers on the keypad to his study. He was changing these numbers daily, for nobody else must ever go in there again. Since accidentally discovering Captain John Biddle's head cocooned inside the marble bust, he had felt energised and inspired. He swung back the door to his inner sanctum.

He surveyed the room; the recent changes were satisfying. The removal of the carpet had allowed the bare boards to be stained a deep and lifeless brown. A soft sofa had been replaced by two dark wooden chairs, slatted and hard. The imposing new mahogany desk had been exchanged for a smaller and cruder version, happily of the right period, the eighteenth-century. Modern drapes and stylish lamps had been removed, and between the old maps and charts on the walls were items gathered from antiques stalls, such as a rusty quadrant, a couple of cracked lanterns – and his latest 'find.' The stallholder had guaranteed that this tight group of leather strips was a *genuine* cat o'nine tails from the Caribbean, still smeared with traces of human flesh and blood. Biddle had been thrilled to believe him.

This old ship's quarters now befitted the sacred remains of his ancestor. Jedekiah absorbed the heavy and brooding atmosphere; it made him feel more needy, inferior even, yet more aggressive. Keenly aware of the venerable presence in the locked cupboard, Jedekiah reflected on him. To a casual reader of 'Gulliver's Travels,' Captain Biddle was merely the person who had rescued the traveller from his troubles in Lilliput. But to his faithful and admiring descendant, he was a hero of immense wisdom and courage, who had for too long been denied his true glory.

Those lost decades, those wasted centuries, were now over; the captain would soon regain his rightful goods and possessions.

Biddle reverently approached the cupboard, produced a key from his pocket and turned the lock in the double doors. Lifting up his hands and opening them, he involuntarily shivered as the face inside appeared once more. Even though the image was imprinted so forcibly on his mind, Jedekiah was nevertheless struck by the crude beauty and vibrant energy of this sacred relic, this skull, blood-red, roughly mended with old plaster and wax. Its veined and piercing glass eyes, peering from below the lifeless grey wisps of hair, held Biddle in their unseeing grip.

Its servant stood there, arms raised, staring at the precious object. He bowed his head, closed his eyes, and yielded to the ancient authority. Thoughts swiftly began to form. Images of his gleaming new laboratory, ready for its first residents, who would welcome its warmth and cleanliness after the miseries of a grey winter and damp spring. The picture was sharp and vivid.

Coming to his senses, he looked up, released his grip from the catches and took a step back. He felt honoured, as if drawn into a deep secret, into hidden mysteries. He himself was no longer the mere descendant trying to rescue a family's reputation or stolen riches. Jedekiah Biddle, the Lord of the Manor, was now an accomplice, a willing servant of an exalted ancestor who could reach out through time and space to still require and receive his service.

Sat behind his desk before a group of eager reporters, General Thorclan felt like a prisoner in his own office. They had initially praised his wise leadership in the Battle of Hawkwell Field, and happily discussed the decorations for bravery given to squirrels. Two of them, Walnut and Smoky, the fearless leaders of the assault on Napoleon's Imperial Guard, had received the 'Order of The Grand Acorn', conferring the privilege of wearing a red and green striped sash around the left foreleg (and another on the right on the anniversary of the battle).

But the atmosphere had now changed. Snoghod (*The Moon*) was asking about the strange light by the Gothic Temple – and rumours of 'Weapons of Mass Diffraction'.

Prompted by a stare from Gniptip, his P.A., who was standing behind the press corps, Thorclan nodded firmly. '*Correct*,' he announced. 'There *are* rumours.'

Even the sweet-tempered Duripaxe was becoming nosey. 'What are we doing about the increased activity of the National Trust within our borders?' she asked.

'I can tell you,' said Thorclan, 'that it's certified.'

'*Classified*,' corrected a female voice at the back.

'That as well,' he added.

'Can I ask, General, whether the recent success of the *combined* forces will persuade you to let other provincials stay in the Grecian army?'

'Yes, you can ask,' said Thorclan. 'And you *just* did. Next question?'

Two sharp knocks on the door halted matters. Gniptip opened it, put her head round, spoke quietly, and looked back. 'General, it's the couple you asked to see.'

'Splendid,' uttered Thorclan, standing up, mightily relieved. 'Ladies and Gentlemen of the Press, do excuse us, it's been a pleasure as always. As you leave, do congratulate two of our courageous soldiers, who have been summoned for a special reason.'

'Which is ?' asked Snoghod, quick as a flash.

'Can't say,' replied Thorclan. 'Do you expect me to tell you everything?'

'Not any more we don't,' mumbled Kul.

Gniptip ushered them out and Thorclan breezily welcomed Yenech and Melanak, both looking uncomfortable. 'Perfect timing,' he announced. 'Do sit down.' He motioned to the arc of chairs, and resumed his seat. 'This might be awkward. . . .'

'General, I can explain,' interrupted Yenech. 'Behind the bike-sheds, the two of us were looking for. . . .'

'Not interested,' said Thorclan.

'And in the long grass by the Eleven-Acre Lake,' burst in Melanak, 'we'd spotted an unusual ants' nest, and. . . .'

'Not relevant,' said Thorclan. 'No, it's about a proposal.' Yenech wanted to speak, but Thorclan carried on. 'From *me*,' he said. Now Melanak looked alarmed. 'I've noted,' he continued, 'that you're a good couple, a *team*.' Melanak blushed and Yenech fidgeted. 'There's growing tension. Rumours. Gossip.' He paced around the room, hands clasped behind his back. 'We need to be *seen* to be doing something.'

'*Seen*, General?' asked Yenech. 'Is that wise?'

'Not seen *exactly*,' said Thorclan. 'I mean, our people need to know we're *prepared*, ready for anything. That's why you're here.' Gniptip handed him a sheet of paper. 'This is a report on your aeronautical abilities. It's impressive. Says you captured the enemy's aircraft, the Firefox, and aimed it at the duck decoy, before jumping out in the nick of time. *Brilliant*.'

'General, it wasn't *quite* like that,' said Yenech. 'I can explain. . . .'

'Don't explain *anything*,' said Thorclan. 'Actions speak louder

than words. I've always said that. Now, this is your mission.'
Yenech and Melanak looked at each other. 'To handpick and
train a team of crack troops. I'm setting up SOS. A Special
Operations Squad. You are its first leaders – promoted to Captain.
Immediately.'

Yenech struggled to reply. 'General, what can I say? I'm s . . .
I'm speechless. . . .'

'Good,' said Thorclan. 'Sign of a real leader; don't say
anything. I've always said that. Now, here's a list of potential
recruits, people who have the necessary expertise on land, *and*
in the air.' He handed over the document and shook their hands.
'Before you go, one further question; ever heard of the Forces
of Destruction?'

They both shrugged their shoulders. 'No, General,' Melanak
replied.

'Good,' enthused Thorclan. '*Another* sign of a real leader;
admit you know *nothing*. I've always said that. Well, good luck
with your recruits and first operation.' On those parting words, he
waved them towards Gniptip and the door, and leant back.

It had been a *very* successful morning.

Apart from seeing the huge balloon, Charlie had not had a
successful morning. In fact it had been *really* annoying, especially
when that mist had appeared. He'd spent two hours crawling
round far too many temples and monuments, searching for
small openings that might be a fairy's front door or window.
He'd seen *some* possibilities, such as suspicious low ventilation
holes (in Concord and Victory), and ill-fitting blocks or crevices
in stonework. And the square holes on the Rotunda's dome
– but could these fairies *fly*? Jamie *had* said they didn't have
wings. . . .

It was all getting ridiculous. It was time to tell John; they'd
have a good laugh about it.

Cycling up to the front gates of Chackmore Manor, Charlie
caught sight of John practising his Frisbee technique on the
long drive. The distance was improving more than the direction.
Noticing Charlie's arrival, John ran up to let him in.

'Hi,' he said, 'what have you been up to?'

'Lots,' said Charlie, pushing his bike through the gap. 'Do you want to hear something really weird?' John looked at him. 'Definitely. What is it?'

'It's Jamie,' said Charlie, trying to adopt his most scornful voice. 'Listen to this. He says there are *fairies* at Malplaquet!'

He waited for John's laugh. It didn't come. Instead he became thoughtful, and then his eyes brightened. 'That's it!' he exclaimed. 'Of course. . . . That's brilliant!'

'What on *earth* are you on about?' asked Charlie, confused and annoyed.

'Footprints – in my bedroom,' continued John. '*Tiny* footprints. In the dust. Last night, after I got back from school. I was going to phone, but . . . anyway. . . . Cool – a real *fairy* in the Manor!'

'You don't actually *believe* it, do you?' Charlie was completely taken aback. 'It could be something else. . . . Like animal tracks. . . .'

'They were *footprints*,' said John firmly. 'Made by a tiny person.'

'Come on, this is ridiculous!' Charlie was floundering. '*Fairy* stories . . . things that aren't true . . . there are *loads* of stories about them!'

'Exactly!' said John, even more excited. 'That's why it's easier to believe in little people, because *everyone* writes about them. But I bet they're not like the books say, wearing cobwebs and lacy stuff.'

'Jamie says it's *normal* things,' said Charlie, wanting to show his knowledge now the topic was a serious matter. 'Granny makes some of it.'

'Of course,' murmured John. 'Like her dolls clothes. . . .'

'Another thing,' said Charlie. 'They're usually in the gardens, in the temples and other places, but I . . . er . . . haven't found any yet.'

'The *gardens* . . . ,' mused John. 'Of course. . . . Had to be. . . . I *knew* it! This is brilliant – come on, let's go and look for some!' He ran back to get his bike.

Charlie groaned inwardly; it was time for lunch, and he didn't want to spend more time looking for fairies at the bottom of the garden – or in *any* part of it. But he might be luckier with John, if a tiny figure *had* already turned up in his bedroom.

He swung his leg over his bike and rode off to catch up with his friend.

A few days later, Snallard was heading towards the Bourbon Tower, the old hunting-lodge just outside the grounds, for one of his regular meetings with Biddle. He liked being wanted by this powerful human, but he also enjoyed being on a mission that no-one else knew about. He knew he himself was regarded as a bit of a waster, but he was sure everyone would come crawling to him once this saga reached its dramatic conclusions – the demise of Nigriff and J. Thompson, and the permanent security of Malplaquet's tiny people. Those two schemers would abjectly admit their foolishness, and ask for his forgiveness and favour.

It was a considerable walk, so Snallard was relieved to find a young male squirrel scrabbling beneath a holly tree. Owing to its youth, it obeyed Snallard's demands, even showing little resistance when its rider forced it down a rocky and treacherous incline. The final stage of the journey, involving it limping and struggling through sharp and dense undergrowth (trying to ignore Snallard's indiscriminate use of a switch of hazel), was almost literally crippling.

When the pair arrived at the gloomy tower, Snallard leapt off and ran into the ruined interior. His mount, in considerable pain, crawled away.

Snallard waited for about twenty minutes before hearing the sound of human breathing and the padding of footsteps on the grass outside. An unmistakeable silhouette blocked out the sunlight as the figure filled the arched doorway.

'Good, you are here again. We are leaving for a very special place. Come.'

Snallard did not enjoy the journey to Chackmore Manor. Lying deep inside Biddle's smart brown briefcase, in cramped, dark and almost airless conditions, he was nauseous from the strong smell of expensive leather and the car's cornering. It was a relief when the briefcase was finally laid on its side and its top curled back. Light flooded in and he put his hands over his eyes against the sudden glare.

A large face appeared across the opening. 'This will be your new home.'

Snallard crawled out, squinting at the sharp light. Standing on the hard metal surface of the worktop, he breathed in a few mouthfuls of sterile processed air, and took in the harsh view of a very large room. Powerfully lit and lacking any windows, it hummed with the quiet pulse of motors. He noticed rows of stainless bars, glaring cupboards, neat piles of boxes, and wall-charts of diagrams and symbols.

This was a marked contrast to his normal world, full of greens and yellows, reds and blues – *life* colours. Instead he was faced with the bland and deadening shades of lead and slate-greys. Similarly, the gentle flow of breezes and softness underfoot, the welcome yielding of nature, had been replaced by a manufactured firmness and permanence, a neutral and faceless vacuum.

He *should* have hated it – but he didn't. It was dry . . . and new . . . and clearly designed just for people like him. It spoke of efficiency, of purpose, of security.

'It's perfect,' said Snallard, in a tone of gratitude and appreciation. 'Is this all just for *me*, I mean, *us*, the Lilliputians?'

'Of course,' said Biddle. 'It's the least I can do.'

The first resident took a few steps along the gleaming surface and surveyed one of the cages. It seemed remarkably vacant and lifeless, with only a square of fabric in one corner and a metal trough hooked to the bars. Snallard, in spite of his enthusiasm and sense of privilege, suddenly remembered his own home comforts; the rugs, the squashy seed-bags, the hearth-glow of charcoal in the depths of winter, the familiar lines on his old elm table. 'Will there . . . be anything *else*?' he asked hesitantly.

Biddle laughed. 'Anything *else*?' he said. 'Plenty! This is just the *beginning*, the way into your new world. In this part, you'll be carefully checked over; you see, some might arrive with contagious viruses, or even genetic faults. You'll be assessed and corrected – *helped* – before you settle down together.'

'So there's *more* space?' said Snallard. 'There are thousands of us.'

'Naturally,' said Biddle, thinking fast. '*This* room is only the first of many. There will be several of these facilities, the best that modern science can provide for such important people.' He meant every word.

Snallard's concerns were fading. 'So we won't need to go scavenging for food any more, or hunting, or growing our own crops?'

Biddle shook his head. 'You will be taken care of *completely*. These boxes contain a balanced dietary programme.' Snallard viewed the rows of semi-transparent containers, containing different coloured pellets.

'Is there one with marzipan?' Biddle had already supplied him with plenty of the stuff in other meetings.

Biddle hesitated; he wondered why he had to converse with this creature. . . . But if it *was* to bring along the others, Biddle knew he had to humour, even flatter, it.

'I believe there *is* one, but there may only be a few lumps. One of my workers has similar . . . good taste.' Finding the relevant box, he handed over a portion. Snallard took it eagerly and began to tear at it. The feast boosted his confidence.

'So when the new Empire starts here, *I'll* be a leader?'

'You will certainly be held up as an *example* to the others.'

'Good,' said Snallard. 'Just what I deserve.' He wiped his mouth.

The tour of the facility over, they went outside to confirm the best routes for bringing in the Lilliputians. Biddle set Snallard down while he reset the door's security code.

With his back to the rest of the kitchen garden, Jedekiah didn't notice the silent approach of the disc as it flew over the old brick wall, but he heard the thump as the yellow Frisbee bounced on the path, and he turned to see it skim straight into the startled Lilliputian. The direct blow caused the poor chap to collapse heavily, his head striking the ground hard.

He lay there, still and unmoving.

Biddle had little time to react before John and Charlie came hurtling round the corner, but he did squat down in front of Snallard and pick up the disc. The boys saw his glowering face and stopped a few paces away.

John was the first to speak. It had been his best-ever throw, so he was pleased that his father had witnessed its flight, but he realised that yet again he had done something wrong. 'I'm sorry. . . . I shouldn't have. . . .'

Jedekiah forced his mouth into the shape of a smile. 'It *could* have been nasty,' he said, 'but there's no harm done.' He grabbed the immobile tiny figure and stood up. 'I just dropped this doll, that's all.'

John visibly relaxed, but Charlie was intrigued. 'Why have you got a *doll*?'

Biddle's speed of thought was impressive. 'It's a gift, for the old lady by Bell Gate.'

'Like her Christmas present?' asked Charlie. 'Although she'd already got that one.'

'So I gather. This one's *very* different,' replied Biddle. 'I found it locally, and immediately thought of her. I was about to wrap it up and post it.'

Both boys were so taken aback by his kindness that Charlie decided to help as well. 'I know,' he said, 'I'll take it for you. I've got to drop off some plants for her that Mum's been splitting up; I can take the doll with me.'

Biddle hesitated. 'Right. I see. I'll, um . . . look for a box in here.' He went back into the cavernous laboratory, pulling the door behind him. He needed time to think.

Inside, he casually looked at the inanimate specimen. Feeling for a tiny pulse was almost impossible, so he shook it slightly, but it didn't stir. He couldn't tell whether it was deeply unconscious or actually dead, and frankly, he didn't care either way.

He considered Charlie's offer. If the little thing *had* died, the old lady could definitely have it; she'd realise what he was prepared to do. However, if it was *alive*, it definitely *wouldn't* betray Biddle; the pathetic being had convinced itself it would benefit from the plans. And its twisted mind could explain being at the Manor.

So that was decided. The boy *could* take it to the old woman.

He found a box, dropped the person inside, and sealed it up, with a small gap for air. Just in case. Snallard probably *would* be more useful alive than dead.

Pleased at his ability to respond to this unusual turn of

events, Biddle strode out and handed the parcel over to the messenger-boy.

'Shall I say who it's from?' said Charlie, putting it under his arm. 'Or is it a surprise?'

'It *is* a surprise, but I think she'll know who it's from.'

'Any other message?' asked Charlie.

'You could say there *might* be more,' replied Biddle.

Charlie said a quick 'cheerio' to John and returned to his bike, happy that with this doll he now had the *perfect* opportunity to ask Granny about fairies. . . .

John was also happy for several reasons. His father had seen his improved Frisbee-throwing, hadn't scolded him for being careless, *and* also had shown real kindness to a local old lady. Watching his retreating back, John knew he was a good man.

Jedekiah was fairly happy, but he was puzzled that the boys had actually *seen* Snallard. Was that because Snallard was somehow different, and lots of people could see him? Or was it that Lilliputians were now becoming more visible?

He certainly hoped it was the latter; it would make everything *so* much easier.

3. Digging up the Past

For the last half-moon Nigriff had been diligently scouring the archives for the name of Gothep (the 'Illustrious'), who might have been his ancestor kidnapped from Lilliput in the eighteenth century. It was not going at all well.

So far he had uncovered some third cousins twice removed, two great-aunts (and two *not*-so-great-uncles), and some fourth cousins once removed and twice re-inserted. He'd read the early sagas, such as *The Painful Song of Surmek, the Flute-Plucker*, or *The Eternal Ramblings of Hegit the Short-Sighted*, and the famous *Five Go Pillaging*. Sadly these had revealed that his background included mole-catchers, bark-scratchers, and even leaf-chewers. Fortunately there were also a good number of doctors, professors, Provincial Representatives – and *three* Listeners.

But he was still stuck one generation away from the original victims. At Lebojel. Hopefully, Lebojel, the son of Gothep.

Today Nigriff was working at the same table as Professor Malowit, a good friend who nevertheless doubted (like almost all the tiny people at Malplaquet) that the old stories about an island home were actually *true*. Nigriff was therefore delighted when Malowit quietly leaned over to mention things about Captain Biddle and Lilliput that could be historical *facts*. 'It's early in my research, and one shouldn't jump to rash conclusions, but . . . well, perhaps it *did* happen after all. Rum thing.' Nigriff wished him well with his work.

The Archivist was now gingerly turning the yellowing and fragile pages of the diary of an early settler at Malplaquet. It described their struggles in the first winter, their problems in growing crops in unfamiliar soils with massive seeds, and a perilous attempt to land the frightening Vazedir fish. Nigriff scanned the thin and flowery writing on each page, looking for a mention of Lebojel.

And after nine or ten pages it appeared. At the bottom of a sheet. *'Went for a night hunt with young Lebojel,'* the entry read, *'and his father. . . .'* The name was overleaf; hopefully it was none other than Gothep. Nigriff nervously turned the delicate page, and read. . . .

'. . . *Gellisleb.'*

'Gellisleb!' exclaimed Nigriff loudly. 'Who on *earth* is Gellisleb?'

'Problems?' inquired Malowit gently, conscious of disturbing others in the Archives.

'Plenty,' said Nigriff, sounding despondent. 'I've been on a wild duck chase.'

'You mean a wild *goose* chase?'

'That as well,' Nigriff replied. Appreciating the concern, he (more quietly) slowly explained about his possible ancestor, Gothep. 'But apparently it's not *him*. It's Gellisleb.'

'*Gellisleb*?' said Malowit. 'Odd, but I'm sure that was the word on an old box I saw recently. Didn't open it, but it stuck in my mind. Down this way, I think. . . .'

With Nigriff in tow, he wandered past rows of shelves, took a right, a second left, squeezed past tall cupboards, down three steps, another right and finally stopped where the roof curved down to the floor. By a pile of dusty and faded boxes. 'Yes, this is it.' He lifted one out, a faded blue colour, and blew on the dust. He read out the word on the top. '*Gellisleb*. The very man.'

Nigriff hesitated, embarrassed that he hadn't yet catalogued this far corner. Nevertheless, he took the box, placed it in a better light on the nearest table, lifted the lid, and took out each document, scanning each page carefully.

'All this material would indicate, Nigriff, that he was a learned gentleman. Even a professor perhaps.'

Nigriff said nothing; he was totally absorbed.

'Well?' Malowit said eventually. 'Am I right? Was Gellisleb a man of letters?'

'No,' replied Nigriff sadly. 'More like a man of *lettuce*. He was a gardener.' He looked up, expecting sympathy. 'My earliest known relative was just a *gardener*.' He held up one sheet. 'Look at this.'

Malowit took it. '*Wilderness Plants; Genista Hispanica. Philadelphus. Viburnum Opulus*,' he read. 'These are difficult words, you know; you do need *some* intelligence for gardening.' Nigriff was crestfallen; Gellisleb's profession, or *trade* rather, cast a dreary shadow over his whole ancestral line. It was humiliating.

Malowit was still rummaging through the box.

'Hello,' he exclaimed, 'this looks interesting.' He placed a sheet on the table. 'It's called *Thoughts on Looking Out from the Wilderness.*' A map of Malplaquet filled the top half, followed by ideas for the new garden. Malowit read it out.

'In all things our Nature should never be forgot. The paths to be curved not straight, valleys to be raised up, eminent places brought low. Plain ground should be stirred up, and rough places softened. Consider the land beyond our bounds; even if the grass withers and the flowers fall, this land, our Nature, will stand for ever.'

'Seems a bit mystical,' Malowit mused. 'Probably been chewing too much bark.' Then he noticed Nigriff's hand gently placed at the bottom, pointing at two words.

Malowit bent over and read the old handwriting. '*Gellisleb*'.

And, after it, in brackets, another word. A name.

'(*Gothep*)'.

'My goodness,' said Malowit. 'So it *is* him after all. Well I never.'

'I *knew* it,' said Nigriff proudly, standing up and smiling broadly. 'Gothep *was* my ancestor, the one from Lilliput.' Then he stopped in mid-flow. 'But why was a gardener termed *Illustrious*?'

'I think another quest has just begun,' said the Professor. 'And if I may offer a few words of advice, bearing in mind Gellisleb's – or rather, *Gothep's* – profession, I would suggest you're not going to find the answer in *here*.'

He pointed beyond him. 'It will be out *there*. In the gardens.'

'You will thank your mother, won't you, Charlie?' said Granny, looking in the plastic bag. 'These Gentians will look lovely on my rockery.'

'Sure,' he replied, untying the box strapped on his bicycle rack. 'Granny, this might sound really stupid, but can I ask you something?'

She guessed what he was about to say. 'Of course; anything you like.'

'Well, Jamie reckons there are *fairies* in the garden.' He hesitated. 'And you make clothes for them.'

She paused and then lovingly laid a hand on his shoulder. 'It's very simple, Charlie,' she said. 'Imagine a mysterious garden. Strange buildings with odd names. Secret paths. An old lady living alone. She collects dolls, makes their clothes.' Charlie was listening. 'People would talk, tell extraordinary stories about the gardens . . . about things that live there.'

He wasn't going to be fobbed off so easily. 'Yeh, okay, but *have* you seen them?'

Granny fixed him with a stare. 'You don't just see with your *eyes*, Charlie. You also see with your *mind*.' Then she winked, as if giving away a huge secret.

That did it. Charlie didn't want to look stupid by asking more questions; if the fairies *did* exist, he'd see one sooner or later anyway. Best just to give her the box.

'Right, I *thought* that was it. This is for you, by the way. From an admirer.' With a grin, he handed it over, suddenly noticing how much her hands were trembling.

Granny took the gift. 'I expect it's a doll,' she said quietly, hoping that Charlie didn't spot the quiver in her voice. 'Thank *you* – or whoever it was that gave it to you.'

'I think you *know* who it was,' he said. Granny nodded and forced a smile.

Charlie swung back on his bike and with a wave set off for home, clear in his mind about this 'fairy theory.' Firstly, Granny's words were sadly the ramblings of an elderly woman who was sadly losing touch with reality. As for Jamie, a brotherly wind-up was still the best explanation.

But *John's* attitude was odd. Then Charlie remembered what Granny had just said about the link between the garden and stories. And, he thought, John *was* obsessed with a children's story about Lilliputians living here. *That* was it. John – often alone in that big house . . . his imagination playing tricks . . . *seeing* things . . . the boy should get out more.

'So many *sad* cases,' thought Charlie. At least *he'd* worked out what was going on. Mightily pleased with himself, he shot up the track.

In her yard, Granny was holding the taped box very gingerly. 'Thank goodness Yenech and Melanak are in the cottage,' she thought. 'At least I'm not alone.'

Ever since Biddle's Christmas present to her with its threatening note, the safety of Nigriff had been a nagging worry. When had she last seen him? Two days ago? Presumably he'd been in the Archives again, but maybe. . . .

Feeling unsteady, she shuffled inside, holding the box like a precious casket.

Melanak sensed her mood as soon as she entered her sitting-room. 'Madam, what's the matter? And what is that box you're carrying?'

The old lady swallowed, her throat dry. 'I don't know. . . . It might be. . . .'

'Do you wish *us* to open it, Madam?' asked Yenech, keen to be gallant.

She nodded. Placing the box on the table, she found her scissors in her sewing-bag and gently snipped the tape along the flaps. She then placed the two people on the top, and sat back as they slowly lifted one half. Yenech lay down and peered into the gloom. His brief silence made Granny even more nervous, until he sat up, smiling.

'He's alive,' he said, 'and it's a Palladian, I mean one of *us*, but from Palladia. A chap called Snallard, I think. Might be injured.'

Very relieved, in spite of the possible injury, Granny leant across and saw the recumbent tiny figure, one leg stretched out, his eyes shut, looking dazed. Yenech jumped down next to Snallard, and quietly talked to him, looking for injuries. Melanak up above was impressed.

'He's definitely hurt,' Yenech concluded. 'Been knocked out. There's a bump and cut on the back of his head.'

Granny reached in and gently lifted Snallard out, then Melanak cleaned and dressed the head wound, checking for any other damage. An area of bruising on the chest looked as if he'd been hit, and cuts and grazes on the face and hands suggested a fight. Snallard slowly regained full consciousness, and pieced together his distressing story.

'It's my fault . . . should have known better . . . but we do need to know more about Biddle. Someone had to go there.'

'Go where?' asked Yenech, always interested in people's travels.

'The Manor,' he uttered, groaning and holding his head.

'You went to the *Manor*?' asked Melanak, incredulous but impressed.

Snallard nodded. 'I'd been once before, and it was okay then.'

Yenech didn't like being overshadowed. 'Wasn't that rather *stupid*?' He was resenting Snallard's presence more and more.

'Maybe, but it was easy hiding in his son's backpack, and I just explored the top rooms.' He winced as Melanak dabbed at a graze on his face. Yenech scowled Snallard continued. 'I didn't find out much then, so I had to try again. We've *got to* discover his plans.'

'Absolutely right,' said Granny. 'So how did you get back again?'

'I saw Biddle being attacked by a demented squirrel near the Bourbon Tower. While he was fighting it off, I hid in his briefcase. When it was over, he picked it up, and was driven home.'

'There *was* a young squirrel badly hurt there recently,' said Melanak 'Two of my friends found it wandering around.'

'When we got to the Manor,' continued Snallard rapidly, 'I crept out unseen and searched his garden and sheds. But he spotted me near a cucumber-frame. I ran through his cabbage-patch, but almost got caught in some netting, then he trapped me under a flowerpot. It struck my head as he slammed it down. Next thing I knew you were waking me up.' It was a convincing performance.

'You've had a real fright, Snallard' said Granny, 'but you've told us something *very* important.'

'I have?' he said, wondering whether she had believed his story.

'Biddle can now actually *see* Lilliputians,' she said gravely. 'You lot have always been invisible to him. This is *really* bad news.'

'Unless *Snallard's* special in some way. . . .' said Melanak.

'That *can't* be it,' interrupted Yenech. 'Why should *he* be different?'

'Yenech is right,' said Snallard. 'If he can see *me*, he can see everyone.'

Granny thought that Snallard could be trusted with their current theories about Biddle. 'We think he wants to breed a new race of Lilliputians.'

'In that case, why didn't he *keep* me?' asked Snallard.

'Quality control,' butted in Yenech. 'He wants the *best* specimens. I was his *first* choice last summer until I got rescued.' He folded his arms in annoyance.

'Whatever the reason, you're jolly brave, Snallard,' said Granny. 'When you've made a full recovery, you'll be perfect for Yenech and Melanak's new team.'

Yenech was about to speak but was interrupted by Snallard, looking quizzical.

'New team?'

There was a short silence, until Melanak nudged Yenech, who reluctantly explained. 'Thorclan's asked us to lead some special operations. We're starting. . . .'

'. . . to recruit,' continued Melanak, 'and you're our first. Congratulations!'

'Hang on a minute!' cut in Yenech. 'We haven't even. . . .'

'Come on, Yenech, think about it,' said Granny. 'Who else is there like him? He's made two lone assaults on Biddle's headquarters already. He's *exactly* who you need.'

Yenech knew he'd been outmanoeuvred, and he was upset. There was something about Snallard that bothered him. However, whilst chatting together after they left Granny's, his suspicions seemed misplaced.

'I couldn't say so in there,' Snallard said, 'because she doesn't want us all to ever *leave* the garden, but I've seen inside one of Biddle's new buildings.'

'*Really*?' said Melanak. 'What's it like?'

'Idyllic,' said Snallard. 'Perfect for Lilliputians – warm, comfortable, safe. Proper houses and facilities for people our size.' He paused. 'You know, I've got to ask, are we *definitely* right about this Biddle?'

The other two, surprised by this question, exchanged glances. Snallard continued with his theory. 'We must consider *all* the possibilities. *Maybe* he *is* trying to help us, to start a new race of Lilliputians . . . like a new Empire, so he's getting our new homeland ready, in case we have to move to it. Actually, I reckon you two would be perfect as the first couple.'

As Melanak talked easily with Snallard, Yenech pondered this new and highly attractive theory.

Maybe he *had* misjudged their new team-member.

Maybe Snallard *was* on to something. Granny *would* find it hard to give them up after caring for them for so long. . . . Did she perhaps want to selfishly keep them to herself, forever? Yenech hated that thought, for she *had* been so good to them, but she *was* becoming possessive about the Lilliputians, especially Nigriff. . . . And Snallard *was* a good judge of character; after all, he knew that he and Melanak made a good couple.

And, Yenech thought, *perhaps* Snallard was right about Biddle as well.

For the moment, he sensibly decided to keep an open mind.

Which had never been too difficult for Yenech.

The National Trust staff and volunteers were being given another lecture in the 'Education, Awareness and Information Exchange Facility,' and were desperately trying to look educated, aware, and informed. Mr. Biddle was away in London, so the Operations Manager was in charge, outlining some astonishing statistics.

State-of-the-art data analysis had revealed, he claimed, that 'our average visitor is aged 33 years 3 months 11 days, 5 foot 6.3 inches tall, and is 58% female 42% male.'

'Never seen anybody *quite* like that,' whispered Vicky to Ralph, who grinned.

Furthermore, this visitor of uncertain gender 'has a journey of 12.7 miles, and arrives with 85% of a car, 12% of a bike, and 3% of a foot. He/she stays here 72.5 minutes and consumes half a fizzy freshly-squeezed coffee, and a prawn and chocolate muffin sandwich, topped off with 21% of an ice-cream. He/she buys 61% of a guidebook and 14% of a postcard. These results show,' said the Manager, 'that our visitors are half an inch taller and 53 days younger than they were last year.'

'I *knew* it,' said a man in the front. 'Working here takes years off your life.'

'Doesn't make you taller though,' said Ralph, turning to Vicky.

'Better than cosmetic surgery,' said Vicky. 'Ask Newbold.'

The Manager handed over to the Learning and Information Officer. The young lady enthusiastically spoke on the unprecedented success of the Trust's recent Activities, especially Mr. Biddle's balloon-ride, which made the local television news. 'Unfortunately, there have been *some* difficulties,' she added, consulting her notes. 'Of the 100 eggs in the Easter Egg Hunt, 81 disappeared before it began.'

Some volunteers fidgeted on their seats. 'Can anyone explain this?' she asked.

'Yes,' said one after a pause. 'Rabbits.'

'Badgers,' said a second.

'And Squirrels,' said a third.

'Hmm,' she said, unconvinced. 'Thank goodness Mr Biddle might extermin. . . . I mean, *reduce* them all to beneficial and environmentally appropriate levels.'

Vicky looked at Ralph, who raised an eyebrow.

The *Grand Balloon Give-Away* had attracted record numbers. Fifty balloons, some labelled with special prizes, had been tied up in the grounds on the Friday night. 'Astonishingly, *all* the prize balloons were found,' she said, 'by four pupils at the school.'

Vicky burst out laughing. The Officer scowled. 'The prizes of a Test-Drive of the new 4x4 Porsche, a Day at Towcester Races, a Case of Champagne, and a full body wax and pedicure have been replaced by suitable alternatives.'

'Shame!' called out Ralph, joining in the fun.

'There have been other *minor* difficulties,' admitted the harassed speaker. 'There were legal problems with the blatant sexism of our *Mother's Day Treats*, the *Kite Weekend* was becalmed, and the RSPCA misunderstood our *Blow-Up Animals Day* and staged a demonstration.' Stifled giggles came from her audience.

'However,' she announced, 'next week is our inaugural *Malplaquet Literature Day*, a planned annual celebration of writings inspired by the gardens. The first to be honoured is that superb children's book, '*Mistress Masham's Repose*', by T.H.White. Final details will be available shortly.'

'This one bothers me,' said Vicky, quietening down.

'Me too,' agreed Ralph.

'Finally,' continued the speaker, 'advance notice of a spectacular event this summer, arranged by Mr Biddle, to mark the final restoration of the temples and the completion of the Ha-Ha. This 'Unveiling of Malplaquet' will be, so he guarantees, an unforgettable experience; the revealing of our *treasures*, as he calls them.'

There was appreciative applause from everyone – apart from Vicky and Ralph.

'It gets worse and worse,' she said.

'Come on,' he said. 'Time to go. We need reinforcements.'

Yenech and Melanak needed to gather a team of, in total, five men and five women. Snallard's swift inclusion left three men to find. Two were easy. Wesel and Hyroc's loyalty and initiative, shown in the Cold Stream Cup, had also been clear in other missions, notably the Lake Kidnap and the Battle of Hawkwell Field.

The final choice was difficult. Cherbut and Trimter in the Grecian Army had many good qualities, and the Cascadian Chamklab was athletic and willing, but finally Yenech opted for Yassek. His profound knowledge of Malplaquet had been invaluable and entertaining when gaining the Capital. He had much to offer.

The first female chosen had been Hamnob. The parting words of her mother had been poignant. 'She's a *blessing* to me,' she said, sniffing back tears, 'but if she can help our people at all, then she must do it.'

The two captains were reflecting on that sacrifice en route to Elysium.

'Makes you feel humble,' said Yenech. 'This place is full of special people.'

'And we're about to meet another,' said Melanak. 'Up by the Shell Bridge.'

'Who's that?'

'Surprise.'

Soon they were pushing through the undergrowth in the centre of the Elysian province. 'She spends a lot of time here since she retired,' said Melanak.

'Retired?' gasped Yenech. 'We're not recruiting for an Old People's Home!'

'Silence!' hissed an authoritative voice nearby. 'Stay where you are!'

Yenech froze. The command had an awfully familiar rasp to it.

'Vingal!' declared Melanak effusively, peering into the shadows. 'How good to see you.' She pushed aside some branches, followed cautiously by Yenech, and offered a hand of welcome to the figure seated at her artist's easel. 'Are you well?'

The ex-Listener nodded fairly politely, then glared at Yenech. 'So, young man, what are you up to? A secret walk in the woods with your girlfriend?'

'No,' replied Yenech. 'Well, yes, sort of, but. . . . We haven't quite yet. . . .'

'*Spit* it out,' she snapped, putting down her brushes. 'Get a grip, man.'

Melanak took over. 'Vingal, the General is creating a new operations unit. We need special people, with leadership skills, with experience. People like you.'

'So, Old Tubby is still saving the world, is he?' She considered the offer, liking the directness and the flattery. 'Hmm. Experience, you say? Someone who can make things happen, put men in their place. Are you sure you want that, Yenech?'

Yenech nodded meekly.

Five minutes later the pair were pressing onwards, with two females to find.

'That woman,' said Yenech, 'is scary.'

'Precisely,' said Melanak. 'She's perfect.'

The four Greek statues in the Temple of Ancient Virtue had heard everything, especially Vingal. They were smiling approvingly.

'Such a lady could have conquered the *entire* peninsula,' said the Theban general, Epaminondas.

'Great political leaders can inspire others,' said the statesman, Lycurgus.

'She deserves a story,' added Homer. 'I can see the first line already; 'Of a woman I sing, and her arms. . . .''

'Her arms?' queried Socrates.

'Arms, as in *weapons*,' explained Epaminondas.

'Women have great virtues,' replied Socrates. 'Take my wife, Xanthippe.'

'No thank you,' said Homer. 'I'd have to be *deaf*, as well as blind,'

Socrates ignored this. 'What a woman! I remember a local trader selling figs that were past their sell-by date. When she found out. . . .' And he was off, expounding yet again her many fine qualities. Of course, he could not tell, from the blank and unseeing eyes of the other statues, if they were listening or not.

They weren't.

Jedekiah Biddle, parked in his car near Malplaquet's entrance, surveyed the long line of vehicles with immense satisfaction. The public were arriving in their hundreds for the widely-advertised *Malplaquet Literature Day*. He smiled; the place was going to be absolutely buzzing, with no quiet corners left untouched. Anybody who lived there would be soon desperate to leave.

This was the work of a genius, he reminded himself, although John had suggested a couple of ideas. The boy clearly knew

White's story well, but Jedekiah winced as he remembered the boy craving his attention as they had talked together; it was unlikely the child would ever develop the unfeeling independence that Jedekiah saw as the mark of all great leaders.

He quietly watched the gatemen handing out information sheets about the book, and once again rubbed his chin, feeling the long scar. He'd only noticed it after shaving that morning. It ran from his right ear lobe along the line of his jaw to the centre of his chin. He assumed that he must have accidentally cut himself.

But this thin and raised white line looked like an *old* wound, not something that had happened that morning.

It was most perplexing. And something about this scar seemed very familiar.

4. The Old Story

On Granny's dining-room table lay Jamie's model of Malplaquet gardens. A sheet of chipboard, cut to the right shape, was covered by large patches of blue gloss paint and green baize, the latter broken by swirls of sandpaper paths and clumps of spongy trees. Simple cardboard versions of the main temples stood in their proper places.

On one side stood four Lilliputian females, namely Prittorc, Welalac, Lenyast, and Gowdoc, each clasping a stick that had a wide t-bar on the other end. Before them was a line of coloured plastic cones with bulbous tops (from a board game of Granny's). She was nervously pacing around, watched by Vicky and Ralph. Nigriff, in his elevated position on the sideboard, was guarding Vicky's mobile phone with a small wooden mallet.

Granny stopped her walk. 'Time to check the system,' she announced.

Nigriff raised the mallet aloft, and Vicky held her breath as he swung it down with a loud 'thump' on the on/off button. To her relief, the screen and its 'Mission Impossible' jingle flickered into life. Nigriff bashed his way around the keyboard and waited for the response. It soon came.

'Hullo, Jamie here, is that Field HQ?'

'It's not the field, sir. It's the Dining-room HQ.'

'The Dining-room *is* the Field HQ, Nigriff. Do you want to check my co-ordinates?'

Nigriff looked bemused. Granny helped him out. 'Ask for his position.'

'What position are you in?' asked Nigriff.

'I'm sitting,' replied Jamie. 'Should I stand up?'

Granny sighed and raised her eyes upwards. Nigriff took the hint. 'No,' he shouted. 'Stay seated.'

It was Vicky's turn. 'Ask him where he is in the *gardens*.'

The reply to that question came through loud and clear. 'I'm in the eastern Lake Pavilion,' Jamie said. 'Just behind the cottage wall.' Prittorc lowered her stick and deftly pushed the white cone to the correct location.

'I'm guessing Jamie Thompson, in a temple, with a mobile phone,' declared Vicky, smiling. 'No, sorry, with the lead piping.' Nigriff looked puzzled. 'Military tactics,' she explained. The little man shouted down the phone again.

'Master Jamie, do you know the whereabouts of Jedekiah Biddle?'

'I can see him near the South Front steps,' he replied. 'Below the Library.'

'With a candlestick?' asked Vicky mischievously, as the black piece was eased across the central green expanse towards the mansion.

'Has he got a candlestick?' asked Nigriff. There was a pause at the other end.

'No. Should he?'

'Miss Vicky wants to know,' said Nigriff. Miss Vicky burst out laughing.

Granny had heard enough. 'Just say goodbye, Nigriff,' she said.

'Goodbye, Nigriff,' said Nigriff, then heard, 'Roger, over and out,' just before wildly thumping the button marked with a little red telephone. 'Why did he call me 'Roger'?' he asked. Granny clasped a hand to her forehead.

'This could be a long day,' stated Ralph.

The weather was being extremely kind for the latter half of May, the sun bearing down on the new temporary buildings in the grounds. The Trust's handymen had worked overtime to build imaginary locations from White's story, including the dungeon and the island-home of the Lilliputians ('Mistress Masham's Repose' itself). There was also the Professor's cottage, a timber construction deep in the woods by the Queen's Temple. This was proving very popular. The school's elderly Head of Classics, playing the role of the otherworldly Professor, assumed that the crowds were attracted by his wonderful leather-bound volumes, their covers recently polished to a glass-like sheen by boys in Detention. A more likely explanation was the generous samples of the advertised '*Professor's Home-made Wine,*' in Cowslip, Dandelion, and Gooseberry flavours.

The dungeon was suitably gloomy. A room in the school's basement had been painted a thick black, and a single red light bulb and bars across the solitary window added to the ambience. Wooden replicas of the named instruments – such as the Rack and the coffin-shaped Virgin of Nuremburg – stood by a notice advising, '*Do not try this at home.*' The book's pile of thighbones and skulls were simply shoulders of lamb. One boy left in tears, sobbing, 'why did they torture *sheep* here?' He clearly hadn't read that, '*No animals have been harmed in the making of this exhibit*'.

For the 'Repose' itself, the Trust was using an island beyond the Palladian Bridge. Mostly overgrown with laurel bushes, the centre had been cleared for a splendid half-size replica of the Rotunda. Although the columns were painted cardboard tubes from inside rolls of carpet, and the dome bore an uncanny resemblance to an upturned fibreglass sandpit, the effect was nevertheless fairly authentic. The designers had even, as the book described, laid the tree-trunk half in the water, with a punt tied to it.

Malplaquet was really buzzing. Costumed re-enactors were wandering around, playing Miss Brown (the bad-tempered governess), the Reverend Hater (the portly vicar), and the lumbago-afflicted PC Dumbledum (with stout truncheon and stout wife). The shop was exchanging pennies for Lilliputian 'gold' Sprugs, and selling Maria's gifts for the little people – silk handkerchiefs and chocolate creams. In the Queen's Temple, redoubtable WI ladies with sewing machines were helping girls (and an enlightened boy) to make dolls' clothes. In a workshop, young boys (and an enlightened girl) were making balsa-wood model aircraft, with the required elastic-band propulsion. Poor flights and crashes were being repeated, just as described in the book. . . .

Elsewhere, one could learn the finer points of lace-making (a particular Lilliputian skill), or enjoy the reminiscences in the Library of those who had been taught by T. H. White himself. From there, Vicky phoned base.

'Nigriff? Vicky. Hawkins, in the Library.'

'Thank you, Miss Vicky. Hawkins, in the Library,' he announced. Welalac pushed the red playing-piece forwards, soon joined by Vicky's green one. 'Over and out, Roger,' declared Nigriff, ending the call with the usual mallet swing.

The phone rang just after he hit it. The voice was clipped and anxious.

'Ralph at Venus. *Emergency* over at Rotunda. Blue, yellow. Tell Jamie.'

As those two coloured figures were slid across, a few sharp blows from Nigriff made contact with the 'white person' some distance away.

'Master Jamie? It's Roger. Code yellow and code blue. Rotunda. *Urgent.*'

The arrival at the Rotunda of the flat-bed truck carrying sections for a scaffolding tower had first alarmed SOS, hiding in a nearby yew. A sign saying, '*The Original Hiding-place? See for Yourself*', confirmed their fears.

Ignoring the clattering of the metal squares being slotted together, SOS slid down an ancient badger run to emerge directly below one of the temple's hollow columns, and jumped into its wind-powered lift for the ascent.

Leaping out at the top, inside the double skin of the Rotunda's dome, they saw that panic had already set in. Dozens of Lilliputians were dashing in and out of rooms, especially those on the first level. These sought-after apartments had square windows that were usually filled with fine views of the golf course.

Or perhaps very soon, filled with the view of a human face.

Yenech delegated tasks. 'Take one level each; Snallard at the top, then Wesel, and Yassek, then Hyroc. Move everyone to the *west*, away from the tower!'

A frightened elderly man clasped his arm. 'We've always been so *safe* up here,' he said, 'It's Yenech, isn't it?'

'Not any more,' said Yenech. 'It's SOS. Anytime. Anywhere.'

Melanak was briefing her team. 'The children will be upset. Distract them, keep them quiet.' The team ran off to control the situation. 'These domes *never* work,' muttered one passing woman. 'Seen it all before.'

The dull thumps outside indicated wooden boards and steps being laid on each level. Almost in a panic, Yenech was rapidly lifting furniture from the nearest rooms, and Melanak was rolling up rugs and ordering the removal of pictures. These fine apartments were fast becoming bare and lifeless concrete spaces.

'One more layer,' shouted a workman outside.

Yenech peered into the empty room. 'Spotless,' he whispered to Melanak.

'You're right,' she replied. 'Quick, mess it up!' She dipped her hands into a box of charcoal ash and hurled it before her. The air currents swirled it through the window, just as a face appeared.

'Yuk!' it exclaimed. 'It's filthy! Can't understand why Biddle wants people to look in it.' The builder wiped his eyes and made his way back down the steps. He'd seen enough.

But two boys down below weren't going to put off by a little dust.

'Can we have a look?' asked Charlie.

'If you don't mind getting dirty,' came the reply.

'Course not,' said Charlie, and eagerly jumped onto the lowest boards and hurried up the scaffolding stairs. John wasn't far behind.

Within seconds they were on the top platform and looking out over the gardens from the final platform. The views were glorious, running down to the lakes in one direction, and towards the mansion in another.

'White said they lived in a temple just like this one,' said John.

'Okay,' said Charlie, 'let's see if they're still here.' He was keen to prove all tales of little people as ridiculous. He peered through a square hole, then cupped his hands and bellowed into the opening.

'*Anybody there? Can you hear me?*'

The terrified occupants, crouching in the distant curves, put their hands over their ears to shut out the noise, some mothers neglecting their own eardrums to hug their children. The reverberation was so awesome as it boomed around the circuit that Charlie repeated the experiment. '*Come out, come out, whoever you are!*'

Melanak and her team played finger games with the youngsters, trying to look calm and unaffected. The intensity of the noise and echoes was making some weaker souls crawl out of the far windows onto the narrow ledge, risking a fall or perhaps being seen.

The calmest person was Vingal, shielding two young girls who had just become separated from their parents. In her old role as the Listener in the Provincial Assembly, she had often faced a torrent of meaningless noise. Eyes narrowed, an awesome combination of Boadicea and Canute, she steadfastly faced this familiar onslaught and inspired many until the blast died away.

'Thought as much,' said Charlie outside. 'Not a sausage.'

'*Oi*, what are you two up to?' came a shout from below. It was his brother, Jamie.

Charlie groaned quietly and peered down. 'Nothing much,' he said. 'Actually, we're hunting fairies. The ones *you* believe in.'

'Any luck?' said Jamie, with genuine interest.

'Hardly,' said Charlie. 'I suppose we frightened them away?'

'You can never tell with fairies,' added John. 'They're very clever.'

'Yeh, sure,' agreed Charlie, sarcastically. This game had to stop soon.

As the two clambered down, Jamie moved away to make a quick phone-call. 'Rotunda clear. Casualties unknown. To Eleven-Acre with yellow and blue.'

He ended the call and looked back over his shoulder. 'Do you two want to come down to the lake? There's a model frigate you can steer.'

'*Definitely*,' replied John. 'Like my famous ancestor. It's in the blood.'

'I hope not,' muttered Jamie.

'Thanks for the lift, Miss Vicky,' said Yenech, crawling out from the ruck-sack's pouch onto the path by the north side of the Eleven-Acre Lake

'No problem,' she replied. 'Jamie said you needed help getting down here.'

Other members of SOS also emerged from the bag, faces still streaked with charcoal dust, and headed to the water for a wash. Vicky shielded her eyes against the glare to look across. 'Jamie's by the jetty,' she announced. 'With John and Charlie. And quite a crowd. Are you sure you know what you're doing?'

'Not completely,' said Yenech, grinning, 'but that's never stopped me before.'

Melanak touched his arm. 'We need to get Wesel going.'

Yenech nodded. 'Excuse us, Miss Vicky, duty calls.' He and Melanak strode off with Wesel. Behind them followed Gniptip, who had relished that first action at the Rotunda. She had just been talking to Snallard, and her brow was heavily furrowed.

Vicky watched the team disappear below the overhanging ferns and grasses, and then retraced her steps. Within seconds a series of undulating and high-pitched whistles brought her to a halt. She knew it was Wesel, using his Palladian skills to send out a message across the waters to distant corners and provinces.

SOS was underway again.

As all readers of White's story know, the frigate was the magnificent vessel built by Lilliputians that was usually hidden beneath dense foliage but used for night-time 'whale-hunts.' On one such occasion, Maria had tried to help the sailors, but had accidentally allowed a fish to escape *and* had caused some damage.

There was to be no hunt this afternoon. And no accidents either.

Just an elegant display on the lake of a model ship, lovingly made by a specialist firm in London, its screw propeller controlled by a radio transmitter on shore.

The beautiful frigate was carried out of the school's sculling hut to a smattering of applause. Hawkins, hobbling as always, was holding the control-box with its imitation ship's wheel, switches and lights. The craft was resplendent; a three-master, gun-ports down each side, an impressive poop deck and forecastle, and plenty of polished mahogany. The sails, unfurled, were flapping sharply in the offshore breeze.

'Now that's what I call a boat,' said John.

'That's what I call a *ship*,' said Charlie, trying to help him to grow up a bit.

'That's what I call a *frigate*,' said Jamie, putting both boys in their place.

'My ancestor would have captained one of those,' added John.

'Six inches high, was he?' said Jamie in irritation, disliking John's naïve admiration for the 'famous Captain Biddle.' He was sorely tempted to tell the kid exactly what sort of a man his great-great-whatever-grandfather actually was.

But it could wait.

He had other plans for John that afternoon.

The plans of SOS were going extremely well. Firstly, they'd found the coil of fishing-line (breaking-point 200lbs) that Jamie had left by the water's edge. Secondly, two swans, responding to Wesel's whistling, had landed nearby with a spectacular flapping and were now making their sedate way to the bank.

Yenech, Gniptip, Snallard and Melanak soon climbed aboard these majestic white vessels, and snuggled under the expanse of wings.

'*This*,' said Yenech, holding one end of the line, 'is what I call a boat.'

'I hate to contradict you,' purred Melanak, trying to keep her eyes open in such cosy surroundings, 'but most people call it a swan. And it's just *gorgeous*. . . .'

'And don't steer it near them ducks,' stressed Hawkins, handing over the control-box. He was seated on the edge of the planking, his bare feet cooling off in the lapping water. John took hold of the unit, and pointed the aerial in the direction of the frigate.

'They're not ducks,' he answered, 'they're swans.'

'Yeh, whatever,' said Hawkins.

John turned the wheel, watching the vessel slowly change course. Captain Biddle would have felt like this three centuries ago, he thought, proud at being in charge of his own ship. It was a splendid sight in the middle of the lake, sails billowing in the breeze.

'Make it go a bit faster,' urged Jamie, looking over the operator's shoulder.

John pushed the small lever, and noticed the slight turbulence at the stern.

'Is that all?' enquired Jamie.

'You've got to be careful with these things,' said John.

'Too right,' agreed Charlie. 'There was this plane once. . . . *Look out!* Mind those swans – you're getting too close!'

'I can't help it,' whined John. 'It's not *me*. They're following it.'

Yenech peered out from his hiding-place and addressed his squad. 'Almost there, people. Boarding-party ready?'

'Aye aye, captain,' replied Snallard.

'At your command,' agreed Gniptip.

Yenech signalled to the other swan, pointing to the island with its boat-hut. Vingal gave a discreet wave in return, and steered the bird northwesterly, taking the other end of the fishing-line with her.

With the slightest of bumps Yenech's craft drew alongside the ship. 'Now!' he hissed. The swan raised its wings, and under cover the team scrambled up the side netting in seconds. They were confident that nobody had seen them.

Crouching behind the balustrade, Yenech issued his commands. 'Melanak, Gniptip – tie the line tight around the mast. Snallard – the electronics.'

The vessel was now doomed; connected by the line to the

boathouse jetty, any progress was impossible. And once Snallard had altered (destroyed) the operational wiring, she would be left floating around. And, like a latter-day Marie-Celeste, of the crew there would be no sign whatsoever. . . .

For about two minutes all was well. The line had been firmly tied to the mast, and Snallard had prised open the wiring-box. Yenech was peering over the balustrade watching the stately progress of the other swan and its four passengers.

Then the plan started to go horribly wrong.

Firstly, Yenech was shocked to see Vingal suddenly dive into the water, or as she later described it, 'pulled.' Fortunately the dear lady was dragged back onto the swan by Hyroc and Wesel, but she no longer had hold of the line.

'It's a thumping great fish!' she exclaimed.

'Not a *Vazedir*?' asked Hyroc.

'Correct,' she panted, '*not* a Vazedir. It was yellow, much bigger, with a huge mouth.' (If she had known her statuary better, she would have recognised the bulbous creature at the base of a Saxon Deity). 'I've no idea where it's gone.'

The answer to that one was 'towards the spectators.'

There then came a dramatic change in the weather, as a sudden squall hurtled across the lake (preceded by a shimmering golden disc). The storm was incredibly localised but fierce. From the shore, it was like a mini-tornado, whipping up the water around the ship into a frenzy of thrashing breakers. The swans moved away in alarm.

The bystanders were stunned, Jamie included. 'Why did that happen?' he thought.

'*Get it out of there!*' shouted Hawkins at John.

'I can't,' he replied. 'The controls aren't working. They must be waterlogged!'

'Give it here,' demanded Hawkins, roughly grabbing the device from his hands.

On board the distressed vessel, the four gallant crew were soaked through, slipping and sliding across the rolling deck, hanging on to loose ropes, and shouting above the crack of the sails and the roar of the water as it swept over the ship. Yenech, slithering and crawling aft, grabbed the wheel, which had been spinning madly. Once he had brought it control, he looked behind and saw a most remarkable sight.

Speeding towards their stern, torpedo-like, just below the water's surface, was a large male figure, maybe twice the normal size. Of a glowing sulphur colour, and with a full tawny beard and straggling hair, it was holding a trident.

'Good grief,' thought Yenech, 'it's the river-god from our temple!'

Usually looking majestic but bored in the pediment, he was now in his natural habitat, and thoroughly enjoying himself. He slammed into the rear of the boat, knocking the four sailors off their feet, and shoved it off across the lake, a huge wash (and a strong fishing-line) streaming out behind as it emerged from the storm.

In the meantime, the 'Saxon Fish' had also been enjoying itself with the other end of the line. Before the storm had really struck, it had spotted a pair of feet happily dangling in the shallows. Twisting one way then another, circling and diving in and out, it had created a loose-fitting yet effective knot around one ankle of the owner.

Hawkins had just taken hold of the controls when his right leg was suddenly yanked forward. This was followed, fortunately perhaps, by the rest of his body, and he set off, fully upright, across the surface of the lake in full pursuit of the frigate.

'Never knew water-skiing was on this afternoon,' said one woman.

'And he's got such a bad leg,' said another. 'Amazing.'

Jamie knew the statues had to be in some way responsible, and joined in the applause as Hawkins made his second pass.

If one had listened carefully, it might have been possible to detect a slight echo of that applause apparently coming from the frigate, which was now gradually slowing down and allowing its pursuing captive to sink into the water.

He didn't stay there for long. He never saw the jab of the trident from behind, encouraging him to splash out of the lake as quickly as possible.

But he certainly felt it.

There was no limit to Biddle's frustration by the end of that day. Not only had he suffered hundreds of people telling him what a wonderful time they were having (and he hated talking to the public), but also Hawkins had become quite demented about his 'problems' on the lake.

Biddle knew it was down to Lilliputian trickery, but had this suspicion that they hadn't been his *only* opponents. He'd known for ages about the squirrels conspiring against him, but from what he could tell, it sounded like the swans had joined forces with them. And were the *fish* now ganging up on him? Certainly last summer Newbold had gabbled on and on about the way that one of the bigger and nastier types in the lake had so viciously and deliberately attacked him.

The fact was that he simply didn't know exactly *how* the Lilliputians had done it. And his hope that he might be able to see them had been proven futile; there had been an occasional glimpse of a small shadow, an outline perhaps, but these had always been very fleeting, probably no more than a trick of the light.

He knew that if he was to fulfil the ambitions of his ancestor, he was going to have to do a great deal more.

5. Too Many Questions

The very next day, Granny was ambling in her buggy past the Rotunda. 'Biddle *might* be around here,' she said, applying the brake and addressing the bag by her side, its folds of material drooping out. 'But I think the coast is clear.'

Nigriff's head popped up. 'I don't know about the *coast*, Madam,' he said, 'but it is very quiet *here*. Except for the small group further off on that rise, we are alone.'

'And there's the man we *really* want,' she said. 'In Dido's cave. Hold on.'

She pushed down the pedal and the vehicle crawled up the slight incline to the small cave-like alcove. Unusually, its wrought-iron gate was open, and the top of a broom handle was darting in and out, as dust and leaves were swept out of the arched shelter. Ralph noticed their slow approach and touched his forehead in an old-fashioned greeting.

'Morning, Miss Maria,' he said. 'Out by yourself?' He spotted the bag and its contents, and touched his forehead again. 'And a good morning to *you*, sir.'

Granny smiled. 'Hello, Ralph, we won't interrupt; just a quick chat.'

'That's fine,' he replied. 'Just tidying up after the big day.

What a day that was.'

She nodded in acknowledgement. 'Can we go inside? Nigriff has some news.'

'Of course; welcome to my 'umble abode.' He gestured with his hand.

They sat down on the bench to one side, limited by the narrow space. Granny looked around at the unusual walls; the sponge-like tufa rock, the mosaic effect of broken coloured tiles, and the bits of broken mirrors, reflecting random images. It had an air of fantasy, of frivolity.

'Haven't been in here for years,' she murmured. 'It's normally locked.' She saw that Nigriff was already taking the piece of paper from his inside pocket. 'It's from the Archives,' she said to Ralph.

'I would ask you, sir, to treat this ancient document with the *utmost* respect,' said Nigriff, cautiously resting a piece of paper the size of a postage stamp on Ralph's open palm. 'It is a *priceless* family heirloom.' The old gentleman gently placed one finger on a corner to stop it blowing away, and squinted at it.

'It's obviously very old,' he said. 'Is that writing?'

'Indeed it is,' said Nigriff proudly. 'It was written by one of my ancestors, an original exile from Lilliput itself. This is a piece of living history, penned by one who trod the earth of that blessed land.'

Ralph was suitably reverential, but had to raise a problem. 'Not being awkward, but even with my glasses I couldn't read it.'

'I will gladly fulfil honour,' said Nigriff. 'Allow me.' He took the paper. 'It was written by Gellisleb, who was only a gardener, but also known as. . . .'

Ralph interrupted. 'Sorry, Nigriff,' he snapped. 'What did you say? *Only* a gardener?'

Nigriff's character had changed a great deal over the last year; he'd even become sporty as well as more tolerant. But sometimes the old and narrow-minded Elysian resurfaced. Like just now.

He realised his mistake. 'I, um, I do beg your pardon. . . . I didn't mean. . . . After all, some of my best friends. . . .'

Ralph wasn't *really* cross, but had to say something. 'Let me tell you a story, Nigriff. About a little boy, about five years old, with his friends in a church Sunday School many years ago, being read a story about the creation of the world. About Adam, the very first person. Adam, made by God, standing alone in the Garden of Eden, naked as the day he was born . . . or the day he was *made*, I suppose. This first human is being given his list of jobs. Now, what do you think was top of the list?'

Nigriff pondered for a moment and then spotted the clue.

'I would imagine, sir, that it was to put some clothes on.'

Granny stifled a laugh, and even Ralph found himself smiling.

'No,' he said, 'that was later.' He paused. 'When the teacher told the children that Adam's *first* task was to look after the garden, that five-year old lad knew there could be no finer job. So that chap's been doing that all his life. And if I had my time again, I'd *still* do the same. So let's have none of this *only* a gardener.'

Elysians were known for their intelligence for good reason. 'I must tell you, sir, that this person, this ancestor, was known as the 'Illustrious'. I believe that he was called that *precisely* because he was a gardener. It is a title deserved by *all* in his profession.'

'Not many get called that,' said Ralph. 'Not even Percy Thrower himself. Anyway, what do these little words actually say?'

Nigriff read out the strange instructions about what should be done to Malplaquet – paths being made curved, rough places being softened. 'It's rather strange. And we thought it might mean more to *you*, as a gardener.'

'Well, there's not much I can say, to be honest,' he replied hesitantly. 'When the Lilliputians came here, that's exactly what was going on – lots of filling in, flattening slopes, digging everywhere.'

'Perhaps Gellisleb was writing about what he saw,' said Granny. 'Maybe he found it interesting.'

'I'm sure he did,' said Ralph. 'Their new home was being knocked about. . . . Shh! What was that?' They listened carefully, hardly daring to move. It was the voice of a tour guide, approaching their hideout. They could hear her strident tones and sharp enunciation. Nigriff crawled back into the bag.

'Dido's cave, with its tufa-encrusted façade, has on its front the dedication 'Mater Amata, Vale,' meaning, 'Farewell,

Beloved Mother,' as a memorial to his mother, the Marchioness of Buckingham. You may know the old story about Dido and a cave, where she was – how shall I put it? – *entertained* by the hero, Aeneas. It still retains its reputation as a secret meeting place for lovers.'

At that exact moment an old lady burst out from the shelter, dragging an embarrassed gardener behind her, much to the surprise (and delight) of the party.

'Don't believe a word,' she exclaimed, as the two sat down in their getaway car. 'Think what you like,' she announced, 'but we're *just* good friends.'

Granny later admitted that she quite enjoyed the round of applause (and even the few cheers) as the pair drove off together up the track.

Jamie's father, who had always nursed blatant ambitions for his elder son to be an architect, was delighted at the gaps that kept appearing in his bookshelves, as numerous tomes on country houses and gardens found their way to his son's bedroom.

Jamie was doing his own research on Malplaquet, knowing he had to find out more, especially about the early eighteenth-century, when the Lilliputians arrived. He read of a Mr. Berkeley, who in 1734 had intended to stop briefly but had actually stayed for three days. He had said it was, *'enchanted ground, and not in people's power to leave when they please.'* Jamie thought 'enchanted' was an interesting word to use.

One Elizabeth Montague had written that, *'Malplaquet is the best idea of Paradise that can be.'* Jamie agreed with that. But it still wasn't what he was after.

Not surprisingly, the breakthrough came via the hand of Alexander Pope. It was an extract from a 1731 letter. *'If anything under Paradise could set me beyond all Earthly cogitations, Malplaquet might do it.'*

The word *Paradise* initially caught Jamie's eye, but after re-reading the line, he realised that Pope was saying that the gardens made him think of a perfect place not *in* this world, but *beyond* this world.

'That,' he thought, 'is *really* interesting.'

'Silence!' The Provincial Assembly in the Gothic Temple that night began with this time-honoured and courteous instruction from the Listener. The Provincial Representatives, squatting on the circular rug's green band in the lofty central room, gave their full attention to Swartet. She was in her usual position in the ring, standing behind the traditional pile of humans' books laid on their side.

By one of the windows stood Granny, who unusually had been asked to be present. Although Jamie was next to her, she wasn't feeling at all relaxed.

'The *timing* of this regular session is fortuitous,' announced Swartet, looking round at the alert faces, 'given that yesterday we witnessed – and indeed some of us took part in – an extraordinary day. A day of remarkable success. Unfortunately it has, however, prompted some important – even *disturbing* – questions.' Granny didn't like the way that the Listener glanced in her direction. 'Let us begin with the positives.'

After a brief silence Thorclan put up his hand. She nodded at him.

'Madam Listener; we've all been worried, especially in recent moons, about *security*. I believe we have a solution in SOS. They performed miracles yesterday.'

His words were met with several grunts of approval. Swartet spoke. 'General Thorclan, please convey in a letter to Yenech and Melanak our appreciation of their bravery – and our hope that the two of them will continue to work closely together.'

'I'm sure that won't be a problem,' said Thorclan, before muttering under his breath, 'but Gniptip won't like it.'

'I beg your pardon, General?'

Thorclan thought rapidly. 'I, er . . . don't think that Gniptip will . . . um, *lick* it.'

'*Lick* it?' queried Swartet.

'Yes,' agreed Thorclan. 'The envelope, for the letter. She won't lick it . . . not my PA anymore. . . . I'll do it myself. . . .'

'Thank you, General, for that generous – and sensible – offer,' replied the bemused Listener. 'Now, were there any other benefits from yesterday?'

Several PRs raised valid and encouraging points. Firstly,

SOS was composed of people from all four provinces – another indication of growing unity, of the new Empire.

Similarly, the weather conditions were particularly favourable yet again – especially that sudden storm which had blown up.

And the animal and bird population, notably the swans, was as helpful as ever.

The two final points for reassurance, for celebration even, were the discomfort of a possible enemy (who had so wonderfully entertained the crowds), and the likely fact that not a single Lilliputian had been seen.

In spite of all this good news, the Listener nevertheless looked pensive. 'There are *issues*,' she said coldly, 'to be discussed. But first I have asked the respected lady on my right to clarify some points. Madam, do take a seat.' She motioned Granny towards a nearby footstool.

'Can you give me a hand down, Jamie?' the old lady whispered. 'It's a bit low with my joints.'

Jamie held her arm as she lowered herself with a groan and a sharp intake of breath, tucking her legs to one side with difficulty. Jamie stepped back.

'Sorry to be awkward,' she said. 'How can I help?'

She sounded apprehensive, and Jamie knew why. Neither of them had ever forgotten how the Assembly had turned on Nigriff last summer. Some of those PRs were still there. You couldn't predict their attitudes; sometimes they took the opposite point of view, or asked absurd questions, almost for the sake of it. Perhaps that was their job.

'For many moons,' intoned the Listener, 'you have been not only our protector but also our comforter. Watched over us. Kept us safe through dangerous winters. Fed and clothed us. Cared for our children. Which is why you have our full confidence.'

Jamie didn't like that last bit. 'This isn't good,' he thought. 'That's what football club chairmen say before they sack their manager.'

Swartet continued. 'Nevertheless . . . following yesterday's events, a few of us cannot place their *entire* trust in you.' Granny, looking confused, twisted round to see Jamie, who was biting his bottom lip. Swartet finished her preamble. 'Once this *little* matter has been cleared up, I am sure we can continue as before.'

'I . . . I'm . . . I'm sorry, I don't understand. . . .' Granny was visibly shaken. Jamie was getting more tense; this was no way to treat this dear person who had dedicated most of her life to them. He wanted to shout out and tell them to stop.

The Listener took a deep breath. 'My apologies; this is not easy for any of us. Let me explain. Yesterday saw the celebration of a *story* about Lilliputians living at Malplaquet. Many of us, probably the majority, had no *idea* at all that this potentially *dangerous* book existed. And so I am sure you will understand when I say that we need to know how it came to be written. I am honour bound to inform you of alarming rumours that *you* yourself were directly involved in its creation. It would be helpful if you could provide sufficient evidence to *refute* those presumably scurrilous rumours.'

There was silence. Granny was slowly wringing her hands together in her lap, trying to find the words to say, but it was all too much for her.

'This is *stupid*!' A voice rang out, a loud voice, loud enough to make some windows rattle. Some Representatives put their hands over their ears and winced. Jamie couldn't stop himself shouting. 'This is ridiculous! You've got it completely *wrong*!'

'Young man, you have forgotten *where* you are, and who *you* are,' came the rebuke from Swartet. 'This is a Provincial Assembly; the central chamber of our self-government. *You* are an invited guest. You should show fitting respect to our ancient traditions and practices.'

'And *you* should show respect to aged *people*, especially *her*,' blurted out Jamie. He felt a hand on his shoulder. Granny had struggled to her feet. 'It's alright, Jamie. It's not their fault. Leave it to me. I'll explain.'

Jamie sat down on the floor, shaking his head, blinking back tears.

Granny composed herself and began her address as calmly as she could.

'I was trying to *help*,' Granny began. 'After the Great Divergence, when you all got scattered round the grounds – and the mansion became a school – I was worried that a few tales might start about little people living here, that crowds of visitors would turn up. So I thought it best if you became . . . well, became a *story* instead.'

'Are we to assume then,' asked the Listener, a distinct air of disbelief in her voice, 'that *you* told this Mr White all about us?' There was absolute silence as they awaited the answer. All eyes were on her.

'No,' she declared boldly. 'Not *all* about you. I gave him some *ideas*. *Ideas*, not information. *Ideas*, not facts. *He* wrote the story, and he did it *without* my help.'

Jamie thought, not for the first time, what an impressive woman she was. He felt slightly relieved, although he was still angry that they were putting her through this. Who did they think they were? Had they no concept of their size? He wished that Nigriff was still a Representative; he would have come to Granny's defence.

One PR (Humelish, Grecian) put up a hand. Swartet nodded. He cleared his throat and adjusted his collar.

'I am *partly* reassured, Madam, but I still partly *confused*. You claim you gave this Mr White – and I quote – 'ideas, not facts.' Hmm.' He looked at his audience. Jamie suddenly remembered, to his horror, that Humelish came from a long line of barristers. This man meant business. He was playing with her, practising his skills. 'Let us be clear about precisely *two* things. Number one; the basic *fact* that you *did* tell him was that tiny people live at Malplaquet. This is not an idea, not a theory, but simply, in all its stark and hard detail – what can only be described as a *fact*.'

Granny was blushing deeply, looking unsteady on her feet. Jamie could hardly believe the cold arrogance of the Representative, despite his skilful use of language and logic.

'Let us consider a second feature of your explanation. There are undoubtedly many *ideas* in this book that are simply just that. *Ideas* – not facts. That *is* helpful to you. Unfortunately, Madam, you and your human companions have spent the past year trying to convince us that some of these 'ideas' are indeed *facts*. Let me remind you of these 'ideas' – or, as *you* say – these *facts*. That we are all Lilliputians. That we are descended from a group kidnapped from our island. That the villain was a Captain Biddle. That his descendant has bought a house in the local village.' He paused for effect. 'So *what* are they? Four *ideas*? Or four *facts*?

Madam, can I ask you, with the greatest of respect, to give us a simple answer to that question?'

And of course she couldn't. Granny was trapped, and she knew it. She took out her handkerchief and dabbed at her eyes, sobbing. 'I'm sorry . . . wanted to help . . . a mess . . . I was only a girl. . . .'

Jamie walked over and put his arm round her shoulders. He glowered at the PRs, some of whom looked guiltily away. This wasn't what they had expected.

The Listener spoke up. She also seemed surprised by events. 'Madam,' she declared. 'I am sure your *motives* in your youth were right, even if the *results* of your actions were unfortunate. Despite this, we have nevertheless lived here in peace and relative safety.' ('Because she's been looking after you all,' thought Jamie.)

'I would suggest that you take your leave to console yourself. We will discuss how to best handle the current situation – and its potential consequences.'

Granny needed no encouragement. She shuffled off towards the door, Jamie supporting her under one arm There was a definite mood of some sympathy in the room, but he didn't notice it, and he stared at everyone on the way out.

Just before they left, they both heard the next question from a PR. 'Madam Listener, now we are clearly no longer safe at Malplaquet, should we discuss the idea of finding more *suitable* accommodation? Somewhere more *secure*?'

Once outside, Jamie swung the heavy door back behind him as hard as he could. It slammed shut with a satisfying thud.

He hoped that it would give the little characters a throbbing headache.

It was the least that they deserved.

Jedekiah Biddle, a cardboard box under his arm, angrily flung open the door that used to be marked *Study* but was now *Captain's Cabin*. He slammed it shut behind him, rattling the oil lamps hanging from the ceiling. He gazed around, at the netting, the charts covering walls and bookcases, the old sailing artefacts. This was where he could feel at home – where they could *both* feel at home. For the moment, however, the scene did little to lighten his mood.

It had been a seriously bad day.

For the last hour, he had been forced to chair a meeting and listen to the fawning of his incompetent team, who were more deferential than ever, telling him what a 'brilliant' and 'inspirational' event the T. H. White day had been.

Biddle knew differently. It had been a disaster. And then he felt the box; today's final insult. A gift from his team. A gift of dolls. To show their 'appreciation'. From the WI stall in town.

His workers had given *dolls* to Jedekiah Biddle.

The man who was on the verge of acquiring thousands of actual living creatures.

The man who had, not long ago, handed a *real* one over to a young boy to give to a crazy old woman.

The man who was now hurling the box with its pathetic contents back across his cabin in violent frustration.

The box thudded into the door, spilling the toys out. He stared at the lifeless bodies, some with their limbs now bent back or broken off. That made him feel better.

He approached the cupboard doors, and reverently swung them back. Inside, preserved from all decay and dissolution, was the precious head. Scarred, discoloured, lightly misshapen, Biddle knew it was a real person – not like those wooden things on the floor. Biddle stared at it, drawing energy from its forceful presence. He shut his eyes, savouring the inspiration.

His mind was becoming clearer. Two things were necessary.

First, the restoration of Malplaquet had to continue as quickly as possible. If Snallard *was* right – and somehow the pathetic creature seemed to know something – then the Temples had to be repaired. And not just those, but the *whole* thing, Malplaquet in its entirety – old pathways, original planting, the ha-ha, the entrance-gates. *Everything. All* of it restored.

The second conclusion was galling. He had to accept that he still couldn't really see any Lilliputians – apart from Snallard. Which left only one option.

Reassured, Biddle gently closed the doors on his ancestor, and turned to admire himself in his old mirror, with its mottled glass and stained frame.

What he saw made him peer more closely at the dull reflection.

And then recoil in shock.

With all the demands of the last few days, Jedekiah hadn't paid much attention to his personal appearance, and to his horror he saw what a mess his face was in.

He knew he had nicked himself shaving a couple of times, and there was that scar he'd noticed yesterday, but where had all those *other* marks come from? He fingered his chin and cheeks cautiously, counting at least six separate lines and long scratches. Near his right eye was an area of discolouration, like a bruise, and in front of his left ear some dry and yellowing skin was starting to peel.

'Damn this weather,' he muttered. He grimaced to get a better view of his tightening skin, and was stunned to see two of his lower teeth beginning to blacken just above the gums. That had to be the fault of the local dentist he'd tried. He'd only gone there to be part of village life. Bad decision. Time to check in with his usual specialist. And find some decent cooks. Clearly the present ones were providing rubbish.

Satisfied with these explanations, Jedekiah strode to the door, kicking the dolls out of the way.

Bad days like this only made him more determined.

He had work to do.

6. A Bunch of Fairies

'It's so unfair,' said Vicky bitterly, looking round the table at the others, especially Granny who was still upset. 'It makes me *so* cross, it really does. Sorry, Nigriff, nothing personal, but some people have such *tiny* minds.'

'I must agree, Miss Vicky,' declared Nigriff. 'It is hard to live amongst those with a limited mental capacity. However, the *quantity* of brain cells matters less than their *quality*. I myself, for example. . . .'

'The fact is, the Assembly is *right*,' sniffed Granny. 'And last summer I said the same thing to you all, but you didn't believe me. It *is* all my fault. It was bound to end like this.' She sighed and shook her head, and hardly noticed when Ralph gently squeezed her hand.

'Maria,' he said, 'you *can't* talk like this. They just don't know the whole picture, that Biddle really *is* after them – and the new Empire's so close.'

'*Is it?*' she snapped back, much to their astonishment. 'Are you sure of it? Because *I'm* not any more.'

There was an embarrassed silence. The prophesied new Empire of Lilliput was the central part of their hopes, the reason for their actions. Yet the very person who had first understood the promises in Pope's poem was now rejecting the whole thing.

'Granny,' said Jamie, searching for a response, 'You *explained* it; said I was *the* person to make it happen, the *Guide*.' He was upset.

Tears were filling up in her eyes. 'I'm sorry, Jamie.' She was now hating herself for encouraging false hopes in this young boy. 'Looks like I was wrong about that as well. It was an *idea*. Not a *fact*. Sorry.' She slowly got to her feet and shuffled off upstairs to her room, closing her bedroom door softly behind her.

The sombre atmosphere was broken by Nigriff. '*I* think she was wrong.'

Jamie turned on him. 'That's rubbish, Nigriff, you agreed. . . .'

'Master Jamie, *you* misunderstand me. I mean she was wrong about being wrong. In other words, she was right.'

'About what?' asked Ralph, making sure *he* understood.

'About Jamie. Being the Guide.' replied Nigriff. 'And the Empire *is* becoming real, I can feel it in my bones – and I have found it in my research.'

'Found it in your research?' asked Vicky. 'How come?'

'It's my family tree. A few points are to be clarified . . . it's hard with a tiny mind,' he said smiling, 'but I have found Gothep. He *was* my first ancestor here, as I had thought.'

'Gothep, the *Illustrious*, right?' asked Jamie, smiling.

'Indeed, sir,' explained Nigriff. 'And I have, in my possession, his ideas for transforming these gardens.'

'Hang on, Nigriff,' burst in Vicky, just before Jamie. 'You're not *seriously* claiming that an ancestor of yours changed this place? Even if *illustrious*, he was still only six inches tall.' Then she had a bizarre thought. 'Wasn't he?'

'I have no indication of his specific height,' said Nigriff, 'but one can assume that he was of normal Lilliputian dimensions.'

'So exactly what *are* you claiming, Nigriff?' said Jamie.

'Nothing,' said the archivist. 'I am presenting evidence. We must see where it leads.'

'At the moment, it leads up the garden path,' said Ralph. 'It doesn't make any sense to me at all. Seems like a perfect mess.'

That last phrase, 'perfect mess', clicked Jamie's mind into gear. 'Oh, yeah, there's *my* research as well.'

'*Yours*, master Jamie?' enquired Nigriff.

'Well, nothing like yours, Nigriff, just some stuff I've found about Malplaquet being perfect, like a paradise.'

'Granny wouldn't call it that at the moment,' said Vicky.

'I hope she dozes off,' said Ralph. 'A nap would do her good.'

'I've got these notes,' continued Jamie, reading from a sheet of paper. 'Mr Berkely arrived from Rousham, wherever that is.'

'Know it well,' said Ralph. 'Small but charming.' He casually nodded at Nigriff, who smiled warmly back, pleased at the apparent compliment.

'He was only going to stop for a bit,' continued Jamie, 'but said he couldn't leave because it was '*enchanted ground*' here.'

'Sounds like an excuse for overstaying his welcome,' said Vicky. 'It's not great though, is it. 'Sorry, I wanted to go but your garden wouldn't let me.' '

'The word *enchanted* shows that even then it was mysterious,' said Nigriff.

'And Alexander Pope wrote loads,' said Jamie. 'Especially this; *if anything under Paradise could set me beyond all Earthly cogitations, Malplaquet might do it.*'

'Earthy cogitations?' said Ralph. 'Is that those new organic potatoes?'

'Earth*ly*,' corrected Vicky, pleased at her English GCSE proving useful. 'He's saying the gardens made him think about another world. Hmm. that's *very* interesting. . . .'

'Makes me even *more* proud to be a gardener,' said Ralph.

'So, to sum up,' said Vicky. 'Nigriff thinks that Gothep. . . .'

'The *Illustrious*,' added Nigriff.

'. . . somehow made a big difference to this garden,' said Vicky. 'And some writers, just like the painters did, said it was like heaven. But it's hardly *heavenly* at the moment. To be honest, it's pretty grim.'

Nobody could argue with that odd contrast. 'Maybe,' offered Jamie, 'it's like Nigriff often says – Restoration and Destruction. Things getting better *and* worse.'

'That's another thing,' said Vicky. 'I've been thinking, and I don't want to make a bad day worse, but we *should* consider every possibility . . . is there a chance that those words mean that Malplaquet gets *restored* and the Lilliputians get *destroyed*? Sorry, but. . . .' Her voice trailed away.

There was no answer from anyone. It was too terrible to contemplate, and Vicky regretted saying it all.

It *had* made a bad day worse.

'Oi, Tinkerbell! I want a word!' The grunted syllables rang out across the forecourt of the mansion. Jamie knew it would be a mistake to turn around, but he also knew it would be a mistake not to. You didn't ignore Will Dunnett. He was in the Fifth Form and about to leave – to 'earn some dosh,' as he put it. Jamie turned slowly, and saw Dunnett, with a couple of his mates, chewing gum and looking menacing.

He was also, much to Jamie's relief, looking not at him but at someone else.

At John Biddle, who had obediently halted. Will Dunnett was still shouting, even though John was near enough to touch, and Jamie heard everything.

'If I say I don't *believe* in you, will *you* drop dead? *Please*?' Will Dunnett laughed at his own wit, and turned to share the joke with his cronies, who were giggling and pretending to collapse.

John's clear tones rang out across the area. 'I do think that's uncalled for and uncharitable. I don't like being teased about serious matters.'

This response confused Will Dunnett. Firstly, the boy didn't seem scared. Secondly, he had used some long words. And finally, the little kid was still standing there, as if he wanted to have a conversation. Which was precisely the case.

'I assume that you are referring to my interest in the possible existence of fairies.' John saw that the three boys had their mouths stuck open. He thought this was very rude, but he ignored it. 'Little people form a significant part in the stories of many cultures – not just fairies, but leprechauns, goblins, elves, and dwarves to name just a few. It therefore seems an open question whether such people exist or not.'

Jamie knew that John was in trouble. But John didn't. 'No doubt you will say,' he continued, 'that you don't believe in them because you've never seen one. Well, you believe in *many* things without seeing them. Like in the person stood behind you.'

Will Dunnett lowered his face inches away from John's, and sneered, 'Who is it, your *fairy godmother*?' In the circumstances (especially from him), that was quite clever, but he literally jumped as he felt the hand on his shoulder.

'Ah, Dunnett again!' said the prefect. (This was one of his favourite lines). 'Is he being a pain, Biddle?'

'No,' said John, 'we were just having a nice chat about fairies.'

The prefect was delighted with this new Dunnett story to spread around, and John continued happily and safely on his way.

'Have you heard how Granny was treated at the Assembly?' asked Yenech, walking with Melanak through the Grecian valley bushes. He had suggested these regular meetings to discuss their strategy and long-term objectives as the two leaders.

'If I'd been there,' she replied, 'I would have said something.'

'Me too,' said Yenech. 'I can't believe that no-one spoke up for her. Y'know, I'm just not sure who you can *trust* nowadays; I'm just glad the two of *us*. . . .'

Melanak had grabbed his hand. 'Yenech,' she said, 'we need to talk. Get a few things sorted out.'

This was a surprise. He hadn't expected things to move so quickly. 'Well, er, yes . . . of course. What things?'

She smiled at him. 'It's a relationship – a *special* relationship.'

Yenech smiled back. The sun was shining; it was going to be a good day.

'It's about Snallard. I should have told you before.'

The sun had suddenly gone behind a cloud; the air was cooler. Yenech stopped, trying to cope with this shattering news. He'd realised Snallard was a *potential* rival; Melanak had always admired bravery and courage, for that had drawn her to Yenech in the first place.

He stumbled out a gracious response. 'That's okay. . . . He's got lots of good qualities. . . . I can't blame you, I mean. . . .'

Melanak laughed, which didn't help. Then she took his other hand, which did.

'No, you *crumpet*, it's not like that, it's the opposite!' She leaned her head back and laughed again, and Yenech watched her hair blowing and her eyes sparkling.

'The opposite?' said Yenech. 'You want to get rid of him?'

'Not exactly. But he needs watching. By both of us.'

Yenech was confused. 'Why?'

Melanak looked around to make sure they were alone. 'I'm not *totally* certain, but I've a hunch he's not working with *us*.'

'What? Why do you say that?'

'When we found him in that box. Didn't trust his story in the slightest. Nor did Granny – that's why she suggested he joined our team.'

'Hang on,' said Yenech, trying to cope with this next twist. 'You're saying you both realised he's . . . working for Biddle?' She nodded. '. . . but you put him in SOS? There's no *way* he's staying.' He raised his voice. 'The little traitor, wait till. . . .'

'Shh!' urged Melanak. 'If we're right – and I'm pretty sure we are – it's better that way. Remember that old saying – keep your friends close, and your enemies closer?'

Before Yenech could reply, a sudden noise not far away made them both turn round. Through the tangled mass of branches they could just see a face at ground level. It was John Biddle, reaching in and pushing aside the stalks and dusty leaves. 'Time to go,' whispered Melanak, and pulled Yenech deeper into the undergrowth. Yenech thought that if *this* was what keeping her friends close meant, it was absolutely fine by him.

'Yeh, I know I said I would,' whispered Charlie into his mobile, 'but it's really dark out there.' Crouched behind the bed in Granny's spare room, he was speaking to John Biddle, and he wasn't in the best of moods. Somehow John had persuaded him into one last attempt to find some fairies, and staying overnight at Granny's was part of the plan.

During the course of that Saturday, in the area below the Temple of Friendship, there had been a 'Festival of the Countryside.' An enormous canvas marquee, surrounded by freshly-painted farming equipment, had shown off all sorts of rural crafts and handiwork. Its tables had groaned under the weight of prize fruit, vegetables and flowers, interspersed with displays of home-made pickles, local pottery, wooden toys and needlework. Granny herself had exhibited some superb dolls' clothes, inevitably receiving the usual compliments.

The marquee was now closed for the night.

John had insisted that the fairies would be there during the hours of darkness. 'It's fairy *heaven*,' he'd said. 'Everything they want and need under one roof.' Charlie had told John that, to be honest, he was fed up of the whole thing, but he'd give it one more go.

'I've got my torch,' continued Charlie. 'I'll creep out when she's asleep. Jamie says she goes to bed early. . . . It's alright, she can't hear me, I'm behind the bed. I'll tell you tomorrow.' He finished, knowing the trip would be an utter waste of time.

Granny's cottage, like many old houses, wasn't soundproof. It had gaps between floorboards, ill-fitting doors, and badly-designed chimney flues that carried voices to anyone seated downstairs. Like Granny.

She soon shouted a cheery, 'Just giving the ducks their supper, Charlie!' and wandered outside. Making contact with Wesel was easy, and squirrels were sent off to find as many of SOS as they could. Job done, she ambled back, said 'Sleep tight' to Charlie, settled down in her own bed and quickly drifted off to sleep.

She was confident that the little people would soon put an end to Charlie's curiosity.

The night was clear and dry, so Charlie should have felt at ease, but in the gloom, places and shadows were less familiar, and the sounds of the night were also unusual. Even as he passed through the entrance-gates, the old bell had clanged a few times, no doubt disturbed by a night-time breeze, and he thought he'd seen a tall figure in the woods, wearing a large crown (or a helmet?), keeping pace with him. He knew it had to be only the outlines of the tree-trunks; a real person would have crackled sticks and leaves underfoot, but around him all was silent.

His torch was lighting up the way ahead, its bright funnel a contrast to the shades around him, but the sudden and sharp black outlines of a disc harrow and an old-fashioned reaper, scything into the night sky, made Charlie halt and take a deep breath. As their vicious and grim shapes of this farm equipment hovered above him, he stepped nervously forward, watching for any movement they might make. They stayed absolutely dead still.

A few metres away stood the looming grey mass of the cavernous tent, its shrouds hanging heavy and lifeless. Using his torch to pick out the guy-ropes and pegs hammered into the ground, Charlie bent down and hauled up the cold and rough canvas. He wriggled underneath, grasping his torch firmly, then looked straight into a pair of dark bulbous eyes. He hardly dared move or even breathe.

The large hedgehog, only a few centimetres away, didn't move a muscle either. Charlie knew that if he made any sudden movement, it might take fright and attack him, and those spines could do some serious damage to his face. He twisted his hand to adjust his torch and noticed, to his horror, that a heavy stick had been driven through the back of this animal, pinning it to the ground. It had been savagely skewered and was well and truly dead.

Charlie looked up to the top of the murder-weapon, and noticed the handle. The handle that you held onto whilst you cleaned your muddy shoes on the brush below. . . . The hedgehog-*shaped* brush. . . .

Charlie tried to laugh quietly, but it came out as a whimper, which surprised him. He squirmed fully in and stood up inside the vast room, and played the torch around, assuming it would light the place up. But it only cast strange dull shadows, lines and angles that danced their way across the roof and into corners.

He was regretting coming here.

He began to walk along the row of tables, feeling uneasy from the almost total silence, an unsettling deadness, broken only by the rhythmic ticking from the far display of clocks.

An orange suddenly rolled off a bowl of fruit, ran along the table and dropped to the floor with a dull thud. It surprised Charlie, all by himself in the dark, and he felt even more nervous, but happily he then saw something familiar – Granny's small dresses and jackets, neatly folded. And in their midst, lying side by side, were three of her dolls. Their unseeing and hard eyes stared blankly upwards, their painted mouths fixed in a grin.

Charlie was relieved to see them. He no longer felt so alone. He walked on to the next display, some jams and chutneys, labelled with spidery writing. He felt slightly calmer; his eyes had adjusted to the light, and he had got used to the almost funereal atmosphere.

Unfortunately something else now dropped off from another table, directly behind him. Turning round, he shone his torch down. Two of the dolls were lying there, legs bent awkwardly underneath them. He shifted the beam upwards and his hands began to shake as he saw the other doll, the one with a puffed-out red dress and black shoes.

The one with pigtails and glasses. Seated bolt upright.

With an arm stuck up at a right angle, as if it was waving, or greeting him.

Charlie now realised two things.

First, his hair *could* stand on end.

Second, that fairies really *did* exist.

Charlie was shaken but also confused. He'd assumed that if there were such things as fairies, they'd sit around in a cosy group making clothes from cobwebs and fluffy dandelion heads. This one was different. It looked weird. Almost deranged.

So he began to run.

Incredibly, he thought he spotted some soft toys running nearby, keeping up with him – first a squirrel, then a baby rabbit, and finally a fat mouse. He bumped into the sweet stall, and read 'GO AWAY' picked out in liquorice sticks on its table-top. A music-box sprang open to play its jaunty tune, and the fading light of his torch briefly picked out a tiny figure twirling round to one side. Then the far end of the tent was suddenly lit up, as candles spluttered into life inside several gap-toothed pumpkin heads.

Charlie was running fast, desperate to get away, and he charged straight into the group of scarecrows, standing crazily together. One of them deliberately fell towards him, its arms outstretched in welcome.

Charlie thrashed about, and became caught up in yards of material, balls of wool unravelling, and scarves and gloves flapping in his face. He hardly noticed the volley of asparagus tips that hurtled across from the vegetable stall, but he certainly felt the walking-stick that grabbed at his ankle as he scuttled under the canvas. . . .

Charlie was very quiet at breakfast next morning. Granny tried to talk to him.

'You didn't sleep well, did you?' she said. 'I heard you tossing and turning all night. Nightmares, was it?'

'Probably,' mumbled Charlie. 'But I'm growing out of them.'

'That's good,' said Granny. 'Those things can be really nasty.'

'Mr Newbold to see you, sir, as requested.' Not looking up, Jedekiah Biddle gave a curt nod at his secretary and prepared himself; this was not going to be pleasant. The door to his cabin opened slowly, and a hesitant figure appeared.

Jedekiah took charge. 'Julius, wonderful to see you. Thank you for coming – and for being on time.'

These kind words of welcome made Newbold even more fearful. What the devil was the scheming crook up to, he wondered – and what on earth had happened to his face? Newbold averted his eyes, and cautiously took the proffered hand of friendship. A seat by the desk was pulled forwards and Julius sat down. He looked at all the old sailing paraphernalia, then saw that Biddle was writing out a cheque.

'I confess that I left you slightly short last time,' said Jedekiah, signing with a flourish and sliding the paper across the polished surface. 'This should *more* than compensate.' Julius stared at the number followed by all the noughts. He didn't reply. Nor pick up the cheque.

'I can understand your reticence,' continued Jedekiah smoothly. 'I can't deny we've had our little disagreements. But that's – how should I put it? – water under the bridge. Or under a *cascade*?' He was trying to lighten the atmosphere, but Julius didn't wish to be reminded of his past humiliations. He still said nothing, but sat looking down and holding his hands tightly together.

'The truth is,' said Jedekiah, 'that I haven't appreciated your *special* qualities.'

Julius knew exactly what he meant. It was his eyes. The eyes that could see Lilliputians. 'So,' he thought, 'Biddle *still* can't see them.' He looked at his patron – and regretted doing so. Apart from the extensive scarring, the eyes were in a really bad way. They had always been empty and cold, but now they were yellowing and bloodshot. One seemed to have a vein creeping across one corner. 'Alcohol,' thought Julius, 'or something worse.'

Jedekiah continued the one-sided conversation, hating the way Newbold was looking at him. 'I've a few little jobs for you. You'll have a team of Trust workers. The restoration *must* be finished. For a Grand Opening – and it's only weeks away.'

Julius, fully aware of Biddle's dependence on him, spoke at last. 'But some of those people – the Volunteers – don't like me. They won't want me around.'

'They won't want an argument with the Property Manager,' replied Biddle. 'There will be no problems.'

Julius considered the offer, and leaned forward to grasp the cheque. Jedekiah swiftly put his own hand on top, held Julius' down, and also leaned across the desk.

'There's another little thing you can do for me,' he whispered, staring straight at Newbold, who was trying not to look at his eyes. 'I want you to find me a person. When the time is right. Soon.'

Julius felt the grip relax slightly, and eased away his hand (with the cheque). He mumbled something in reply, and got up to leave. He'd nearly made it to the door when he heard, 'The first job, Julius, is to finish the wall. The ha-ha. We're behind schedule.' Newbold halted briefly and then left, glad to escape the grim surroundings.

Jedekiah sat back, relieved it was over. He hated having to use such people, but to *depend* upon them was humiliating. Nevertheless, he thought, it will soon be different.

He opened a drawer, took hold of the bottle and crystal tumbler, and poured himself a large rum. Holding it up, he gazed at the golden liquid for a few seconds before nodding his head in deference to his ancestor's shrine. He felt energised and invincible.

'Apparently the look on his face was priceless,' chuckled Granny, in her living-room with some friends. 'I shouldn't laugh, but I've never known anybody be scared of a hedgehog boot-scraper before!'

'Or an orange!' added Yenech.

'Scarecrows *can* be creepy in the dark,' said Thorclan.

'Perhaps they should be 'scareboys'!' said Granny, chuckling merrily. 'Oh dear, we shouldn't laugh, it's not funny really.'

'Yes, it is,' said Jamie. 'Serves him right for being so nosey.'

'Well, that's solved that problem,' suggested Granny. 'I'm sure he thinks it was all a bad dream. Anyway, he knows these characters aren't always as sweet as they look.' She paused, and the others knew exactly what she was thinking.

The door opening broke the pensive silence. It was Vicky, carrying Nigriff in her jacket pocket. 'Hi,' she said, with a distinct lack of enthusiasm.

'Morning, Vicky, do come in,' invited Granny. 'And hello to you too, Nigriff. What brings you both here?'

Vicky looked down at Nigriff to prompt him. Holding the top of the pocket, he cleared his throat and spoke steadily and deliberately, staring straight at her. 'On my person, Madam, I am carrying a sealed envelope addressed to your good self. It is from the senior members of the Provincial Assembly. I do not know its contents. I am under *strict* instructions to deliver it to you.'

With that, he reached down and held out the tiny oblong item.

7. Prizes and Rewards

Everyone looked at Granny, wondering how she was going to react. Her words came out quickly and sharply. 'There's no *way* that I'll read anything from that lot,' she declared, which surprised nobody. But then she added, 'Their writing is *far* too small. Even with my glasses on. Nigriff, would you do the honours?'

Nigriff nodded slowly, impressed at her readiness to learn her fate. He motioned to Vicky to place him on the table. 'Madam,' he began, with an air of solemnity, 'I fear that this message may be a *private* and personal matter. It may even, given the tenor of the last Assembly, contain unsettling, even *distressing*, news. Do you really wish this missive to be divulged to all those present?'

'You are not 'all those present,' Nigriff,' corrected Granny. 'You are my *friends*. And you should all hear whatever it says. Please do read it.'

Nigriff prised open the envelope, unfolded the paper and began. '*Dear lady, concerned as we are with the welfare of all those living at Malplaquet, it has been brought to our attention. . . .*'

'Smug bunch!' grunted Vicky. 'Who do they think they are?' Three small faces looked up. 'Sorry, but they're *so* full of themselves. . . . I mean, they're only. . . .'

'Vicky, dear, let's hear the rest of it,' interrupted Granny. 'I know you're upset, but that's just the way they are I'm afraid.'

Nigriff carried on. '. . . *brought to our attention,*' he repeated, '*that you have recently uncovered a human plot to reveal our existence.*'

Yenech and Melanak both clapped. Granny nodded graciously at them. Vicky shook her head in frustration at the pomposity of the letter. Jamie felt the same, but thought this opening was a good sign.

'*Thus in the light of those events, insofar as they give a presumably accurate indication of your character and wishes, it would be more reasonable. . . .*'

'Nigriff, get on with it,' moaned Vicky. 'This is *so* long-winded.'

Nigriff was shocked. 'Long-winded, Madam? I can assure you, that in my many years of experience of the considered deliberations of the Provincial Assembly, this necessary preamble is a model of brevity, precision, and succinctness.'

'That's a 'no',' said Yenech, looking at Vicky. 'I think.'

'What's the rest of it say, Nigriff?' asked Granny, now feeling fairly positive.

'. . . *more reasonable to concentrate upon your historic intentions rather than upon the unforeseen consequences. Thus, we are pleased to announce a resumption of our normal working relationship, and we look forward to further joint ventures.*' He quietly folded the letter in half.

'Very good of them to say so, I'm sure,' said Granny and stood up, brushing her apron, apparently untroubled. 'Right, now that's dealt with, who's for some refreshments? I've a batch of lemonade left.' She looked at the circle of faces.

'But Granny,' blurted Vicky, 'are you going to leave it at that?'

Before she could answer, Jamie spoke up. 'What choice have we got, Vicky? We all know they've been really unfair to her, but what else can we do?'

Nigriff joined in. 'I can only apologise for the attitude of my countrymen,' he said. Yenech and Melanak murmured their agreement. 'Nevertheless, Master Jamie is correct. There is no alternative but to continue with our task, regardless of whether we receive criticism or appreciation.'

Vicky found this hard, but shrugged her shoulders and looked sympathetically at the old lady. The tiny people meant the world to Granny. Being on friendly terms with them, however ungracious they were, was so important. 'It doesn't matter,' said Granny. 'It really doesn't.' She began to move towards her kitchen.

'I'll give you a hand,' Vicky said, and the pair left the room.

'This *task* you mentioned, Nigriff,' said Jamie. 'It would be a lot easier if we knew exactly what it is. . . . Okay, it's to defeat Biddle, but all we're doing is waiting for his next move and then spoiling it for him. And I'm meant to be the great Guide, but I've no idea how to help you lot.'

Nigriff thought for a few seconds. 'This may be a good moment to reflect on a few matters. Let us consider. Pope's poem links the arrival of the new Empire with the restoration of the garden temples.'

'But if we're *near* the restored ones,' added Yenech, 'we become more visible.'

'Though they do make us more similar to each other,' said Melanak, nudging him with the slightest of contacts. 'Closer. That's a *good* thing, right?'

Yenech nodded. 'That's what the New Empire means,' he said. 'Which is fine by me.'

Nigriff summed up. 'The restoration of the temples leads to the restoration of the Empire. The link is clear. Our enemy is playing right into our hands. Although he may need our help. . . .'

'Our *help*?' asked Jamie.

'The vast ha-ha, as a construction in the gardens, should *also* be regarded as a temple that needs to be restored. Unfortunately, given current progress, this is many weeks away for Biddle. Unless of course we come to his assistance.'

'Lemonade,' announced Granny, entering the room. 'And I'm glad to say that it's gone a bit flat, so we shouldn't have any more of those burps, Nigriff.'

'Madam,' said Nigriff. 'Your kindness, unlike Malplaquet, has no bounds.'

'Should I say, ha ha?' asked Granny. 'I just caught the end of what you were chatting about. Perhaps the ha-ha should be a *'joint venture,'* like the letter said.'

'I thought that meant an invite to Sunday lunch,' said Yenech. 'But I prefer casseroles, not joints. . . . What? What's so funny?' He didn't get an answer because of all the laughter, but he did get a nice hug from Melanak, so that was fine.

'I dunno whevver it'sh troo or nort,' slurred Snallard, leaning heavily on his fourth mug of a heavily-diluted (but still potent) Australian Shiraz. 'Orl ah'm sayin is wot I've hurrd.' He was offering his opinions to a group of fellow Palladians in his local, the 'Spotted Cow,' in the old kitchen basement of the Temple of Friendship. The wine had been unwittingly supplied by a group of fourth-form boys who had suddenly abandoned it one afternoon in the ha-ha. Snallard had developed a taste for it.

'I don't agree,' objected one companion, holding the more traditional Dandelion Cordial. 'She's been our protector for as long as any of us can remember.'

'She came to me with a lovely blanket when my little girl was born,' said another. 'Even though it was blowing a gale outside.'

'She made me a grand carrot and coriander soup when I was ill,' said a third. 'It was so delicious, I wanted to have a bath in it.'

'Yeh, f . . . f . . . fine.' replied Snallard. 'But . . . but *why*, eh? Ansurr me thaat.' His eyes were glazing over, and he was finding it hard to focus, or keep his drooping head up.

'Most of us think that she really cares for us,' replied one.

'Not . . . not . . . the Asseb. . . . the assum . . . the reps,' said Snallard, fighting to get the words out. 'Them knows . . . knows she told the Whiter white . . . that wit write . . . that Mashum man. . . .' He was staring blankly ahead, searching for the words in his scrambled brain. He took another long draught of wine. The audience silently rose and left.

It took Snallard a few minutes (after checking under the table and peering behind the curtains) before he realised that he was alone. He got unsteadily to his feet, gazed at the open doorway, which seemed to be swaying. He made a dash for it, and lurched forward, scarcely noticing the dull pain as his shoulder slammed into the doorpost.

And he was only dimly aware, as he staggered outside and

paused to take a deep gulp of fresh air, of a hard object smashing down across the back of his head and knocking him out.

'There's a . . . er . . . *gentleman* to see you, Mr Biddle. It's not an appointment, I'm afraid, but he says it's extremely urgent. Shall I show him in?'

Jedekiah, sat at his desk in his office at Home Farm, grumpily nodded. He was working on what would be the most brilliant occasion at Malplaquet since the 21st birthday celebrations of the Third Duke in Victoria's reign. For *that* event, reflected Biddle, the grounds were full of local farmers and villagers; for his event, the Grand Unveiling, people – *important* people – would come from all over Britain. The hand-written letter he was composing to Lord McMillan was a typical such invite.

With dismay, Biddle watched Newbold's slight frame insinuate its way into his room. What on earth could *he* possibly want? Biddle remembered to adjust his features into some sort of smile. He even considered shaking his hand, but Newbold was proudly carrying – holding firmly out in front of him – a large shoebox.

'We've had our differences, Mr Biddle,' he began, pleased with himself, 'but I'm glad to be back in your payment – I mean, working with you, sir. So I've brought you a present. But I doubt you'll be able to see what's in this box. You'll have to trust me.'

Biddle ignored that last instruction, but he was now intrigued by his arrival. Such positive hopes faded when the fool ostentatiously placed the gift on Lord M's letter, smearing the ink across the cream vellum.

Newbold lifted the lid. 'There you are, Mr Biddle; what do you reckon?' He expected his employer to say something like, 'I can't see anything, Julius,' or just possibly, 'It's a doll, Julius.' So he was surprised at the actual response.

'It's a Lilliputian. Asleep – or unconscious.'

Julius was shocked. 'You can *see* it?'

'I can not only *see* it, I *know* it. It's called Snallard. It's been like this before.'

Julius was dumbfounded. 'But I thought you *couldn't* see them?'

Biddle hated having to talk about his difficulties, especially with Newbold, but he had no choice. He aimed to keep it brief.

'I can see *this* one, but no others. Not yet.'

'But why can you see this one?'

Jedekiah paused. 'I don't have that answer.'

Newbold thought. 'So how do you know . . . what's his name? Snailhead?'

'Snall-ard,' pronounced Biddle irritably. Somehow, Newbold had in only a few seconds revealed Biddle's inabilities, his ignorance, and his poor communication skills. Time to prove who was the master. 'He works for me . . . but I may . . . *dispense* with him soon. Judging by the smell of alcohol, he's serving another master.'

'So you don't want him?' asked Newbold. 'You asked me to catch any of them, like last summer. . . .'

'Not *any* of them, Julius,' came the reply. The use of the first name was somehow both friendly and chilling. 'And certainly not *this* one. Tip him out where you found him, and without being seen. No-one must know he's working for me.'

He watched as Newbold replaced the lid. How long had this creep been back, not yet two days? And he's already spoiled one of his best plans. Was there no end to this man's stupidity? But there was some vital information to pass on. 'Things have changed since last year, Julius. I don't need *any* Lilliputians – I want *all* of them, though not quite yet. But a particular one to begin with. The key person.' He paused to emphasise the next sentence.

'His name's Nigriff.'

'It says here,' said Mr Thompson, reading *The Advertiser* at the table after supper, 'that Malplaquet School has its Founder's Day this coming Saturday. Prizegiving, Inter-House Sports Competition, and a picnic. Why didn't we know about this?'

Mrs Thompson looked blankly at him, and got up to fetch her diary from her drawer in the kitchen.

'You *did*,' their son insisted. 'I brought back a note last week.'

'That wouldn't,' said his mother, returning to the room, 'be the same as, 'I brought back a note which is still in my jacket pocket' by any chance?'

'Hang on,' said Jamie, excusing himself.

'I know what it is,' said Mr Thompson quietly. 'He doesn't want us to go because he hasn't got a prize. Or he's not in any Sports events.'

'Or he doesn't want a picnic with his parents,' said Mum. 'In front of his school friends.'

'Pity,' said Dad. 'I'd like to meet Floorclean and Midriff.'

'Sorry,' said a breathless Jamie, returning with a scrunched piece of paper that resembled a bad origami day. 'My fault.'

Mr Thompson unwrapped and scanned it. 'So,' he said, trying to make light of his son's academic failings, 'there isn't a '*Third Form English prize for Knowing More about Alexander Pope than Anybody Else in the Western Hemisphere*'?'

'No,' said Jamie. 'Should there be?'

'And I don't expect,' added Mum, not to be outdone, 'there's a '*Junior Design Prize for Imagination, Creativity and Commitment with Cardboard*'?'

Jamie thought it best to humour them. 'No, but I did win the PSHE prize.'

His parents were shocked and delighted. 'Wonderful!' they chorused. 'We knew you deserved something,' said Mum. 'What was that for – visiting Granny?'

'Not quite,' said Jamie. 'For '*Coping Heroically with a Challenging Domestic Environment*'.'

'Hmm,' said Dad. 'Okay, quits. So, are you okay about not getting a prize?'

'Yeh, fine, especially as I *did* get one.'

'Is this another of your wind-ups?' said Mum. 'You *honestly* got one?'

'Honestly,' he replied. Well, *half* of one. I'm sharing the Vis Ed Award with John Biddle.'

'Oh darling, that's brilliant,' exclaimed Mum, and rushed over to give him a hug. Jamie flinched and decided he really did deserve that PSHE prize.

'Well done, son,' said his father. 'So all that history I told you was useful?'

'Er, maybe . . . but Mr Merryman said it was mainly for my model. They're displaying it in the Marble Saloon on Saturday.'

'Well, that's just as good,' said Dad, putting a brave face on it. Mum thought that the months of a cardboard-strewn bedroom floor had been worth it after all. . . .

'But I don't know if I'm in the Sports,' said Jamie. 'The House Prefects are sorting out who's doing what.'

'Well, you can't be good at everything,' said Mr Thompson. 'and it's fun watching others anyway. I don't suppose that . . . er . . . Floorclean and Midriff are in it?'

'I don't *think* they will be,' said Jamie, 'but you never know. . . . There's always a *few* surprises.'

'I have in my hand a piece of paper,' announced General Thorclan to the members of SOS, seated in a semi-circle. 'It is signed by Swartet herself, to thank us for preserving our peaceful lives here.' He looked at his squad with pride, particularly pleased to see Gniptip back in his office. There was so much filing to be done, and several buttons on his Mess Dress were coming loose. And his trousers needed letting-out again. Maybe the material was shrinking. Or had he put it on the wrong wash?

'Exactly what does it say, General?' Yenech's question interrupted his train of thought.

Thorclan squinted at it. The light didn't seem to be good. 'It says, *Dear General, please pass on to your team my strangest coagulations for their brewery and corsage.* Bit odd. Perhaps it's in code.'

Gniptip was already at his elbow, ushering him gently to one side. 'Allow me, General,' she said. 'It's an emotional moment for you.' Thorclan was happy to do as he was told, and Gniptip conveyed the Assembly's strong congratulations for their bravery and courage in frightening Charlie so successfully in the marquee.

Thorclan stood up to resume the briefing. 'Even though I myself have risen to the exalted heights of Glob, Scab and Plop,' he said, underlining his military status, 'I'm delighted that you're all matching my own high standards. Tomorrow, however, we will be raising the bar – and some of you will be for the high jump.'

Yenech got it. 'This is the School Sports Competition, General, isn't it?'

'Of course, Yenech, like I've said, always keep the message simple. This is your next mission. Nigriff and I, in consultation with the bigger people, have decided that this annual gathering could be a useful target for the disruption and confusion of the enemy.'

Melanak put her hand up. 'But it's a *school* event, not one of Biddle's.'

Hyroc leaned across. 'All the same thing,' he said. 'It's no good getting rid of the Trust visitors if Malplaquet's still full of schoolkids and parents. They've *all* got to go.'

'So this year,' added Thorclan, 'we're going to be *really* offensive.'

'*On* the offensive,' corrected Gniptip.

Thorclan pondered. 'Can we do both?'

Yenech was struggling with a few doubts. 'Another mission is all very well – and I do love going places – but isn't this *really* dangerous? Broad daylight, in the open, the place crawling with visitors. . . . And with *us*, I suppose.'

'*If* I understand Nigriff,' offered Thorclan, 'and *if* Nigriff is right (both big 'ifs,' thought Snallard), we shouldn't be nervous. The visitors are *parents* – they're hardly ever here, so they're not aware of the garden's hidden beauties. Like us.'

'I like being a hidden beauty,' whispered Melanak to Yenech.

'I wouldn't say *hidden*,' came the smooth reply.

'Anyway,' said Thorclan, 'the sports track isn't near a temple, so you're even *less* likely to be seen. Now, is everyone clear about the primary school objective?'

Hyroc was confused. 'Isn't Malplaquet a *secondary* school? What's this primary one?'

Gniptip cleared up that little difficulty, and Thorclan drew the meeting to a close, telling them to plan their tactics. 'Oh, yes,' he concluded. 'Almost forgot. Nigriff wants us to do lots of work on the ha-ha. It's got to be finished, and fast. He says it's important.'

Snallard's ears pricked up. 'Does he?' he thought. 'That's interesting. Very interesting indeed.'

'It's a *cracking* day for your Sports, Jamie. Just a pity you're not in anything.' Jamie murmured a non-committal reply; he genuinely didn't mind that much. He was with his parents on the woodland path to the sports area – a large elliptical clearing, almost surrounded by trees. As they reached the top of the slope, they came across Granny, seated in her buggy with Ralph.

'Good morning, Granny,' said Mum breezily. 'And you must be . . . um . . . the gentleman friend? Ralph, isn't it? Jamie's told me lots about you.'

Ralph touched his forehead, and lifted himself slightly out of his seat. 'That's right, Mrs Thompson. Ralph it is. I'm pleased to make your acquaintance. Jamie's told me a lot about you as well.'

'I'm sure he has,' she replied, not at all sure about what Jamie had said but charmed by the display of manners.

'I didn't know you were a sports fan, Granny,' said Mr Thompson.

'I'm not really,' she agreed, 'but I like being in the fresh air with little – I mean, *young* – people when they're enjoying themselves. Better than being inside on a day like this.'

'Of course,' he said. 'And you've got your sewing with you?' he added, glancing at her case on the rear of the buggy.

'Always with me,' said Granny. 'Never go anywhere without it.'

Jamie had been looking around during the conversation. He knew Thorclan and Nigriff planned to deploy SOS for maximum disruption. 'SOS,' Nigriff had told Jamie, 'normally means *Special Operations Squad*. But today it can stand for *Spoil Our Sports*.'

'And *Silly Old Sausage*,' Thorclan had added. 'Just thought I'd mention it.'

Until now far all had been predictable; boys in running shorts and white vests, teachers looking important with clipboards, hurdles being carried out from a hut, parents greeting each other with handshakes or polite kisses, dogs scampering around in excitement. Then Jamie spotted SOS.

At the far end of the site, beyond the running-track in the shadows of the bushes, he could make out some tiny people. It was an aerobics class, led by one figure, who was leaping up, bending over, lunging forward, arms stretching. 'If they're *lucky*,' thought Jamie, 'that's Melanak. If they're *unlucky*, that's Vingal.'

Suddenly there was a momentary flash of light from beyond the trees to his left, making him squint in that direction. A few seconds later there was another, then another. This was feeling awfully familiar. . . .

From another direction, way off to his right, came more bursts – and the ground beneath his feet had a faint dull and rhythmic thumping. Jamie moved to give himself a better view, and there they were, recognisable through an opening in the trees. Standing in a line, just as invisible to the common eye as they were at the Battle of Hawkwell Field, were the Saxon Deities. Six of them were standing attentive and dignified, and the half-sized one was peering over a bush.

Instinctively Jamie looked around, and there was another group, wonderfully unnoticed by the adults before them. The awesome Roman soldier from the top of the Cobham Monument. The regal George I, normally on horseback but now astride a turtle. Queen Caroline, looking grim. A camel. Two gryphons. And most frightening of all, Hercules and Antaeus from the Grecian Valley, normally fiercely entwined in a fighting hold, but now standing together like a pair of tag-wrestlers.

They were all flexing their muscles. Even the turtle.

'Well, let's find a good place to watch,' said Dad, suddenly by Jamie's side.

'Yes,' said Jamie. 'Let's.'

In spite of Jamie's expectations of excitement, it was all initially very quiet. The assorted statues simply posed and stretched, like body-builders parading their assets before a competition. SOS also affected an air of nonchalance – or was it exhaustion? 'Maybe they've overheated from Vingal's exercises,' thought Jamie, watching the casual team-members with hands on hips or in pockets, idly chatting and even yawning. 'They're not doing very much.'

Then it became clear that SOS had done their work during the hours of darkness.

The heats for the track races were the first indication. Jamie heard the Head of PE instructing the boys who were fanned out in staggered starts on the first bend. 'Remember, in the 400 metres, stay in *your* lane. If you enter another one, you'll be disqualified.' After nods from the nervous competitors, he held up his aerosol klaxon, shouted, 'On your marks . . . get set . . .' and braced himself for its foghorn blast.

A steady hiss emerged above his head, followed by a stream of white foam that shot in a graceful arc from the can and, in a substantial dollop, deposited itself across the head and shoulders of the nearest boy.

This prompted amused applause from the ranks of parents and boys, glares from the Headmaster at the usual suspects, and the backslapping of Wesel by his impressed comrades.

'How did that happen?' asked an incredulous Mr Thompson.

'Kids messing about,' suggested Jamie.

The runner was de-foamed, the Head of PE resorted to his trusty whistle, and the race began. All was going smoothly and properly until the third corner of the circuit, when the boy in the outside lane suddenly slowed down, and without warning swerved to his right off the track and disappeared at speed amongst the nearby trees. After twenty seconds of cracking and stamping, he re-emerged, dishevelled and frustrated, and inevitably jogged in some way behind all the others, complaining loudly about his lane.

An examination of the area proved the boy to be correct. Somebody *had* painted his track going off into the trees, and not wanting to be disqualified, he had dutifully followed it.

Lines were hastily re-drawn, and the races continued with few interruptions – well, *most* of them did. Jamie watched the camel lazily clopping over to the start of the 1500 metres, carefully taking up its place at one end of the line of runners. Just before the whistle, it leaned hard over, thumping into the first boy, who set off a chain reaction of collapsed athletes. It was also bad luck for the boy whose foot was trodden on by the same beast; a severely bruised and sprained ankle, acquired whilst standing still, was the day's most *unusual* sports injury.

Similar tactics occurred in the 100 metres heats. One boy was pushed from behind (nudged by an unseen horse) just as 'get set. . . .' was announced. 'False start, Lane 3,' shouted the marshal. Next time it was lane 1. Then Lane 4. And finally Lane 2 – who actually achieved the fastest false start of them all, courtesy of the sword prodded by the Saxon Deity.

SOS were responsible for a remarkable period when the laces of several boys in the starting-blocks behaved in bizarre ways. Some came undone, others disappeared altogether (their owners discarded their shoes and ran in socks instead), and some actually became tangled (even *knotted*) with their neighbours'. Two boys staged a remarkable three-legged start before collapsing in a heap.

There were heated exchanges of opinions between the sports staff, pinning the blame for these embarrassing mishaps on each other, on the Grounds staff, or on other teachers. Some disgruntled parents wanted 'a quiet word' with the Headmaster, only returning to find that rabbits had stolen their nutritious salad picnic – or a large crow was seated in the trees with a ham roll jammed in its beak. Other visitors, seated under trees, found that nuts and berries were landing with unerring accuracy in their drinks. The *Shot of the Day* belonged to Smoky, who added some fruit to a glass jug already full of iced Pimms. His sizeable whole cooking-apple had the glorious impact of a belly-flop, and was a worthy winner.

And then the reinforcements turned up.

8. Good and Bad Sports

Jamie has never forgotten his first sight of the three angels, standing side by side and with wings folded, floating a couple of metres above the ground. Of noble bearing and gold-bronze in colour, confident and authoritative, they each held a large disc that Jamie recognised immediately. Set high in the nave in the school chapel, these stone roundels depicted Creation's weather forces. And now these objects were outside. And were being released.

A Wind disc, hurled by its angelic owner like a Greek discus-thrower, swirled around the site, pulling air behind it in turbulent gusts. Its *first* circuit caused few difficulties; hats blew off, paper plates spun away, sheets were plucked from clipboards to dance across the track. Its *second* circuit was far more impressive. The awesome blast caught the refreshment tent full on, straining its ancient guy ropes and wooden pegs, and pulling at its fading canvas. The ropes quickly gave way, neatly snapped by the force of the gale (or, as Jamie noticed, scythed in half by the disc).

When weather forecasters say things like, 'the odd drop or two of local rain,' *local* means roughly the area of a town. At Malplaquet on its Sports Day, 'local' rain emptied itself on a group of about ten visitors, before the relevant disc returned like a circular boomerang to the hand of its smiling and angel-faced owner.

'Weather's a bit funny,' said John, sitting beside Jamie and watching drenched and dismayed picnickers re-arranging their soggy spreads. The Thompson's spot was utterly dry.

'Yeh, I've thought that,' agreed Jamie. 'Really weird. Can't explain it.'

'Are you *sure* you can't?' asked John.

'Dad, I'm just going for a walk with John,' said Jamie to his father nearby.

'Right, but look out for these sudden showers.'

'Okay, back soon. I'll be fine.'

John grabbed Jamie's arm when they were out of earshot. '*You'll* be fine,' he urged. 'That's the *point*, isn't it? It's the fairies.'

Jamie was thinking fast. Either he could put this kid off the scent for good, or he could tell him the truth. Or then again, maybe he could do a bit of both. . . .

He looked around the two of them furtively, and then cupped one hand over his mouth before leaning forward whispering to John:

'You *must* listen to me. Charlie wouldn't, and it was really bad for him.' Jamie shook his head and pretended to grimace. '*Don't* get involved. Do what I do – believe in them – but *leave them alone*. They have allies. Strange allies. Between them, they can do. . . .' (he paused) '. . . *anything*.'

Jamie tried to look afraid – or at least anxious – but he needn't have bothered.

They both heard it. A faint whistling sound, getting louder and louder, nearer and nearer. It ended with a loud '*kerwhump!*' as the front half of a school javelin split the air between them and landed at John's feet. Strictly speaking, it was almost *in* his feet, nicking the front of his left shoe. Jamie looked up, and saw about fifty metres away the archer from the Saxon Deities tucking his bow under his arm, pleased at his ability to intercept a piece of sports equipment in flight.

John had gone pale, beads of sweat standing on his forehead. He swallowed hard, trying to speak but nothing came out. He stood there, immobile apart from a frantic nodding, which was either agreeing with Jamie's request or trembling from sheer terror. Probably it was both.

A teacher ran over and picked up the missile. 'Sorry, you

two,' he said. 'Haven't a clue how that happened – we'll have to report it.'

'It's alright,' said Jamie. 'Accidents happen. We'll keep quiet, won't we, John?' John carried on with his nodding.

The Field events were underway, or *should* have been. To the consternation of the Headmaster, there were unaccountable difficulties with much of the equipment.

The high-jump bar was behaving weirdly. Sometimes, even when a jumper had made no visible contact, it just fell off. Last year's senior champion was incensed at his three no-jumps (and dismissal) in the very first round, when he *knew* he'd missed the bar by at least thirty centimetres. At other times, the bar lived a charmed life, rejecting any attempts to dislodge it; one 'no-hoper,' who had been persuaded (bullied) into taking part, performed a bizarre scissors kick, which launched the bar up in the air, spinning and twirling madly. It somehow landed neatly and precisely back onto its ledges, quivering and yet stable.

This was impossible to explain. Except by an 8-foot tall Queen Caroline, consort of George II, standing mischievously by a post and having the time of her life.

Hercules was really throwing his weight around. Having (presumably) spent so long tangled up with Antaeus on a plinth in the Grecian Valley, he was making the most of his freedom. He loved kneeling down and grabbing the ankle of some boys at the end of the first phase (the hop) of the Triple Jump. Their excuses such as, 'my foot got stuck!' were plainly ridiculous. Anybody could see the runway was clear.

Hercules' favourite playground was the Shot area. It was full of wonderful possibilities.

There were the simple but rewarding games. Tickling the athlete under the arm as he lifted the shot to place it under his chin. Giving him a yank as he crouched on one foot, hoping to dart backwards, spin round and thrust the shot upwards. It didn't look the same as the thrower toppled awkwardly out the back of the circle.

The more difficult tricks were wonders to behold. If the shot was successfully launched, its graceful arc could be halted as if by an invisible hand and it would plummet to the ground. Others 'rebounded' (or were thrown back, to be accurate), so that they scored 'minus two' metres. But some plucky efforts, almost dropped by the weaker boys, kept going horizontally to land well beyond the normal range. The one that buckled the roof of a brand-new Jaguar was particularly difficult to measure.

The badgers had been doing sterling work underneath the shot-putt area, so that an occasional ball disappeared into the tunnels below, and as the competition ended, the fragile surface collapsed completely, two teachers scrambling around in the craters and trenches.

'They should do *something* about all the animals here,' said Mrs Thompson, watching a line of squirrels playing 'Follow my Leader' along a row of hurdles. 'Did you see that third-former being chased by a Muntjac deer earlier on? By the way,' she added, 'have you seen Floorclean and Midriff anywhere?'

Jamie shook his head. 'I'm sure they're around, Mum. Their friends are.' He was looking towards the newly repaired Refreshment Tent, where Melanak was helpfully putting extra cubes of sugar in the cups of tea, and Yenech was salting the strawberries. 'Anyway, it must be the final two races soon.'

Mr Thompson consulted his watch and programme, and looked up to see the runners taking their positions. 'You're right. Steeplechase, and then the Senior 4 x 100 metres relay. Come on, let's stand by the water jump. Not *too* close obviously.'

As they walked over, Jamie saw that they were being overtaken by the crocodile from the Grecian Temple pediment. A lustrous amber colour and at least four metres in length, the magnificent specimen was padding along at a good speed, its head and tail swinging alternately in rhythm. It reached the ditch, and slithered in under the water, the slight ripples easily mistaken for a breeze on the surface.

The race had started. 'Goodness me, that'll hurt in the morning!' exclaimed Dad. The leading boy had gone absolutely flying, legs cartwheeling in the air. That's what happens when you run into a large immovable (and invisible) turtle slumped in front of you.

As the runners careered round the corner, the sun suddenly emerged from a bank of cloud. The leader, trying to judge the distance to the water jump's hurdle, looked ahead between its bars – and noticed that a shaft of sunlight had picked out a long body in the water. A body with a pair of globular and cold eyes. The boy didn't stop to think that Buckinghamshire wasn't their natural habitat; in fact, he didn't stop at all. He swerved violently to his right, and headed off through groups of startled parents and across the car park. Other runners also caught the briefest of glimpses. Most turned and ran back the way they had come, but one slipped on the hurdle as he spied the creature, overbalanced and splashed into the water, and as he left in a panic-stricken hurry, somehow tore his shorts. . . .

'Well, what a shambles,' said Mum. 'Anybody fancy a bite? I'm peckish.'

'After this last race,' replied Dad. 'There's loads of strawberries left anyway.'

Granny and Ralph were handily parked by the belt of trees near the track. They were well placed for seeing the athletes as they sprinted round the first bend, and also for having a chat with some tiny people who were very pleased with themselves.

'I assume you've got something special planned for this one,' said Granny. 'The Senior Relay is always the highlight.'

'Naturally,' said Yenech. 'We've called up extra help.'

'Locals,' said Melanak. 'Some little surprises.'

The whistle sounded and four boys sprinted off, batons pumping up and down in their right hands. But only for a few metres. One boy suddenly looked down at his baton, and with a yell hurled it as far as he could over the nearby bushes (and with unerring accuracy through the windscreen of a Governor's car).

'Does that count as *dropping* it?' asked Ralph.

The other three competitors were determined to hang on to theirs, but were clearly not very happy about it. Each one had his right arm extended, keeping the baton at arm's length.

'Those red ants can be really nasty,' said Hyroc.

'I reckon Stag Beetles look worse,' said Yassek.

'I wouldn't want a slowworm wrapped round my wrist,' said Thirkatew. 'Even if it is harmless. It *looks* like a snake.'

That particular runner couldn't give his baton, entwined by the reptile, to his number two, who shot up the straight, followed by the first boy shouting at him.

'Those handovers can be tricky,' offered Ralph. 'Seen it happen lots of times.'

'The other two managed,' said Granny. Indeed they had, and the two new boys were now staring in disbelief at the insects crawling up their forearms. To their credit, they were still holding the batons. And screaming.

It was hard to see who actually won. The likeliest candidate was the pupil fleeing the snake, but with no baton he would have been disqualified. The problem was that in the final straight, a deep mist – almost a smog, to be honest – suddenly drifted down and totally hid the action on the track. Although everyone *heard* the loud yells of the runners cut short by an almighty 'thump!' – followed by silence. Absolute silence. A baton slowly rolled out of the thickest part of the fog. It came to a halt right by the finish, and a stag beetle emerged from one end and scurried across the line.

In spite of the chaos (and the early departure of many disgruntled parents – and of some PE staff to the 'Queen's Head'), there were still two prize-giving ceremonies. The first was the presentation of the athletics cups, and in his speech the Chairman of Governors said he was delighted that some 'outsiders' had done well ('Is that us?' said Yenech to Melanak), and that some long-standing records had been broken.

'I didn't see the Long Standing one,' said Ralph, 'but the Long Jumping was great.'

As a final contribution, SOS were delighted to see that several handles fell off some cups on being handed over, but their piéce de resistance, however, came with the presentation of the magnificent lidded silver cup to the winning house. As the captain held it aloft, raising the lid with one hand, a white rabbit peered over its rim.

'Now that's what I call magic,' said Granny. 'Absolute magic.'

The second ceremony was the awarding of the academic prizes in one of the State Rooms, and Jamie walked up (with a quiet John Biddle) to receive the Visual Education Prize. It would have been better perhaps, if his parents hadn't leapt to their feet at that moment and applauded wildly, but he could understand their reaction.

It had, after all, been a very successful day.

For Jamie's class, the lesson wasn't just the first one on a Monday morning, it was also the first one after half-term. There was a distinct lack of intellectual sharpness in the room. Too many late nights were taking their revenge on adolescent minds and bodies, which were befuddled, befogged and becalmed. The RS teacher, Mr Cooper, was trying to inject some life into this torpor as he distributed exercise books on his tour round the room.

'I'd like to say, Chris, that your work is excellent.'

The boy stirred himself and looked up in vague surprise.

Mr Cooper paused briefly. 'That's what I'd *like* to say. Unfortunately. . . .' and he dropped the book with a dismissive thud onto the desk, '. . . I can't.'

The teacher stopped at the next pupil. 'Good work here, James.' The boy perked up. 'Sadly, none of it's *yours*.' The book was dropped elsewhere.

These preliminaries over, Mr Cooper stood at the front and with the slightest of smiles, eyeballed one particular pupil.

'Sam, *your* work is outstanding.'

Sam was taken aback by this compliment. 'Really? Thank you, sir, I wasn't. . . .'

'No, Sam, *outstanding* as in 'not yet handed in'. Any sign of it?'

Sniggers started. Sam delved into his bag and the lesson got underway.

'Let's recap. Remember those carefree days before the holiday interrupted your intellectual ambitions? We were studying '*Life in the Ancient World*' – although we really shouldn't have been discussing the staff-room.' He paused, anticipating an amused response. He'd have to wait a long time. Some boys shifted position or glanced at their neighbour. They *were* stirring, but the lesson might be over before they woke up.

'We were talking about Greek temples. Can anyone remember why they were built? Yes, John?'

'Homes for the gods,' said John Biddle. 'They had a statue of the god or goddess inside.' Jamie stifled a yawn.

'Good,' said Mr Cooper. 'A *dwelling* for the deity.' Jamie felt another yawn coming. 'The temples linked the people with the gods and their powers.'

Jamie sat bolt upright, slamming his chair against the desk and fingers of the boy behind, who had been slumped across it. This boy now yelped, thrusting his bruised fingers into his mouth, sucking hard.

'A problem, Charles?' inquired the teacher. Charles shook his head, his fist still stuck in his mouth, and his eyes slightly watering. 'Yes, Jamie?'

Jamie tried not to betray too much interest in his voice. 'Did you say, sir, that the temples – the Greek ones, that is – had *powers* in them?'

'Absolutely,' enthused Mr Cooper, pleased to have a discussion. 'It's a simple idea, starting with primitive and *animistic* beliefs. Quick test. Animistic. What is it? Yes, Sam?'

'Annie Mystic was that weird woman. She spoke in chapel recently.'

'Not exactly,' corrected Mr Cooper, but enjoying the mistake. '*Animus*, Latin, for 'spirit.' Animism is the belief that spirits, or strange forces, exist in nature. Like wind, thunder, or the fertility in the ground. But the Greeks later identified these forces with gods and goddesses, and so the mysterious powers of nature were no longer out in the open but were instead concentrated. . . .'

'. . . in the *temples*,' concluded Jamie loudly, mainly talking to himself. 'Contact with *another* world. . . . Of *course*. . . .' Everyone was looking at him.

'Well, I'm glad you think so,' said Mr Cooper, pleased that one boy had understood. 'Now, let's deal with Plato.'

'*Amazing*,' whispered Jamie. 'Absolutely amazing.'

'This is *indeed* good news,' said Nigriff to Jamie later that day in Ancient Virtue, keeping eyes (and ears) open for any intruders. 'Although this knowledge only confirms what we already know, that the temples have strong links with Lilliput itself.'

'But there's *more*,' said Jamie, looking excited. '*Seriously* good news. You're going to love this about Plato.'

Above them, Socrates leaned slightly forward at this mention of his best pupil, and smiled. It was a long time since he had heard anyone speak that great name.

'We had to read about him for prep, and I've made some

notes.' He took out a piece of paper and began. 'There are perfect Forms. . . .'

'Do you mean like your Form 3A?' asked Nigriff. 'Are *they* perfect?'

'No, they're. . . . Well, they're. . . . Okay, I'll start again. There are three beds. . . .'

'Only *three*?' said Nigriff. 'I'm sure. . . .'

Jamie sighed. 'Nigriff, you've *got* to let me explain.'

'My apologies, master, but to ask questions is the best way to knowledge.' Above them, Socrates nodded in agreement. 'But I will certainly now listen.'

'Imagine there are three beds,' said Jamie. 'The first one is a *painting* of a bed. That's a *copy* of what we call a *real* bed – which is the second one. Okay?'

Nigriff made a zipping movement across his mouth and nodded silently.

'And Plato said this second bed, which we lie on, is *also* a copy of another, a third. And this third bed's even *more* real.'

Nigriff couldn't stop himself talking. '*More* real? How can it be *more* real?'

Jamie had to consult his notes. 'Because unlike the second, which will – hang on a minute, here it is – *decay and rot*, the third is everlasting. It's the *perfect Form* of a bed.'

'And where might one see this perfect *Form* of a bed?' inquired Nigriff.

'Plato said it's in another world,' explained Jamie. 'The world of Forms. The *real* world, beyond this one. The world where everything stays perfect forever.'

Nigriff was deep in thought, his sharp Elysian mind coming to all the right conclusions. He wasn't thinking of beds, but gardens. Three gardens. Of *paintings* of the garden of Malplaquet that were copies of an actual garden. A garden they were living in. And this garden, this beautiful 'island' in the middle of the countryside, was apparently a copy of a third, a *perfect* one in another world.

His homeland. Lilliput.

Standing on the inner bench, Nigriff leant back, dabbing his eyes with his tiny handkerchief. Tears were rolling down his cheeks.

And the same was also true for the group of four statues that were sharing this sacred place with them.

'If you ask me,' said the Head Gardener to Vicky and Ralph, hunched over a pile of stones with hammers and chisels, 'it's a waste of time with that bunch of young lads he's brought in. What an absolute *shower*!'

The pair stood up to stretch their backs. 'Not working, are they?' asked Ralph.

'You'd think they'd never seen a *wall* before, never mind a ha-ha,' moaned the gardener. 'I really don't know why Mr Biddle wants it finished so quickly. I know his big 'do' is coming up, but that's all about the temples, not this bit.'

'It *is* part of the garden,' offered Vicky. 'Defines it.'

Their boss wasn't convinced. 'Ours not to reason why,' he intoned, and wandered back, shouting, 'Come on, break's over, time for some real work!'

Ralph and Vicky smiled. 'It's good to get extra help anyway,' said Ralph. 'But I can't work it out either. Nigriff says we should get this finished – so *all* the temples are restored – and Biddle's *also* saying that. . . . How come they both want the same thing? Doesn't make any sense to me.'

Vicky nodded in agreement. 'Me neither. And there's no *way* that it'll be done for the big night.'

'Remember,' said Ralph grinning, 'that Yenech said SOS would help. You'd forgotten that.'

'Actually,' said Vicky, 'I hadn't.'

They both knew that the little man's thoughtful gesture was no more than that. A group of Lilliputians, even if incredibly keen and willing, couldn't quickly construct a wall that was over two metres high and one hundred metres long. The task was impossible.

'Hmm,' said Yassek, staring at their task that evening. 'Big job.' Even though normally optimistic, he and SOS were finding it hard to be cheerful about the final stretch of the ha-ha. The supporting wall had split and collapsed years ago. Many of the dressed stones from its face had cracked apart as they had tumbled down, and the exposed earthen edge had slumped forwards. Weeds, brambles and small trees had taken root, so that the ditch itself had all but disappeared.

'No-one said it would be easy,' said Yenech. Vingal purposefully strode up to the huge overgrown slope, a teaspoon gripped in her hands. She was, as ever, ready for a challenge.

Melanak tapped Yenech on the shoulder. 'I've seen Thorclan recently. He'd been talking to Nigriff; they might have an idea.'

Yenech smiled in appreciation, but even with his respect for the experience of the old soldier, and of course for the brains of the archivist, he couldn't imagine what they meant. 'Maybe a platoon from the Grecian Army,' he pondered. 'Or it's a training-exercise for the new recruits. . . .' His voice then trailed away.

For he'd noticed that the light had changed, the gloom of dusk being sharpened by a few more shadows, as if a full moon had been switched on across the landscape. But it wasn't that cold and flat light; it had a warmth and energy to it, more like a glow than a beam. And it was accompanied by a rhythmic thumping that could be felt underfoot, coming from beyond the trees.

SOS peered in the direction of the sound and the growing light.

9. Famous Ancestors

As the crowd appeared over the rise, SOS initially saw the tops of spears, of military standards, and plumes bobbing up and down. Soon the horses and the men came into sight. A vast troop of Roman soldiers, the size of humans, were marching in unison, purposeful and disciplined. Their bodies glowed golden with light and easy movement as they swept irresistibly on, causing dozens of squirrels and rabbits to scurry away.

At the head of this magnificent column was a single chariot, two-wheeled, pulled by a pair of powerful horses and driven by a toga-clad woman. In her left hand lay the reins, and her right was held aloft, its upward palm supporting a small object the length of her hand. Yenech squinted at it, and soon realised it was a person, standing bolt upright, hands on hips, swaying slightly. Like a proud general at the head of his army.

Which is precisely what he was.

General Thorclan.

He held up a hand, and the signal was instantly obeyed, the whole army coming to a swift halt. Thorclan turned, and spoke with the lady who was his driver and bearer. She stepped down, and deposited her leader gently on the grass in front of the astonished (and understandably apprehensive) Lilliputians.

Yenech and Melanak had the presence of mind (and training) to salute. Thorclan responded in kind.

'Been recruiting,' he said nonchalantly. 'Found them hanging around in the Marble Saloon. Weren't doing much. Nigriff's idea really.'

SOS said nothing. They had never seen such figures – or had never seen them 'alive' before. Row upon row of armoured Roman soldiers, as far as the eye could see, towered over them, swords and daggers slung around their waists. A few were equipped with the stock tools of an army on the march – spades and shovels, even pick-axes. Two men carried a stretcher, partly draped in a tarpaulin, under which could be seen some buckets and spikes.

'These lads should be useful,' continued Thorclan. 'Had to knock them into shape – they haven't seen action for centuries. And they know the score; dig foundations, cut away undergrowth, shape stones. A bit each night; can't arouse suspicions.'

Yenech nodded. Thorclan leaned over and whispered. 'I know *you're* my driver, Yenech, and our little jeep *has* been very reliable, even without an engine – but I must say. . . .' and he looked back at the goddess-like figure, plumed horses and glowing chariot. 'I must say, Yenech, there really *is* only *one* way to travel.'

The person in SOS who was most delighted by this extraordinary turn of events was, of course, Snallard. Relieved that he no longer had to do any hard labour, he was also thrilled at this astonishing sight. At first, like the others, he'd felt intimidated by this military display, but once he had seen these ethereal soldiers obeying Thorclan's orders, he realised that they weren't a real threat. They were vague and insubstantial creatures, mere will o' the wisps that would melt into the landscape at the first sign of true strength and authority. The authority that his master had.

Having thus easily discounted them, Snallard watched them work, knowing that at some point he might mention them to Jedekiah Biddle.

But he was in no hurry to do so.

'I apologise for the request to meet me here in the church, sir,' said Nigriff, 'but I have encountered a mystery that may be better solved by *two* brains.'

Jamie smiled; Nigriff really *had* changed, to ask for such help.
'That's fine, it's better than stuffing my face in the Grot – I mean,
Tuck – Shop.'

'Indeed,' agreed Nigriff. 'Now, allow me to swiftly explain.
In some other human documents, I have found other mentions of
my ancestor, Gothep. These writings have two *peculiar* features.'
Jamie nodded, but was still thinking about food. 'The first,'
continued Nigriff, 'is that the word, *consult*, is often linked with
him, usually on garden design.' He pulled out a tiny piece of paper.
'Here are two examples; *Consult Gothep on levelling slope. . . .
Consult Gothep on damming stream.*' He returned the paper to his
pocket. 'He was clearly meeting an influential person, a human,
to discuss the layout of the garden.'

This was very familiar. 'Nigriff, you've said all this before,'
exclaimed Jamie, 'that Gothep did something to this place. Do
you *still* honestly believe it?'

'It is far-fetched,' acknowledged Nigriff, 'but here is the
evidence. And, as I said before, we must see where it leads us.'

Jamie had to agree. 'So who was this '*influential person,*' this
human?'

'His identity is not clear,' admitted Nigriff. 'Indeed, there is
also an issue over the identity of Gothep himself.'

'What do you mean?'

'His name often has an 'f' in the middle, so it is written as
Gofthep.'

'Does that matter?' asked Jamie. 'My English teacher said
Shakespeare spelt his name *sixteen* different ways.'

'It's about *accuracy*,' replied the archivist. 'It has taken me
so long to find him, and now I don't even know his proper name.
It's *very* frustrating.'

A small head popped up round the pew. 'Crosswords,' it said.

They both turned. 'Hi Yenech,' said Jamie, 'what are you
doing here?'

'Oh, I'm . . . er . . . meeting . . . a friend.'

'Good,' said Jamie. 'How is Melanak?'

'Fine,' said Yenech. 'Happy.'

'And,' said Nigriff, 'why are my words *cross*? I may be
confused, but. . . .'

'Wrong,' said Yenech. '*Crosswords*. Not *two* words, but one. That's what *Gothep* is, a crossword device. Like a *cat o 'nine tails* is a cat of nine tails.'

'I fail to understand how a grossly deformed feline can shed any light on my ancestor,' said Nigriff, who really was now becoming cross.

'That name,' offered Yenech, 'sounds like an abbreviation. It's got *of the* in the middle – or *o 'the* for short.'

Jamie understood the idea. 'So Gothep is really *g of the p*?'

Yenech shrugged his shoulders. 'Could be,' he said. 'It fits.'

Nigriff was feeling shocked, even humiliated, at such logical dexterity but realised that the church, at the heart of Elysium, had to be transmitting intellectual energies to Yenech. The building could take the credit. Time to show his own skills.

'We are thus faced,' he suggested, 'with Gellisleb, also known as *g of the p*, who is often consulted about the garden. We must first ask what the 'g' stands for.'

Jamie gasped. 'Genius,' he said quietly.

'Thank you, Master Jamie,' responded Nigriff. 'I appreciate the compliment.'

'Alexander Pope,' continued Jamie, as if in a trance. 'Gellisleb *knew* Pope. . . . And the two of them planned this garden. . . . How have I *not* seen this before?'

Nigriff and Yenech looked at each other, both feeling ignorant.

'It's in one of Pope's poems,' Jamie said. 'Mr Merryman kept quoting the line at us, he said it was the most important thing Pope ever said about gardens. It's amazing. . . .'

'And that line,' said Nigriff, 'is what?'

Jamie paused before replying. 'It's simple; *Consult the genius of the place*.' He knew he had to explain further. '*Genius* is a Latin word,' he said. 'It means the real character, or true spirit, of a place. So people have always thought that to *consult the genius* sounds like respecting the character of each site, but we now know that it really means talk to the *g of the p* – Gofthep or Gothep, in other words, Gellisleb. . . .'

It was Nigriff's moment to shine. 'You are suggesting – and I see no flaws in your logic – that my ancestor worked closely with

Pope? That he created for the exiled Lilliputians a garden that was a true reminder of their homeland?' He paused, and then spoke out solemnly. 'My ancestor was the *Genius of the Place*,' he stated, pride evident in his voice. 'I *knew* he wasn't just a gardener.'

Yenech walked over to Nigriff and shook his hand. 'You're a chip off the old block as well,' he said warmly, '*You're* a genius.'

Nigriff accepted the compliment. 'Yenech,' he replied, 'I can honestly say the same about *you*.' They gave each other a congratulatory hug.

Jamie knew this had been a remarkable day. What was going to happen next?

Next Saturday was the eagerly anticipated 'Summer Fete' at Chackmore Manor. After the success of Biddle's Christmas party, it was no surprise to see crowds swarming through the gates that morning, the event happily coinciding with a spell of warm and settled sunshine.

With the theme of a 'Medieval Fayre', the grounds were full of conical tents, trestle tables of local crafts, brightly-coloured standards fluttering in the soft breezes, and handsome minstrels and troubadours serenading young damsels (none of whom were distressed). A Jousting Demonstration was the main event, but there were also opportunities to *Hold a Hawk*, *Bend a Bow*, *'Ammer some Armour*, and *Brew your Beer*. Mr Thompson was heading to that last one, until Mrs Thompson saw Granny on her WI stall. The family was shepherded away from any temptations.

'Morning, Granny,' she greeted her. 'Lovely day.'

'Super,' she said. 'Hello, Jamie. Enjoying the Fayre?'

Jamie couldn't help scowling slightly. Coming to the Manor just put him in a bad mood. 'There's nothing *fair* about Biddle,' he grumbled.

Mr Thompson took up the challenge of this word-play. 'I don't know,' he said. 'After all, it's a fair *day*, and there's plenty of medieval *fare* to eat. Though we didn't pay an *entry* fare to come in. Perhaps we should call it a *fete* instead.'

'Definitely,' said Jamie. 'A fete worse than death.'

Mrs Thompson shook her head. 'I don't know why I bother,' she said to Granny, then noticed something familiar on the stall.

Amongst the beautifully tailored jackets and embroidered dresses
was a shoebox. Inside it was a doll. An older male doll, wearing
long yellow socks. She looked quizzically at Granny. 'Didn't Mr
Biddle give you that at Christmas?'

The old lady nodded, her jaw firm. 'It's a swap,' she declared,
quickly adding, 'And it's *very* inferior to my other one. I'll give
it back to Biddle myself if I see him.' Her words were spoken
sharply.

Mrs Thompson was taken aback by her strength of feeling. 'I
see,' she said meekly. 'I didn't realise. And I'd heard he's been
unwell, not showing his face much in Chackmore. Well, must be
off, I'm after a hedgehog boot-scraper.'

'No!' shouted Charlie, loudly enough to alarm bystanders.
'Absolutely no way!' He began to back off.

'Charlie, what's the matter?' asked his embarrassed mother,
wondering if she was the only normal person present. 'They're
just over there by those scarecrows.'

She was shocked by his reaction. He just stood there, the
colour draining from his cheeks and his lips quivering. 'Are you
alright?' she asked. 'You don't look at all well. . . .' Noticing the
St John's Ambulance stall in one corner, she grabbed him by
the hand. 'Come on, this way.' She gently walked him over, but
unfortunately it was past a stall of soft toys – moles, badgers,
rabbits and the dreaded squirrels. Charlie's eyes rolled in his
head, his legs gave way and he slumped to the ground. Medical
helpers quickly ran over.

Jamie and Granny exchanged knowing smiles. Mr Thompson
groaned. 'I don't believe it,' he said. 'We'll have to take him home.
Just when I was feeling thirsty. . . .'

Jedekiah Biddle was watching the Fayre from the security of his
cabin. He hated chit-chat with inconsequential people, but he
also felt self-conscious about his face. More lines had appeared
on his cheeks, and what looked like old scars had mysteriously
surfaced along his chin. There were slight ridges on his scalp.
A private doctor had stated with bewilderment and scarcely-
disguised distaste that he'd 'never seen anything like it in my
life, Mr Biddle'.

There was a timid knock at the door. Jedekiah shouted, 'Enter!' and a young boy stepped forward.

'Ah, John, my son, come in.' John took a few paces, looking anxious. This was a strange situation for him, being *invited* into this room – this dark place, full of old ships' furniture and rusted sea-faring objects. He'd also never seen his father look so awful – so frightening. And he'd certainly never heard him say, 'John, my son'.

'It's about time you grew up – I mean, took on more responsibilities,' said Jedekiah, placing an arm firmly around his shoulders to pull him in. 'I want to tell you about something that's very dear to me – to *both* of us perhaps.'

John tried to relax as he was eased into a rough chair. His father leaned over. John wanted to feel close, but found himself drawing back from the grim face.

'I've a little job for you,' it said. 'With the Thompsons and that old woman.'

'My father wanted me to take all of you,' said John. 'It's a pity that Charlie and your parents are going to miss it.' Jamie nodded and looked with some concern at Granny, who was equally serious. The three of them had left the Fayre and were now passing through a brick archway into the walled kitchen garden. Or what used to be the kitchen garden. It had been almost entirely concreted over, and was dominated by an imposing green metallic structure, rather like a huge windowless garage.

Jamie and Granny simply stopped, stunned at the sight. 'I had no idea this was here,' said Granny quietly.

'Nor me,' whispered Jamie.

'It's where he's doing his research, or will be soon,' said John proudly. 'I've not been inside, but he just told me all about it, and wants me to show you round. I've got the code for the door.' He looked at the numbers and letters written on his palm.

'What sort of research?' asked Granny. She already knew the answer.

'On some small mammals,' replied John. 'They live at Malplaquet.'

'I see,' said Jamie quietly. 'What sort of mammals?'

'I suppose they're voles or field-mice, something like that,' said John. 'He said our ancestor, John Biddle, had discovered them and brought them here.'

'He should have left them alone,' muttered Granny, shaking her head. 'Left them with their families.'

Now at the door, John tapped in the code. Jamie looked round at a couple of security guards making themselves obvious in a far corner.

'My father says their habitat is under threat,' explained John. 'With the restoration and all the extra visitors. He doesn't want them to die out.' He twisted the brass handle, pushed the heavy door, and they stared into the gloomy interior.

'This is the new home for the animals,' he announced. 'Once my father has captured them all. It won't be long, he said.' John slid his hand along the wall to find the light-switch, and the fluorescent tubes clicked and hummed on.

Jamie and Granny squinted into the harsh and soulless space as the bright metallic surfaces threw back the unforgiving light. As their eyes adjusted, they took note of the cages, the stainless-steel cupboards, the microscopes, the glass boxes, and (perhaps worst of all) the antiseptic and dead atmosphere.

'Wow, this is *cool*,' enthused John. 'He can *really* take care of them here.'

Granny was too upset to speak. Jamie was simply angry. He managed to grit his teeth and just agree with John's conclusion. 'You're right,' he said slowly. 'You're absolutely right.'

'Why did that scheming monster want us to see that awful place?' asked Jamie, as he and Granny made their way home along the main street of Chackmore.

'Because he's a scheming monster,' she said. 'And,' she added, 'he thinks he can't fail. And he wants us to know he's won.'

Jamie was pondering this. 'It might be,' he said, 'that he's trying to *persuade* us. That his place *is* best for them. Because of the restoration, like John said. But that *can't* be the case.'

'Of *course* it isn't,' agreed Granny sadly. 'But the trouble is, Jamie, that I'm not getting any younger. That's why I got you involved, to help me out.' She stopped and Jamie saw that her eyes were moistening. 'But *you* won't be around here much longer either. . . . It's just your school-days, and then. . . .'

'It'll be four or five years,' he said defiantly. 'And then it depends. I can always find work round here.'

Granny was gently squeezing his arm. 'Jamie,' she said. 'You're very kind and very sweet. But maybe . . . maybe . . . it's time to accept the inevitable. . . ?'

She was startled by Jamie's reaction as he pulled away. 'No *way*!' he shouted. 'There's no way they're going to end up with him!' Curtains twitched in a couple of houses. Granny gently led him along the path.

'I'm sorry,' she said, 'it's just that he seems so *powerful*. And I know that *factory* is no home for them. But what *can* we do?'

'*I* don't know,' said Jamie, 'but I think *Pope* does. And *Gothep*.' Granny raised her eyebrows. 'Biddle may be powerful,' said Jamie, 'but he's *no* idea exactly what these gardens are. Nigriff and I have just found something out. . . .' He put his arm through hers and they continued their walk, Jamie jabbering away and Granny's mood lightening with each step.

Years later people still talked about the *Great June Storm*, the one that appeared from nowhere at the end of the month. Up until it broke in the late afternoon, the day had been thoroughly pleasant, with scarcely a breath of wind; a *settled* day, as if the world was quietly pleased with itself. The weather reports had been indicating that an area of high pressure was 'happily hovering' over Britain, promising a spell of sunny weather.

The onset of the storm was extraordinary. It was unexpected, struck savagely, and was incredibly localised. Its epicentre was in north Buckinghamshire, perhaps even Malplaquet itself.

Possibly even in one particular building.

In a chapel. A chapel with large circular reliefs of angels holding symbols of dramatic weather conditions. A chapel that, without any warning, suddenly had its main doors flung back in an explosion of energy as a wave of determined angelic figures swept out en masse, twisting and twirling upwards and outwards in a boiling golden torrent. Behind them poured forth a veritable cyclone of climatic forces – impenetrable dark rain clouds, volleys of hailstones, violent gusts of wind, searing and crackling bolts of lightning, and deafening thunderclaps. Their angelic guardians finally hurled them, swelling and heaving, into the four corners of Malplaquet and beyond, so that within minutes the gardens and nearby villages were shrouded and swamped by thick and malevolent storm-clouds. The ground shook under this onslaught, as people and animals dived for cover and stared upwards at this crash of the heavens.

It was no surprise that people talked about the *Great June Storm* for years to come.

'This is perfect,' purred Melanak, inspecting the sparkling ancient glass and sea-shells of the grotto walls in Elysium. 'It's beautiful here. Okay, beautiful in a *decaying* sort of way, but still. . . .'

'. . . beautiful,' breathed Yenech. Melanak was leaning forward, shaking her head and long hair free of raindrops, her eyes shining after their dash for cover. Yenech turned away to look at the gentle valley and its stream, shrouded in mist and steady rain and framed by the grotto's rough arch. The only sounds were the steady splashes in the water, or occasional drips that splattered across the front of the shimmering rain-curtain before them. The pair of them were safe within, and this quiet refuge made their friendship all the more special, all the more a shared secret.

There was no need for words. Yenech took her hand in both of his and gently held it. He was pleased to sense Melanak gently leaning into and against him, and Yenech knew at that moment that nothing was ever going to disturb their quiet joy, their togetherness. Not even the bolt of lightning which seared down and split an ancient oak in the churchyard to their right, an ancient oak that in its final act smashed into a row of old tombstones, breaking two in half and gouging up the hallowed turf.

Yenech and Melanak hardly noticed it.

It made Nigriff jump though. He was in the church porch, gazing with incredulity at the fury and power of nature. He would have preferred to go in and hide, not stand there bracing himself against the mad gusts that threatened to hurl him against the cold stone walls. Trickles of rainwater were turning into large puddles or definite streams, which ran between the flagstones and under the old door. Nigriff pulled his coat around him and stared up at the grim sight – heavy rainclouds occasionally lit up by flashes of light, branches of venerable trees creaking under the windswept weight of their sodden leaves and fruits.

Nigriff knew that he had to be here, knew that he had to face this onslaught. This was no freak of the weather. He had lived in the gardens long enough to know that the air that he breathed and the ground that he walked on were shot through with deep mystery, alive with potent energy. This world of Malplaquet was not dead matter, but something vibrant and alive. This storm was no mere unusual conjunction of weather systems.

Malplaquet was heaving, churning itself up into a great finale, after which it would never be the same again.

What it would become, Nigriff did not know. But he knew that *he* had to be ready, and to be strong, and he knew what he had to do.

Something that he couldn't explain to any other person.

And that was why he was standing there, all alone, facing the storm.

For the storm meant danger. Very soon.

10. Seeing the Truth

From the shelter of his front porch, Jedekiah Biddle watched his men scurrying around in the lashing wind and rain. They were desperately tying down covers over garden furniture, driving quad-bikes into garages, closing windows on greenhouses, and stuffing rakes and spades under their sodden arms. He found it all mildly amusing – his minions dashing around in a panic, heavy rain bouncing off tarmac paths and pouring over clothes, the frantic instructions shouted in the chaos.

He stopped smiling when, to his left, he noticed a figure slithering round the corner by the conservatory. From the walk and build, Jedekiah guessed that it was Newbold, but he couldn't be absolutely sure. The wind and rain were making visibility difficult, the man was dressed head-to-toe in what looked like a camouflage jacket and trousers, and his head was almost totally encased in a large rounded military helmet. From the front of this item hung a bulky pair of binoculars that obscured the top half of his face.

Biddle continued to look as Hawkins appeared on the scene and thrust his walking-stick across the newcomer's midriff. Words were exchanged; Newbold pointed towards the house, waving cheerily at Biddle. Hawkins looked at his master, waiting for a response.

Jedekiah was tempted to leave them for a few minutes, but he gave a curt nod in their direction. Hawkins lowered his stick, and Newbold passed on, his heavy army boots scrunching on the gravel drive. The sodden apparition soon reached the first step.

'I've been shopping,' said the mouth below the binoculars in a cheery tone. 'At an army depot. I thought you'd like to see it. Can I come in?'

Jedekiah disliked the cocky manner, and thought the visit was pointless. Newbold obviously only had with him some military wet-weather gear and a ridiculous pair of bolt-on binoculars. 'Out here will do,' he replied. 'You're far too wet for the house.'

The momentary slump of the shoulders indicated Newbold's disappointment at this rebuttal, and he nervously looked down before lifting his head and speaking with renewed confidence. 'You're right; these lenses work better outside.'

Jedekiah wasn't going to discuss binoculars with this fool. 'I *know* how they. . . .' To his astonishment, Newbold interrupted him. Bluntly.

'Not *these* you don't.'

This curt arrogance so shook Biddle that he didn't snap back at him. Instead, he coldly asked the masked face, 'Really? So what is that stuck below your helmet?'

'It's an MRD-1R / FC-5,' said Newbold.

Again a pause. 'Which is *what* exactly?'

'It's a Thermal Infrared Binocular Goggle System,' said Newbold. 'The sensor is a 7-14 micron uncoded amorphous silicon microbolometer, and its resolution is 320 x 420 with 2D interpolation.'

'Fascinating,' said Biddle, tempted to turn on his heels and slam the door.

'The highest quality Germanium optics,' continued Newbold's mouth. '*And* you get a free lens cloth with every purchase.' He pulled out this free gift, a damp lump of cream material, and wiped the rag across both lenses.

'Why *would* I purchase one?' said Biddle, somehow intrigued.

'It gives high-resolution digital thermal imaging,' said Newbold. 'You can *see* heat. I know, for example, that your face has been getting hotter these last few minutes.'

Jedekiah ignored the impertinence; he had suddenly understood. 'This equipment can see *anything* that is hot? Any living creatures?'

'*Exactly*,' said Newbold. 'Clever, isn't it? Heat has infrared wavelengths. We can't see it. Except with these on. Even at night.'

Biddle gestured to Newbold to hand over the helmet, and he placed it on his own head, adjusting the mounting and eyepieces. He was amazed at the effect. Now in front were glowing bodies of different levels of orange and red; a large human shape was directly before him, and smaller ones were clustered further away in a garage. All apparently lit from within by a smouldering fire.

Stepping down carefully from his porch, and ignoring the rain running down his neck and soaking into his naval jacket, he walked to the nearest shrubbery. He swivelled up the binoculars for a normal look, peering along the base of the hedge; no signs of life. Replacing the equipment over his eyes, he scanned the same area.

There they were; a family of (probably) mice. Invisible to the naked eye amongst the twisted stems and leaves, with these binoculars they were blobs of molten lava. Jedekiah stooped down, picked up a large stone, and lobbed it into the hedge. It crashed down through the branches, scattering the glowing shapes.

He grinned broadly. Newbold was a genius – well, this was a clever idea anyway.

As Biddle returned, Newbold spoke up. 'With your . . . *disadvantage*, I thought. . . .' Biddle held up his hand. 'Enough,' he stated firmly. 'Order twenty. To arrive within 48 hours. My men will need training.'

'If you want,' said Newbold cheerily, pleased with his success, 'I can get you something else as well.'

'Not a free *lens cloth*?' replied Biddle, realising to his irritation that he was joking and exchanging pleasantries with this servant.

'No, of course not,' said Newbold. 'They're part of the package. No, *this* is what you *really* want.'

Jedekiah was ready to guess, but couldn't hope too much with this character. He raised an eyebrow. 'And that would be. . . ?'

'*Nigriff.* Snallard and I have an arrangement.'

This was an enticing prospect, but he wasn't convinced Newbold could do it. 'Delighted,' he said. 'Sounds like things are definitely *hotting* up, Julius.'

With that, he swiftly strode indoors, pleased with his witticism, but annoyed at sharing it with Newbold – especially as he had used his first name. . . .

Newbold's cheery, 'Bye, Jedekiah, see you soon!' was more than the Lord of the Manor could take, but the idea of the goggles spared Newbold from his anger.

For the moment.

'I hope that storm yesterday didn't wash away any of the ha-ha.' Granny was enjoying her elevenses with Ralph. 'You and Vicky have worked so hard on it recently.'

'Don't you worry,' said Ralph. 'Built to last, it is – and almost finished. Not surprising, mind, seeing as a Roman army has been helping most nights.'

'Thorclan is really pleased,' she added. 'He said that leading such fine men is the pinnacle of his career.'

'Especially when they're ten times his size,' smiled Ralph. 'And he's taken a shine to that goddess and her chariot. Can't blame him – I'd follow her into battle any day. Absolute corker, she is.'

Granny looked across at him in mild (and pretend) disapproval. Ralph smiled back. 'Not that she's a patch on *you*, Miss M.' Granny accepted the compliment for what it was – kind, but perhaps not strictly true. She swallowed a sip of tea, and put her cup down, looking thoughtful. 'What I don't understand,' she said slowly, 'is what the other workers make of it. They go home every evening, having built a few yards that day, and then turn up next morning to find more done.'

'They're easy,' said Ralph. 'They reckon Biddle sends in more chaps at night. Anyway, that's what I told them, and they're happy with that. They don't ask questions – so long as they get paid. They'll get it done.'

Granny shook her head. 'That's what worries me,' she said. 'Biddle's determined to get it finished, for the big 'Unveiling' I suppose. But Nigriff *also* wants it done. Why does it matter so much? And Nigriff's doing just what Biddle wants.'

'Or Biddle is doing what *Nigriff* wants,' suggested Ralph. 'I wouldn't worry about him, with all his Elysian *brains*. And I reckon he's picked up some Grecian *brawn* as well. Nigriff can look after himself.'

'Maybe,' said Granny, 'but just *recently*, I've wondered if the temples are *diluting* their special qualities. Thorclan wouldn't normally let a woman affect him, and is Nigriff still as clever as he was. . . .? I don't know. . . . I just hope you're right.'

Ralph leaned over and squeezed a hand. 'We've got to be brave, Miss M,' he said. '*And* look after each other. None of us can do this on our own.' Granny's eyes expressed her appreciation. As each day passed, she was more and more grateful for his companionship and support.

'I don't *fully* understand why you have brought me here,' said Nigriff to his companion, as they struggled through the grass above the cascade to Copper Bottom Lake. Ahead, built into the rocky mound at the top of the waterfall, and almost obscured by undergrowth, stood an old wooden door. Few visitors knew of it, or of the room behind. A room that contained an ancient water-wheel. Indeed, few Lilliputians ever went in there. It was known to be dangerous.

'It's an idea of mine,' said Snallard. 'And you're the best – the *brightest* – person I know for an opinion. I think it could give huge amounts of simple energy, with no extra effort. I need to know whether it will work.'

'I hate to disappoint you straightaway,' said Nigriff, 'but it hasn't worked for years. The mechanism ground to a halt long ago. You can tell by that lever.' Standing by the door, they looked up at the rusty metal bar sticking out from the wall. It operated the sluice-gate for the upper lake, and in the past allowed water through a grilled opening and onto the water-wheel. Linked to a series of cogs, drive-shafts and gears, this revolving wheel had entertained the third Duke's children by pulling them in boats towards the cascade. But that was all in the dim and distant past.

'I think *something* can be done,' urged Snallard. 'We'll have a look; come on, we can squeeze under here.' And he did so. Nigriff also ducked down amongst the moss and damp earth, crawled under the door, and entered the gloom.

There was so little light inside that their eyes took some time to adjust, but they were in a chamber about two metres square, lined by grey and leaden bricks that were streaked by a dirty and crusty mortar. High to their left was the slit of the sluice-gate, their only source of light. The damp and glistening walls were pockmarked with feeble and straggling ferns.

The huge and forbidding water-wheel, with its spars of thin metal, looking spidery and immobile, dominated the room. Around its circle were the scoop-like troughs to catch the falling water and rotate the machine. It had an air of menace, but also neglect – an impressive piece of engineering that had been long forgotten.

'*Fantastic*, isn't it?' enthused Snallard. Nigriff gave no reply. He was too preoccupied with what lay below; a grim chasm, a deep blackness that contained metallic teeth and ratchets. He'd been here once before, as a young man, fully aware of the dangers. He now walked gingerly onwards along the narrow and musty brick walkway.

The crash of the door bursting open behind almost made Nigriff lose his balance. The room flooded with light, and Nigriff turned, shielding his eyes from the sudden glare. He thought he recognised the tall figure silhouetted in the doorway, and definitely did so when it spoke.

'*Splendid*,' said Julius Newbold. 'I'm delighted when people keep their appointments. Allow me to offer a hand of welcome.' He stooped down. There was nowhere for Nigriff to go as he backed into the far corner, but he needn't have worried yet. Newbold grabbed hold of Snallard and dumped him unceremoniously in the nearest trough on the water-wheel. Snallard was surprised, and not a little frightened. He peered over the edge.

'Be careful – it's . . . it's an awful long way down,' he said to his accomplice.

'Yes, it is,' replied Newbold. 'That's why I've put you in there.

Wouldn't it be a *pity* if you fell in?' Both Nigriff and Snallard noted the sneer in his voice. 'I really should take care of you, after all this help, like I said. But first things first.' He bent down and picked up Nigriff in his fist, stuffing him in his coat pocket. Then he turned to leave. A cry from Snallard halted him.

'What about our *plans*? And you can't leave me here! How can I get out?'

'I'm sure you'll think of something,' he said. 'As ever. Or maybe *I* can help.' Outside, he grabbed hold of the rusted lever and yanked it down hard. With a massive crescendo of noise, the old sluice groaned downwards and the full torrent powered its way through the grille and crashed over the wheel. It began to creak and groan slightly, forcing the machinery to move for the first time in a hundred years.

Newbold walked off with his prize. 'Well, I said I would take care of him,' he remarked to himself casually. He was surprised to be spoken to by the figure in his pocket.

'Was that *necessary*?' asked Nigriff, bouncing along.

Newbold pondered the question. 'Competition,' he soon replied. 'He was becoming too useful to Biddle. I don't need that.'

'But you *do* need some Lilliputians,' said Nigriff. 'You always have done.'

Newbold stopped, looked around and moved off the path into the shelter of some bushes. He put Nigriff down on the grass. 'What's your point?' he demanded.

'It won't be good for you, turning up with only *one*,' Nigriff said. 'Admittedly, Biddle will obviously regard *my* capture as an undoubted advantage, but you have merely lost one, gained one. The mathematics are not in your favour.' Julius screwed his face. He knew this little man was correct. 'I have a suggestion,' continued Nigriff, 'for there may come a time when we can help each other. And I know where my people live. In return for my safety. . . .'

The conversation soon ended with Newbold grinning and offering a finger for Nigriff to shake.

And so it was that Newbold arrived at Jedekiah's house, proudly bearing the prized Lilliputian, lamenting the accidental and sad loss of Snallard. He also handed over two more of Nigriff's kinfolk, a young married couple. His master was indeed thrilled, as Nigriff had correctly judged.

'It's a simple question,' snapped Swartet, looking at the sea of faces whose owners were seated cross-legged around the rug in front. 'And there should be a simple answer. I will say it one more time; does anybody know why Nigriff is so late? He is due to present a report.'

The Representatives looked to left and right, as puzzled as each other. One was particularly anxious, his eyes scanning the room, hoping for the slightest piece of information; General Thorclan. He wanted an answer even more than Swartet did.

After a few whispers, a meek hand was gingerly raised. Swartet noticed. 'Yehvar, you have something to tell us? You know the reason?'

'I'm not sure I know the *reason*, Madam Listener, but I did see him a few hours ago down by the Eleven-Acre cascade. He was with Snallard, I think.'

Thorclan reacted immediately. '*Snallard*?' His voice was louder than he had intended. 'Are you *sure*?'

Swartet was intrigued by the response. 'You are surprised, General? Can you explain?'

Thorclan regretted his unthinking outburst. 'It's . . . er . . . it's nothing. It's just that. . . . Snallard has never really been his friend. It's surprising.'

'It certainly is,' agreed Swartet, fascinated by the conversation. 'Especially when one considers that Snallard is a member of the SOS. Which mainly consists of Nigriff's *close* friends. It is *very* surprising.'

'There's something else about Snallard, Madam Listener,' offered another PR, Warlek. 'He got a bit drunk recently, but said Biddle was trying to help us.'

Swartet raised an eyebrow. Thorclan shook his head. 'Snallard's an utter *liar*,' he stated, getting to his feet. 'Madam Listener, I must tell you a matter of great importance.'

'Go on, General,' she said. 'It sounds as if we are getting somewhere.'

Thorclan spoke earnestly. 'We – SOS – have been having doubts about Snallard,' he explained, his hands clasped together. 'The more I hear about him, the more convinced I am that he is working with Biddle, against us. To be blunt, I believe him to be a *traitor*.'

'Someone told me,' added Sneaten, 'that he was by the Bourbon Tower when Biddle was there.'

'These *may* be highly damaging conclusions,' said Swartet. 'Which makes me wonder, General, why he was chosen for SOS. Can you give a simple – and *honest* – answer?'

Thorclan thought. 'I don't regard this as a *military* strategy, Madam, but it helps to keep enemies closer than friends. We could keep an eye on him.'

'You were happy to harbour a traitor in your midst?'

Thorclan became flustered. 'No, not at all . . . or rather, yes . . . but not to agree with him . . . or listen.'

'But wasn't that what Nigriff was doing?'

Yehvar interrupted. 'I should mention the two of them weren't alone. There was a human there.' A disquiet murmur arose. 'He went in afterwards.'

'Went in *where*?' asked Thorclan, confused. 'You said they were by the cascade.'

'They were,' replied Yehvar, 'In the wheel-house. The human kicked in the door, and when he came out, he pulled the lever. Water was splashing everywhere. I heard it.'

'What about Nigriff and Snallard?' asked Thorclan urgently. 'Did you see them?'

Yehvar shook his head. 'The man went away by himself, I think. Then I heard the machinery grinding – working. I tried to go in, but it was too dangerous, all that water.' He looked at them all for support. 'I'm sorry – I should have told you earlier.'

'You are not to be ashamed' reassured Swartet. 'You have probably acted more nobly than those you have just described.'

Thorclan quickly shot her a glance. 'Madam, if you're suggesting that Nigriff. . . .'

'General Thorclan, please compose yourself. You are in danger of forgetting your position.' Thorclan said nothing but was clearly unhappy. 'I am not suggesting *anything*, General. We

have recently come to greatly respect Nigriff, despite previous
. . . *misunderstandings*. But I am duty bound to consider several
explanations for his behaviour.' She cleared her throat.

'First – and perhaps the most acceptable idea – is that he
has simply been kidnapped by this human. A second theory,
unfortunately *less* respectful to him, is that he has been deceived
by Snallard, who may be in league with the person often described
by Nigriff himself as our enemy. Which, I am sure you will agree,
is rather *odd*.' She paused.

'Thirdly, Nigriff has not been led astray at all, but has himself
been working with Biddle, devising a plan to trap us, presumably
for his own personal gain.' She let the murmurs of disapproval
settle down before continuing. 'The final possibility makes the
others irrelevant; simply that he is dead. It is difficult to know
what our conclusion should be.'

'No, it *isn't*,' stated Thorclan firmly, 'not in the *slightest*.' He
gathered himself together. 'Nearly all those ideas are *appalling*.
Only *one* of them pays *any* respect to the bravest, most resourceful,
most loyal comrade I have ever known. You all call yourselves
Honourable Representatives. Nigriff is the representative of all
that is best about Lilliput and its history, and the most honourable
man that I know. And I *refuse* to believe that he's dead.'

'*We* would like to believe the same,' said Swartet. 'We have
come to know and respect him ourselves, it's just that. . . .'

'It's just *nothing*,' said Thorclan. 'As I say, the only *possible*
explanation is that Nigriff has been kidnapped. And this is *my*
conclusion; I'm no longer prepared to serve in this Assembly.
I've not always been blessed with the sharpest of minds, but this
decision is the most *intelligent* thing I've ever done. I'm leaving;
and I won't be coming back. I'm off to look for my friend.'

In the stunned silence that followed, all that could be heard
was the smart clip of the General's shoes as he strode across the
floor and left the room.

The old soldier was on a mission, his most important yet.

'I ought to go and see somebody at the school about it,' insisted
Mr Thompson to his wife as they emptied the dishwasher that
evening. 'It's got to be boys from the school. Probably looking

for somewhere to hide and get up to no good.'

'You can't blame them,' said Mrs Thompson. 'You'd have done exactly the same at their age.'

'No, I wouldn't,' he said. 'Well, maybe . . . but not damage like that. The door was completely off its hinges.'

'The last time I saw it,' she said, 'it was rotten anyway – on that afternoon when you spent two hours explaining the history of the water-wheel. Including the merits of the under- and over-shot types. . . . I bet the door just fell to pieces.'

'Well, maybe,' he replied, pleased she'd remembered that fun they'd had. He'd honestly wondered at the time if she was getting bored. 'But if *I* hadn't shut that sluice-gate. . . . It was chaos inside – and those old workings couldn't have taken much more. They've been locked solid for ages.'

'Well, I'm just glad I married a hero,' she said, turning to him and smiling. 'I *knew* I was right to turn down Sean Connery.' She planted an affectionate kiss on his cheek and returned to gathering up the cutlery.

Mr Thompson enjoyed the moment but said nothing. It never ceased to surprise him, he thought, what he didn't know about his wife; when had she met Sean Connery? Anyway, perhaps he needn't bother the school after all.

'I have been wanting to see you for some time,' said Jedekiah Biddle to the small person encased in the old lantern on his desk, and adjusting the goggles below his helmet. 'And now at last we meet face to face.'

Nigriff thought 'face to face' was definitely an exaggeration; he could see hardly any of Biddle's. The lower half was disfigured by several macabre scars and lines, but the upper part was almost totally obscured by the headgear. Nigriff had quickly realised that presumably the wearer needed this to fully detect him. Biddle could obviously see *something*, for without it, he had initially squinted at Nigriff with delight when Newbold had placed him on the desk, but the lenses had made a real difference. The focus of the eyes had become sharper, the direction more settled.

Nigriff glanced around the room again. The grim and antiquated seafaring décor showed that Jedekiah Biddle clearly was the descendant of the Lilliputians' kidnapper – of *Gellisleb*'s kidnapper. Nigriff shivered involuntarily at the thought. He had never expected to find himself in such a room. With such a person. But he mustn't forget the task he had set himself.

'This is indeed a moment to remember, Jedekiah Biddle,' he declared from behind the glass. 'There are many matters to discuss. But first I must ascertain that my kinsfolk are being treated well.'

Biddle smiled. It was a relief to deal with a Lilliputian who had both manners *and* a proper sense of deference. 'Your people are *fine*,' he replied. 'They're enjoying my hospitality.'

Nigriff nodded in acknowledgement. 'That is much appreciated,' he said. 'As would be, with your permission, a *private* conversation.' Jedekiah was liking this more and more; this tiny person even knew how to treat minions like Newbold. 'Of course; that is no problem.' Jedekiah snapped his fingers, and was pleased to detect a warm rash spread across Julius' face. He watched as he reluctantly sloped out of the room.

'Thank you,' said Nigriff. 'And now we can proceed to our business.'

11. Matters of Trust

'It would be of considerable help,' said Nigriff, 'if I didn't have to stand behind this glass to conduct our conversation. It is creating an awkward echo. It also makes me feel like a *prisoner*, and I do not regard that as my true status.'

Jedekiah smiled. He had to hand it to these people; whatever they lacked in size, they more than made up for it in confidence. 'Of course. Allow me.' Biddle gradually tipped over the lantern so that Nigriff could creep out on to the desk, and he watched him brush down his jacket to make himself more presentable.

'Thank you,' said Nigriff. 'This will make matters a great deal easier. Allow me to present my various, and I hope *acceptable*, suggestions.' Jedekiah nodded, amused by the notion of this tiny character trying to seize the initiative; he would allow it to have its say, and then he would outline its fate.

'You have a problem of some magnitude with Julius Newbold,' said Nigriff. 'To be absolutely blunt, he cannot be trusted. He's no more than a maverick, what is sometimes rather oddly described as a *loose cannon*.'

This was a perceptive start, thought Jedekiah. 'Really? Why?'

'His rare ability to see us so easily has made him hungry for power; he will *never* remain content with simply handing us over to you. The capture of those two people today shows that he can pick off as many as he wants, *and* when he chooses. If you retain him – if you do not banish him – I am in no doubt that in time you *will* regret it. My considered opinion is that he *has* to go. Immediately. Permanently.'

This wasn't in Jedekiah's current plans. He had intended that Newbold *would* go at some point, but he still had some uses. Yet this analysis of Newbold's nature and actions was perceptive. And persuasive. Biddle couldn't admit it, but he would act on the advice. 'I'll think about it,' he replied.

'Without wishing to be impertinent, that is unfortunately insufficient,' replied Nigriff thoughtfully. 'I regret to say that I need your guarantee – your *word* – that Newbold *will* be kept far away from Malplaquet and its inhabitants.'

Jedekiah was changing his mind about this tiny person, who was now reminding him of Snallard. For although Nigriff had asked for Jedekiah's word, which showed proper respect, his tone was wrong. He needed reminding. 'You forget your position, Nigriff.'

'Please forgive me, but I am fully aware of my position, which is this, Mr Biddle. I can supply you with as many Lilliputians as I – and *you* – wish, as I have just proven.'

'You just told me that Newbold had *taken* them!' retorted Jedekiah.

Nigriff replied quickly. 'Indeed he *had*. But I was going to supply you with *one*. Newbold greedily took another. His motive was none other than to show his own power.' The explanation seemed to be accepted, and Nigriff continued. 'This initial transfer of these people should be regarded as a *deposit*, a pledge by me if you like.'

Jedekiah understood. 'So you're promising a few more?'

Nigriff stared straight at him. 'Mr Biddle, please do not misunderstand me. I am not promising you a *few* more. I am promising you *thousands* more.'

Jedekiah tried to take this in. The ticking of the mariner's clock on the mantelpiece suddenly seemed sharp, counting off seconds as if adding up numbers. He was intrigued, shocked by the sudden announcement of his hopes and dreams. But he kept his wits about him – and his pride. 'You can't *possibly* do that,' he retorted, 'and I can do it *myself* anyway.'

'Again, forgive my rebuttal, but you are wrong on both counts,' said Nigriff. 'You will no doubt be able to capture *hundreds* by your plans. But certainly *not* thousands. And those that escape will inevitably devalue the worth of the ones that you have managed to capture.' Jedekiah knew this was right. 'And secondly, the people almost implicitly trust me in this matter. If I were to suggest that they should turn up at a certain place and time – for their safety – they will do it.'

Jedekiah couldn't see a flaw in the logic, but he wanted reassurance. 'But why should *I* trust you?'

'Because I have already *helped* you,' said Nigriff calmly. 'In the vital matter of the ha-ha, encircling Malplaquet itself. I have ensured that the wall is finished on time, as you wished.'

'You think *you* did it?' barked Jedekiah. 'You're out of your tiny mind!'

'That insult and reaction are unfortunate and misplaced,' replied Nigriff. 'Your men would still be digging and scraping if it were not for my decision to bring in our troops. At night. By the hundreds.'

Jedekiah considered this. He had never given that job much attention. He had simply given the order and expected it done. Perhaps it *was* remarkable that these vagabonds of his had finished it. 'So what's your plan? You say your people *almost* trust you. That isn't good enough.'

'You are right, of course. And they also need to trust *you*.'

This was more like it, thought Jedekiah.

'My suggestion is that tomorrow morning you will drive the two Cascadians back to their homes and release them. You will explain to them they were taken by one of your men, who acted ahead of time *against* your orders before our splendid new homes here at the Manor were finished. That I, Nigriff, was wrong in my earlier denunciations of you. That we are now working *together* for the greater happiness and security of Lilliput – for a new and glorious stage in its history. For its New Empire.'

Jedekiah was hooked and he knew it. He didn't even raise an

objection to that idea of giving back two Lilliputians, one male, one female, his very dream of last summer. He was about to say something but Nigriff spoke first.

'I can give you one further test and proof of my trustworthiness. Now that I am here, I know my brave and reckless friends will try to rescue me, almost certainly tonight. It will aid their progress considerably if you were to leave a window slightly open for them in this . . . this *study*.' He wasn't sure if that was the correct description.

Jedekiah laughed loudly. 'Do you take me for an absolute *fool*?'

Nigriff didn't answer this question. 'Naturally you will also be in this room with me. You will pretend to be asleep, but you will be able to watch events unfolding. You will hear me talking to them, and then you will see them leave – *without* me.'

'And suppose you *do* try to leave?'

'You will 'wake up' and prevent us. And thus you will gain even more of my people. I think, if you consider this proposal, that you will realise that you have nothing to lose.'

Jedekiah wished that Nigriff was full-size, a human. He was *more* capable, more intelligent, more crafty than the whole of his team put together. It was going to be satisfying working with him. And in the meantime, he deserved a reward. 'I like it. And I'd like to meet your friends. And now you can meet one of mine. Please re-enter the lantern.'

Nigriff of course had no idea what Jedekiah was up to, but he had no choice. He did as he was bidden, and steadied himself against the glass sides as he was carried to a nearby cupboard, glancing at Biddle's discoloured eyes, pale and sallow skin, and the blackened teeth in his smile.

And then Nigriff saw it; an object shaped like a head, a moulded and chaotic jigsaw, appalling and chilling. He was shocked by the grim sight, but less than he might have been, for he had already been prepared by Biddle's own face. There were astonishing similarities in all manner of details, even in the ruby-coloured blotches on one cheek. Biddle spoke. 'Nigriff, it gives me the *greatest* pleasure to present you to Captain John Biddle. I know you've heard of him.'

As the lantern was set down beside it, Nigriff stared at the relic. In spite of his revulsion, in spite of his anger at this captain's crime, he was fascinated by it. For this figure – this *head*, anyway – had known his ancestor, Gellisleb, Gothep the Illustrious himself. Nigriff was in the presence of his family's history, and this moment was poignant and memorable.

These thoughts were interrupted. 'You need some time together – you'll have lots to talk about.' He pushed the doors almost closed and left Nigriff alone with this historic creator of Lilliputian distress.

In the silence, Nigriff gently sat down. He thought again of Gellisleb being torn from his homeland, separated from his friends. And Nigriff now felt the same; that he was far from all that he held dear, removed from his companions.

And he was now realising, looking at this macabre head, that he had probably underestimated Jedekiah Biddle.

And Nigriff wondered if he really *was* doing the right thing.

'I *knew* this would happen,' sniffed Granny. 'Ever since that wretched Christmas present. It was just a question of time – I should never have let him out of my sight.' She shook her head sadly and dabbed at her eyes with her handkerchief. Ralph, seated by her in her sitting-room and holding her hand, looked at her sympathetically and at the others, all trying to cope with Thorclan's news and wondering what to do next.

Vicky spoke up. 'I can't see any way that Nigriff is . . . well, dead. I mean, Biddle needs him alive. There'd be no point in just killing him, would there?'

Thorclan responded first. 'Usually, Ma'am, I would agree. A normal commander would capture and then question – interrogate, if you like – such a valuable opponent, but that's what a *normal* person would do.'

'Fair enough,' said Jamie, 'but I'm with Vicky on this. I'm *sure* Nigriff is still alive – although I can't believe we're talking like this – and if I know him at all, he knows what he's doing. He might even have gone with Snallard on purpose, just to meet Biddle, or something like that.'

'Never trusted that *Snallard*,' said Yenech, pronouncing his name with disgust. 'Always knew he'd be trouble, from the moment I met him. If I *ever* see him again. . . .'

'You may not have the opportunity,' added Thorclan. 'Yehvar saw Newbold open the sluices – there was water everywhere. My guess is that Newbold got what Biddle wanted, and Snallard got. . . .'

'. . . *exactly* what he deserved,' continued Yenech coldly.

Granny butted in. 'I'm sorry,' she said, 'but this isn't helping. Our best friend has been captured and a Lilliputian – whatever his faults – may have been killed. And we should have been looking after them both.' She paused, then looked across at the young man, the one who had been identified as the Guide. 'Jamie, have you. . . ?' She stopped in mid-sentence as they all heard the sound of tapping on her outside door and looked at each other.

Ralph was the first to get up. He walked over, turned the handle, and as he opened the door, looked down. He caught a brief sight of a tiny person before it was knocked to the ground and it disappeared under a mass of flailing arms and legs. Yenech had shot across the room and thrown himself on top of the bedraggled Snallard, and was now laying into him with all his might, his pent-up anger and distress bursting forth in a wild onslaught of kicks and blows. Snallard was doing little, if anything to protect himself; he was just accepting this punishment.

Thorclan ran over, issuing stern commands for his man to stop, which the attacker either didn't hear or ignored. Ralph bent down and pulled the frenzied Yenech off Snallard, placing him out of harm's way on the table, where he paced around, glaring at Snallard and even at Ralph. Nobody had ever known Yenech to be so angry.

Snallard got to his feet slowly, and stood there, his clothes wet and now very dishevelled, his head hung low, the very picture of shame and disgrace. Every eye was on him.

'Is Nigriff alive?' asked Jamie.

Without looking up, Snallard replied, 'I think so.'

'You *think* so?' shouted Yenech, staring angrily at him. 'What sort of an answer's that?'

'And he's at the manor?' said Jamie. Snallard nodded.

'So why are you here?' asked Vicky. 'You knew you wouldn't be welcome.'

For the first time Snallard raised his head and looked at each of them in turn, his eyes full of regret and guilt. 'I've made the most awful mistake. . . ,' he began.

'No? *Really*?' said Yenech. 'It's a bit late now.' He noticed Granny looking at him with a finger to her lips, and he held up his hands in frustration.

'I'm sorry,' said Snallard. '*Really* sorry. I don't know why I did it . . . and it sounds so stupid . . . but I thought Biddle would help us . . . and Nigriff was. . . . I'm sorry, I was wrong.' He lowered his head again, and covered his eyes with one hand. His remorse was clearly genuine and heart-felt.

'We must do something,' said Granny. 'Nigriff needs us.'

The nods and low murmurs indicated agreement, but there were no immediate ideas.

'Can I suggest something?' The quiet voice was Snallard's. 'But you probably won't trust me.'

'Can't imagine why not. . . .' said Yenech sarcastically.

Snallard accepted the rebuke. 'I think I know *where* Biddle will be keeping him. And I might be able to get us in.'

'How do you know all this?' asked Thorclan, glad for a conversation about tactics.

'I've . . . er . . . been there before,' said Snallard. 'As you know.' The others remembered him being brought from the manor in a box a few months back. 'I could go with a small group, some of the best soldiers, maybe SOS.'

'Not a *chance*,' interrupted Yenech. 'You'll go with *one* person. Me.'

Vicky reacted first. 'Hang on, Yenech, that's crazy. For one thing, Snallard *sounds* like he's learnt his lesson, but it could *still* be a trap.'

'Ma'am, can I say. . . ?' began Snallard, but then noticing Yenech staring hard at him, one finger over his mouth, didn't finish.

'And,' Vicky said, 'surely it'll need more than two of you to rescue Nigriff?'

Granny knew that they needed a professional opinion. 'General?'

Thorclan ruminated for a few seconds, and then spoke thoughtfully. 'For this type of operation, Yenech's tactics *are* a classic means of success – small numbers, high levels of motivation, and the element of surprise. Unfortunately,' he continued, 'they are *also* the classic means of *failure* – outnumbered, foolhardy enthusiasm, and lack of planning.' He then delivered his verdict. 'But it may be our best shot.'

Jamie expressed what he took to be their considered view. 'So that's settled then?'

'Not quite. I have one question for Yenech,' said Thorclan, turning to his faithful soldier. 'Yenech, if Snallard *is* still being a traitor – leading you into a trap in other words – will you be safe? I could have some back-up ready.'

Yenech said nothing, but simply stood his ground, standing upright, legs apart, his hands folded across his chest in defiance.

'Wrong question,' whispered Jamie to Thorclan. 'You should ask if Snallard would be safe.'

From Yenech's slow grin, Jamie knew that was the *right* question.

The National Trust team at Malplaquet weren't happy. With less than three days to go before what had been billed as 'The Grand Unveiling – Bucks Biggest Spectacle,' there was far too much to sort out. The Great Storm had been a real setback. A marquee had been shredded, three portable toilets had been caught by a freak whirlwind and were last seen cruising at 10,000 feet over North Oxfordshire, flash-floods meant that a lorry-full of bread was stuck in Towcester, and the rain had soaked into a batch of fireworks, turning them into damp squibs. There was also no sign this afternoon of their Property Manager, the one who had dreamed up this idea.

'Rumour has it,' said the full-figured Director of Expansion, munching his way through his mid-morning snack (an hour after his just-started-work snack), 'that he's getting fitted for his new costume.'

'Hmph,' snorted Sonia Bill, the Regional Financial Controller. 'I've seen what he's ordered, and if you ask me, he's got the wrong idea entirely. It's alright him saying 'come in 18th century costume,' but to most people that means colourful waistcoats, smart breeches, and billowing dresses. Not a scruffy dark coat, tatty leather boots and a revolting dank wig that hides his face – though I *am* grateful for that.'

'I don't know why he's made such a mess of it,' said Bill Board, the Marketing Manager. 'Says it makes him feel more in character, but he's been adding gruesome bits for weeks now – all those cuts and cracks, it'll only frighten people.'

'Rumour *also* has it,' said the Director of Expansion, 'that it's not *just* make-up.' The others looked at him quizzically. '*I've* heard that those marks, those scars, are real, absolutely genuine.'

'So what are they then?'

He winked ostentatiously, as if to indicate this was a huge secret. 'Surgery,' he said. 'Cosmetic stuff. Wants to make himself look like one of his ancestors – some sea-captain or other. But it's gone horribly wrong – botched job.'

'Like this Unveiling,' said the Visitor Services Manager, Toyah Letts-Close. 'Though it'll be alright on the night, as long as the musicians and performers do their stuff – and the weather's okay. But I don't get some of it – like all that fuss about the ha-ha.'

'Oh, I quite like that,' said the Head of Catering, Gary Baldiss. 'Leaving it until that evening for the final coping-stone. It's symbolic. Ties it together.'

'Symbolic of a lack of planning,' grunted Sonia. 'And what's going to happen when that it goes in? Applause? Very exciting. Fireworks? That'll be different.'

'He'll think of something,' said Noel Facks, the Information Officer. 'He normally does. And don't forget his twenty Security guards he's bringing to patrol the perimeter. He must have something big planned.'

'Which reminds me,' said the Director of Expansion. 'Is it lunch-time yet?'

'*This* room?' said Yenech bluntly, standing at the base of an ivy-covered wall and looking up at the sash-windows. The night was dry, but not clear, for there was no moon to speak of and plenty of cloud cover to hide the stars.

'It's his special one,' answered Snallard. 'He keeps all his valuables there.'

'So why's that window *open*?' asked Yenech, indicating a gap at the base of one.

Snallard shook his head. 'I don't know,' he muttered. 'It's not right. It could be a trap. Biddle might think that Nigriff's friends will try to rescue him and. . . .'

'Forget it,' said Yenech brusquely. 'There's no point me listening to you going on about traps, or Biddle. If I had my way. . . . The fact is, the window's open, Nigriff's probably inside, and I'm going in. Come on, start climbing.'

Yenech pushed through the stems and mass of dusty leaves, determined to help his friend. Snallard followed obediently, but also anxiously, recalling Biddle's words the last time he was here. That Snallard shouldn't come back because it was 'too dangerous'. Words of advice – or words of warning? Either way, he was here.

At windowsill level, they stealthily emerged from the ivy. Yenech motioned to Snallard to stay in the shadows, whilst he crept along and peered into the room. It was very gloomy inside, with only a little light coming from one direction – from a cupboard above a bookcase. This cupboard had double doors, one of which was open enough to show a lantern behind it. Inside that, curled up in a ball, was a small figure. Yenech knew it was Nigriff.

He considered the possibilities. Using the shelves and netting that hung alongside, he could imagine himself climbing up, waking Nigriff, tipping over the lantern, releasing the catch. . . .

Then, as his eyes got accustomed to the light, Yenech noticed the human shape slumped in an armchair in the far corner of the room, its head nestled against one wing. It could only be Jedekiah Biddle. With a very odd helmet on his head, binoculars over his eyes – that were pointing straight at Yenech.

Yenech didn't dare move for a few seconds, and then with relief he heard this prone figure emit deep and rhythmic breathing. He was asleep.

Warning Snallard to stay hidden, Yenech bent down to crawl under the window frame. Even for a person his size, it was a tight squeeze. The vertical bars just inside were less of a problem; they were far enough apart.

Once through, Yenech ran along to the curtain on one side and looked around him. The room was very odd, even creepy. Faded maps and charts hung on the walls amongst yards of draped black netting and coils of rope. Displayed at intervals were guns, swords, polished brass equipment, a couple of telescopes – and a ship's wheel on the floor in one corner. 'Weird,' thought Yenech, 'completely weird.'

The close folds of the heavy curtain material allowed Yenech to safely slide down between them to the ground, and he was soon scurrying across the floor towards the cupboard.

12. Difficult Interviews

The ascent was as easy as Yenech had anticipated. The nets were perfect for climbing, just as if he was training in the Grecian Temple. He wouldn't have been surprised to hear Thorclan's voice, shouting instructions and encouragement. What did surprise him, as he was about halfway up the climb, was the sight of the lantern suddenly being swung into view above him, then his own waist being grabbed by a large hand. A human hand.

Yenech squirmed around in the fist and saw in the half-light the figure that had been asleep in the chair – Jedekiah Biddle, looking badly cut-up and ill-kempt, but also grinning. The smile was cruel and full.

'Well, well, so Nigriff *was* right. As I have already come to expect.' Biddle placed the lantern and Yenech on the floor, and sat down on a nearby footstool. Nigriff was by now awake, rubbing his eyes and simply looking at his friend. Yenech had no idea what to think or do. He was greatly relieved to see Nigriff again, pleased to see him alive and apparently in good shape, but now they were *both* trapped.

Nigriff was thinking hard, trying to sort out his thoughts so soon after being woken from his fitful sleep. His relief at seeing Yenech – and even his satisfaction at correctly predicting the response of his friends – was tempered by the sight of Biddle lurking over them. That hadn't been part of the agreement; Biddle was meant to stay 'asleep,' simply to watch Nigriff sending Yenech away. It only confirmed that Biddle wasn't to be trusted in the slightest.

But now Nigriff realised that Biddle wouldn't simply capture Yenech; he'd still want the promised *thousands* of Lilliputians, not just the couple in front of him . . . and the couple elsewhere. Nigriff hoped that those two were being treated well.

'Yenech,' he said, 'it is *very* good to see you again. Can I introduce you to Mr Jedekiah Biddle?'

Yenech stood there open-mouthed, unable to believe Nigriff's calm civility, his poise in the midst of this desperate situation. Yenech looked up at the man. 'I *know* who he is, Nigriff. And I *don't* want to be introduced.'

Jedekiah again thought how determined, how fearless these Lilliputians were. 'Come, come, my good man – *Yenech*,' he said. 'Things are not always what they seem – *are* they, Nigriff?'

'Indeed not,' agreed Nigriff. 'Who, for example, would believe that I was so *wrong*?' Yenech flinched; Nigriff *never* said anything like that. The remark was surely meant to shock him, he thought, to make him pay attention. Perhaps Nigriff was up to something. . . . 'I am staying here for a while,' Nigriff continued. 'You, however, must return to tell the others about Mr Biddle and his ideas.' Yenech nodded thoughtfully but sadly; he didn't want to leave without Nigriff. Jedekiah was hunched over, very attentive.

Nigriff spoke carefully. 'We have developed a warmth in friendship, and so the great empire for the Lilliputians will begin at the Grand Unveiling. You will all be leaving Malplaquet for the true home of our hearts.' Jedekiah thought this description of their new accommodation was over-stating it, but it did make it sound highly desirable.

Yenech, despite his hunch that Nigriff was plotting something, burst out in anger. 'This is *ridiculous*! It's *nothing* like a true home here!'

Nigriff smiled, which shocked Yenech. 'We have had our cross words in the past, Yenech, but *now* is the time to listen.' Yenech shook his head. *Whatever* Nigriff was up to, it wasn't

making any sense. He couldn't think of any cross words they'd
had. Unless. . . .

'At the Unveiling, the Lilliputians can leave by any way. *Any*
way. But you need a guide. I will be near the Octagon Lake.
Victoria, to use her *old* name, will not be with Mr Biddle.'

'Why should that *girl* be coming?' asked Jedekiah sharply.

'She won't,' replied Nigriff. 'But she might want to. I'm
emphasising the fact that Victoria *won't* be with you.'

'Good,' said Biddle. 'And now I will say something to your
friend. There's been a mistake; two of your people have been
collected ahead of schedule. By one of my men, who was just
being . . . let us say, *keen*. He's been sacked of course. The pair
will soon be returned to Malplaquet.'

'*Who* are they?' asked Yenech, naturally worried. Jedekiah
looked blank.

'Maneroc and Cirep,' answered Nigriff. 'They lived on the
western frontier. In an old disused burrow. They have only
been together a few weeks, and were starting to make the place
look. . . .'

'I think that's *enough*,' interrupted Jedekiah, then remembering
he was meant to be the model of courtesy and kindness. 'There'll
be *lots* of opportunities to chat soon. Now, Nigriff, is there
anything else you want to say to Wretch?'

'*Yenech*,' corrected the man himself. 'It's a name you should
remember.'

'My apologies,' came the reply. 'I certainly *won't* forget you.
As I was saying, Nigriff, anything else to say before he leaves?'

'Only that Yenech shouldn't forget what a pope said,' said
Nigriff. Yenech looked puzzled. 'In brief, God be with you,'
said Nigriff.

'Charming,' said Jedekiah. 'And I'll say good night,' He bent
down and gripped Yenech again and moved over to the window. 'I
see you've brought some friends.' Through his infra-red binoculars,
he'd noticed dozens of glowing blobs scattered under the bushes
and around the plants. Some were shaped like small humans, and
some were obviously squirrels. There was even a huge badger with
a couple of tiny people on its back, and a pair of rats side by side
with a tubbier figure seated on something behind them.

As promised, Thorclan had brought the cavalry.

'Well, I won't say *goodbye*, but *au revoir*. See you soon. In your new home. The true home of your hearts, I believe Nigriff called it.'

Yenech walked along the windowsill to Snallard, who had seen much of what had happened by peering in at one corner. 'I really thought you were gone,' he exclaimed with some relief. 'I can't believe you got out.'

'*I* did,' replied Yenech. 'But Nigriff *didn't*. Just remember that.' He took a deep breath. 'Right, we're heading back – and *don't* try anything. There's a lot of people here who aren't happy with you – and plenty of animals that aren't too pleased either.'

It had been a very confusing few hours for Maneroc and Cirep. It had all started in the early afternoon. They had been having an open, honest and emotional exchange of views (what people who aren't newly-weds might call an 'argument') about how to make-over their new home. They knew they'd been very lucky to find it. Disused burrows with a south-facing slope, considerable privacy and no signs of rising damp were often occupied even before being advertised as vacant, but Cirep's mum knew the expanding rabbit family in question and had heard about this one becoming available.

'I'm surprised by all this earth,' said Cirep, looking forlornly around inside. 'Mum said there was rushed matting here.'

'What she *actually* said, my dear,' explained Maneroc, 'was rushed *mating*. That's why the rabbits needed bigger accommodation.'

'Oh, I see,' said Cirep, giggling.

'But then again, perhaps rushed. . . .' Maneroc began.

'Carpets are better anyway,' said Cirep. '100% wool only. We'll collect some this afternoon. There's loads on a fence by Venus. Come up lovely in a wash, it will.'

'I've always thought wool a bit, well, *fluffy*,' said Maneroc. 'And it's not in many magazines. Wood is the new look. And metal. Minimalism – you know, big open spaces. Dead easy to afford as well.'

'Any 'new look' is already on the way out,' observed Cirep.

'And anyway, it's cold. Unless you're going to instal some charcoal-burners for the winter.'

'I was planning to hire a family of hibernating dormice,' said Maneroc. 'We really need to tackle the garden this autumn.'

'Speaking of which,' said Cirep, 'I've had a couple of ideas. Let me show you where the herb garden's going.'

They never made it beyond their front arch. A pair of large hands appeared from above and dropped them quickly into the bag that was slung over Julius Newbold's shoulder.

'I don't really want to have another discussion,' said Cirep, 'but what about this *minimalist* look now? Like it?' She looked around the cage. Barred on all four sides, it had a small 'house' in one corner, a plastic cube with a door and a round window cut out on one side. A food trough and an upended water-bottle tied to the bars completed the dismal scene. It looked remarkably like a hamster cage. As indeed it was.

The pair were trying to keep their spirits up. They had no idea where they were and their arrival had been curt and officious. Their best guess so far was that it was something to do with Biddle, but they hadn't seen him. In fact the only people they had seen – apart from Newbold – were the two white-coated ones, wearing the most extraordinary headgear. They had weighed, measured and prodded the little people. Notes had been made on a clipboard, entries made on a computer, and occasional 'hmms' had been uttered. But it was all very secretive. And frustrating.

Cirep and Maneroc weren't exactly scared, for they felt that if any harm was intended, it would already have happened. But they were apprehensive, for it seemed likely that they were part of some ongoing research. They didn't want to be there.

Sometime later a man walked in and bent down to stare at them. Again, wearing an odd helmet that hid his face. 'There's been a mistake,' said the unattractive mouth under the goggles.

'I thought so,' said Maneroc before Cirep could stop him. 'It's not finished, not by a long way. I was trying to tell my wife earlier, minimalism doesn't mean *cold and empty*, it means subtle but sparse features, creative spaces that. . . .'

The man seemed bemused. 'Not *exactly*,' he said. 'But we're a bit behind schedule. The apartments need fitting out. A few luxuries, some comforts. . . .'

'Carpets?' inquired Cirep. '100% wool?'

Biddle was almost lost for words. These tiny characters never ceased to amaze and amuse him. They would, eventually, make fine specimens to work with.

'Of course,' he reassured her. 'Whatever is thought suitable. But in the meantime, you will need to return home. My driver is waiting. I can reassure you that those responsible for this mistake have been disciplined, and next time you come to stay, it will be more to your liking. And mine.'

It wasn't just the final afternoon of term, it was the final few *minutes* of term. Jamie was standing towards the end of a long and restless line of boys in their school uniform that urgently needed the loving touch of a Dry-cleaners. The queue snaked its way along most of South Front of Malplaquet House. It was Call Over.

At the start of the line stood a very important quartet; the Chairman of Governors, the Headmaster, the Deputy Head, and the senior boy who had just been announced as the new Head of School. That boy, clutching the prized silver-tipped cane, his badge of office, read out the names of the pupils as they filed past in alphabetical and year-group order, to confirm their presence and signify their 'release' from the care of the school into the hands of their parents. It was a rare schoolboy who didn't have a spring in his step as he neared the crucial point, hurrying onwards to the holidays. They had been told to give a passing nod in the general direction of the four personages on their left, but most boys' minds were elsewhere (usually a beach in North Cornwall or the South of France).

Jamie was fidgeting nervously at the back, his inevitable position given his year-group and surname. He was desperate for news about Nigriff, but he'd been ridiculously busy at school all day, totally occupied with the return of textbooks, the clearing of lockers, and meetings with his new tutor and subject teachers. He'd also only just got back his mobile phone from his Housemaster; it had been confiscated first thing that morning when

Jamie had been trying to use it near a classroom. He would ring Granny as soon as he had been 'called-over.'

The line now began to slowly shuffle onwards, accompanied by an occasional cheer whenever the name of a boy in Bell House was mentioned (one of those customs that has plenty of history but no explanation). Up ahead, Jamie could see lots of excited parents (mothers, to be exact) craning their necks to catch sight of their offspring. Soon the line began to move onwards and to lengthen out, and he was walking swiftly forwards, arms swinging and eyes directly ahead. 'Not long now,' he thought.

It's the odd thing about mobile phones, that they can look perfectly innocuous and dead to the world, but can also spring into life at a moment's notice. Jamie had, as he admitted later, made the mistake of switching his on when he began to walk, so he could make a call as soon as he was in the clear. He'd never expected it to ring just a few seconds later while he was still in the line, especially at the precise moment when his name was called and he was alongside the Chairman of Governors.

If Jamie had had his wits about him, he would have carried on, probably more quickly and possibly even staring at nearby spectators to try to shift the blame, but Jamie was too anxious about losing his phone again. He came to a halt immediately, slapped his right hand across his chest to his inside top pocket to deaden the ring-tone, and turned his head firmly sideways to look the Chairman fully in the face, in an act of apparent military respect and deference. This sudden halt caused a buckling in the line behind, with squashed toes and bumped noses in the Williams, Wood and Wright section – and the Head of School, stuttering and embarrassed, lost his place in his written list of largely unfamiliar younger boys.

The Chairman (unlike the Headmaster), unperturbed by this interruption in the normal slick process, was delighted to receive this smart and unexpected salute. He leaned forward to Jamie. 'Thank you, young man,' he whispered. 'Thompson, was it? Good show.'

Jamie nodded, his hand still held across his chest. The phone was still ringing, and at such close quarters, despite Jamie's best efforts, it could easily be heard by the Chairman. He winked at the apprehensive boy. 'Good friend?'

Jamie nodded again.

'*Female*?' he asked. Jamie smiled.

'Best not to keep her waiting,' said the kindly man. 'Fall out.'

Jamie needed no encouragement. Picking up speed and ignoring the sniggers from senior boys around him (and applause from Bell House staff, who rated his performance as worthy of honorary membership for the day), he dashed forwards to the edge of the belt of trees. He was just grateful that his mum hadn't thought it worthwhile coming to what she said was 'just a roll-call, isn't it?'

He flicked his phone open. As suspected, it was Granny. 'Jamie, thank goodness, I've been trying to get you all day.'

'Sorry, problems. What's the news on Nigriff? Did we get him?'

'No, he's still at Biddle's, but he's okay. Yenech did talk to him though. And met Biddle.'

'What did they say?'

'I can't explain on the phone, Jamie, it's too complicated. We need to meet. I've got Ralph here as well. When can you come?'

'Right now. You're sure Nigriff's alright?'

There was a pause then a simple, '*Sort* of.'

Jamie didn't like either that odd response or its tone of sadness. 'I'm on my way,' he replied. He snapped the phone shut and began to run.

'Charlie? Come down quick, tell John his Dad's on TV.' From above came the familiar sound of two boys jumping to their feet and dropping their Games controllers next to the monitor, followed by a rhythmic and rapid thumping as they leapt down the stairs and hurtled into the lounge. Mr Thompson was watching the local news, leaning forward with interest and pointing – which Charlie thought wasn't really necessary, as he'd had years of practice in locating the television.

'They're about to interview him,' he explained. 'About the Unveiling tomorrow night.' He turned to look at John. 'Did you know he was going to be on the television?' he asked.

'No,' he replied, shaking his head, 'he's too busy to tell me everything. But last time I saw him he said that he will one day.'

'Will what?' said Charlie.

'Tell me everything.'

'*Everything*?' queried Charlie, knowing this was a lot. 'About what?'

'About Malplaquet, the gardens. He promised me.'

Charlie wasn't interested in continuing the conversation, but Mr Thompson picked up on it. 'Sounds like a man after my own heart,' he said. 'What every good father wants. . . .' He didn't finish, as his wife wandered in and spotted Malplaquet's temples flash up on the screen. 'Shh, here it is,' she announced, and they all watched the interviewer walk across the South Front towards a man dressed extravagantly in a frock coat and a full curly dark wig. 'We're delighted that Mr Jedekiah Biddle, the Property Manager, could spare us the time in the final preparations for the spectacle,' he explained, 'although I should perhaps warn viewers that his appearance is not for those of a *nervous* disposition. Fancy dress is the order of the day, is that right, Mr Biddle?' The camera zoomed in on the face of his subject.

'Good grief,' exclaimed Mr Thompson. 'What on earth has he done?'

'It's alright,' said John. 'It's *just* make-up.'

'It's not the stuff you buy in Boots,' said Mrs Thompson.

Jedekiah smiled at the interviewer. 'You are right about the costume,' he confirmed. 'I thought I should set the standard. I can't see me being beaten.'

'He's *already* been beaten,' said Charlie. 'Beaten up. His face is a right mess.'

'Charlie!' scolded his mum. 'Remember *John's* here.' John didn't mind; he was really impressed at the effort his dad had made.

'And your *disguise*,' continued the man with the mike, 'are you meant to be anybody in particular?'

'An ancestor of mine,' Jedekiah explained. 'A sea-captain. John Biddle.'

John sat up at this mention. He was increasingly proud of his family-line.

'He was a pirate, was he?'

Sharp-eyed viewers would have noticed the tiniest hint of irritation flash across Biddle's face, but he quickly hid it with a smile. 'No, no, I'm afraid not. He was highly *respected*, transporting extremely valuable cargoes back to Britain. He was a man of honour – which is why I named my son after him.'

John sat up even straighter, moved by his father's words and this explicit public acknowledgement of his worth and status. At that moment he wanted nothing more than to become a man just like his father, especially as the three others in the room looked towards him and smiled. He felt like a celebrity.

Pictures of the restored temples now appeared, and the interview adopted a tone of direct flattery. 'It is of course *remarkable* what you have achieved here over the last few months, Mr Biddle. Some have said that it is one of the most astonishing programmes of restoration in modern times. And that in the process you've uncovered lots of hitherto secret information about the gardens?'

'People are *too* kind,' he replied, almost sounding humble. 'Malplaquet is an extraordinary place, and what we have achieved here is a *true* restoration.'

'A *true* restoration?'

'Yes, a restoration shouldn't be just about buildings, bricks and mortar, or uncovering early features and, er . . . not losing them again. It's about the *spirit* of the place, what's at the heart of it. Something that you can't see but gives it its character.'

Now Mr Thompson sat up. 'That's interesting,' he said slowly. 'I've never really thought of it like that. He's right. He's absolutely right.' He had a far-away look in his eye.

'And Mr Biddle, we can assume that all this is safe in your hands?'

'Absolutely,' he said. 'As we will see tomorrow night.'

'Can you tell us anything about what you're planning, the entertainments? There are lots of rumours flying about.'

Jedekiah smiled. 'I don't want to reveal too many details, but it will be a night that the local people will never forget. A night to end all nights.'

The interviewer nodded keenly. 'So they will be. . . . impressed?'

'I believe the most appropriate word is *captivated*.'

The programme returned to the presenters in the studio. Mr Thompson turned down the volume on the handset and sat back against the sofa. 'He's a great man,' he said. 'Amazing what he's done for the place. A great man.'

John said nothing, but deep down he also knew it. He absolutely knew it.

13. Arrivals and Departures

Thorclan was speaking. 'You *did* all you could, Yenech,' he said. 'I have never been more proud of *any* of my men. I can guarantee that from now on, your example of extraordinary bravery will be described in the foreword to our Officer Training Manuals, and. . . .'

'General, you're right about Yenech,' agreed Melanak. 'And we all know – and me more than anybody – that Yenech is special. But we won't *need* training manuals in the future. . . .' Her voice trailed sadly away as their likely fate impressed itself on her mind. She hadn't meant to sound upset, only efficient, but. . . .

Jamie burst into the room. 'So, what's the news? How is he?' He quickly scanned the faces of Granny, Ralph and Vicky, whilst also acknowledging the three Lilliputians.

Granny and Vicky didn't reply; both had eyes full of sorrow, and Jamie thought that they had probably been weeping. Ralph spoke up. 'Nigriff's fine, Jamie,' he said. 'Not injured or anything. And Biddle seems to be giving him food and drink.'

Jamie let out an audible sigh of relief. 'Well, that's *something*. So are we going to try to rescue him again? And what's Biddle going to do with him? And why did you say it's *complicated*, Granny?'

'It's best if Yenech explains.'

He spoke up. 'I managed to get into the study, sir, but Biddle was already there. I couldn't help Nigriff escape. We had a chat – but Biddle was always listening and watching.'

'So what did Nigriff say?'

'Like I said, sir, we had to be careful. Couldn't say what we wanted to. Nigriff said something to make me listen carefully.'

'What was that?'

'Said he'd been *wrong*, sir.'

'Brilliant,' said Jamie. 'That would make you sit up. Good old Nigriff. Then what?'

Granny, feeling happier now Jamie was there, joined in. 'He said lots about the Prophecy. He obviously still believes it's coming true.'

Yenech explained. 'Nigriff used some of its phrases. Like 'Warmth in Friendship.' The 'Great Empire.' And the 'True Home of our Hearts.' That's when I got cross, thinking he meant Biddle's place – but it would have fooled Biddle as well.'

'He's a genius,' said Jamie. 'Obviously runs in the family. And Biddle won't have understood any of it. But. . . . Nigriff's *always* believed the Prophecy *would* be fulfilled. . . . Did he say *how* it might happen? Any details?'

'He gave us some clues, I think,' said Yenech. 'He told me, when I got angry, to remember the cross words we'd had.'

'Which were what?' asked Jamie.

'With respect, sir, you also should remember. In the church. The *crossword*. *One* word, not two.'

'Right, sorry. So what *were* these clues?'

'Miss Vicky?' said Yenech, looking in her direction. She explained. 'We've got *one*. Nigriff said that I, or 'Victoria, to use her old name,' would not be with Biddle.'

'Meaning. . . ?' said Jamie.

'*I* got this one,' said Thorclan, joining in. 'On my temple's pediment. The *old* word 'Victoria,' the *Latin* one – 'Victory.' Won't be Biddle's. Clever stuff.'

Jamie smiled. He liked the idea of Nigriff predicting Biddle's defeat right under his nose. 'But we need a *plan*,' he said. 'Nigriff must have something else up his sleeve.'

'Odd place to keep it,' said Thorclan, very puzzled, 'though I have read that spies. . . .'

Yenech interrupted. 'Nigriff did tell me, 'now was the time to listen' and then said, 'At the Unveiling, the Lilliputians can leave by any way.' Then he repeated it. 'Any way.' That's *got* to be another clue. . . .'

Ralph agreed. 'I don't know much about crosswords, but it sounds like it.'

Yenech suddenly started. 'Of course!' he exclaimed. '*Sounds like*! Nigriff said *listen* because it *sounds like*. . . !'

The others looked at him in puzzlement. 'It's a standard crossword device,' he explained, 'a key word in the clue that has the same sound as the answer.'

'So what's the key word?' asked Ralph, pleased with himself and wanting to learn more about this crossword business.

'*Any*,' answered Yenech. 'Sounds like NE. *North East*. Nigriff is telling us to leave at the north-east.' He was most excited and looked round at all the others.

'The end of the Grecian Valley,' mused Vicky. 'There's lots of tree cover, slight breaks in the ha-ha, lots of bushes leading to Malplaquet Ridings. . . . Biddle and everybody will be busy elsewhere. . . . It *does* make sense.'

Ralph was thinking out loud about the practicalities. 'You can get two or three families on one badger. We've not tried out the Muntjac deer before. And there's the statues. They *might* help; look what they did to that ha-ha.'

'I don't know, to be honest,' said Granny. 'It'll be a mass exodus. Little people, badgers, rabbits, squirrels. . . . And there'll be dangers; local farmers out late, unfamiliar tracks, owls.' She shook her head, not at all happy. Her precious people did need to begin a new empire, wherever and whenever it might be, but it was hard to accept that they were leaving Malplaquet.

'And Nigriff?' said Jamie. 'Suppose you do all escape and set out in the dark across the fields? How will he join us?'

There was silence. Nobody knew what the answer was – at least, nobody had the answer they all wanted. After a few seconds Yenech spoke up. 'I think I know the *final* clue,' he said. They looked at him, aware from his tone of voice that it wasn't good news. 'Right at the end. He told me that I shouldn't forget what a pope said.'

'Clever,' remarked Jamie. 'Meaning the prophecy by A

– Alexander – Pope.'

'He said, 'in brief, God be with you.' Nothing else.'

'Is that so bad?' asked Jamie.

'It's the crosswords again, sir. *In brief* is a hint to abbreviate.'

That was all that was said in that room for a few minutes. They all knew that 'God be with you' in its shortened form became one word. A simple word. Goodbye.

Nigriff had said his farewell.

Word about Nigriff travelled quickly around Malplaquet. The message that went out with Thorclan, Yenech and Melanak was simple and to the point; Nigriff was in the hands of Biddle, who was expecting him to lead the Lilliputians to their new 'home' at the Manor that same evening. Nigriff would do no such thing; instead, he was encouraging his fellow countrymen to leave Malplaquet and find another homeland elsewhere, a new empire.

And he had already cleverly given the Lilliputians an actual glimpse of Biddle's plans. Cirep and Maneroc now spent many hours giving precise and grim descriptions of the cages.

As the trio wandered down dark tunnels and squeezed themselves into narrow crevices, talking to who ever they bumped into and telling them to spread the news, they were much reassured and heartened by many of the reactions and comments of their compatriots.

'He's such a good man, always thinking about his friends.'

'Typical Nigriff, always looking ahead and working things out.'

'I'm not sure about it *all*, but if Nigriff reckons it's the best idea, that's good enough for me.'

Sadly, however, they were sometimes startled – and even annoyed – by a handful of other comments.

'Hang on, let me get this straight,' said one grumpy old chap in Palladia, emerging from the stone face of the ha-ha and brushing crumbly white flakes of limestone damp from his sleeves. 'You're telling me that waiting for us is a purpose-built, air-conditioned unit, sparkling new, with food and drink on tap?'

'Well, yes,' replied Yenech, 'but there's no guarantee, in fact, there's good reason to believe that Biddle will. . . .'

'And instead of such longed-for comforts,' he continued,

warming to his theme, 'Nigriff wants us to wander around the fields in the dark to goodness-knows-where? And he calls that being *safe*?'

Yenech nodded, but not as confidently as he wanted.

'Personally, I call that being *stupid*,' concluded the man, disappearing back into his hole.

Melanak had a difficult conversation with a young woman by the Eleven-Acre.

'You've got to see my point of view,' she said, 'being *Cascadian* and him being *Elysian*. Oh yes, I know we're all *meant* to be the same deep-down, but that's only an *opinion*, and what I know for a *fact* is that our two provinces haven't always got on well.' Melanak wanted to interrupt, but the cynicism and distrust was pouring out. 'And isn't it a little *odd*, that this Nigriff – and, don't get me wrong, I'm not saying it's *definitely* happened – who may have been wined and dined in comfort for the last few days, is now telling everybody else to clear off? If I was the *suspicious* sort – and I've known a few like it, I really have – I'd be thinking that he's quids in and he doesn't want to share his good fortune. And I know what he'll say to Biddle. 'I *did* tell them,' he'll say, 'but hardly anybody wanted to come.' It'll just be his close friends who are in on it. I mean, you *are* one of his close friends, aren't you?'

Melanak wanted to shake the twisted logic out of her, but instead simply said, 'I *am*. And I count it as one of the great privileges of my life.'

The reply was predictable. 'I'm *sure* it is my dear, I'm sure it *is*. Now, as I was saying. . . .' Melanak sadly turned around and quickly walked away.

The information and warning had gone out. Malplaquet, with its scattered population of tiny inhabitants, was buzzing. The little people now knew that they had to prepare themselves for the unfolding of an evening, which was likely to shape their future for evermore.

The National Trust's preparations were now over. For days, if not weeks, the lanes and roads around Malplaquet had been full of lorries and vans and cars, bringing everything necessary for a major public spectacle. Lorries that were crammed full of scaffolding poles, or extendable tiers of seats; others that pulled fairground rides painted in garish and brash designs, or trailers of straw bales from local farms, and some trucks that held yards and yards of cables on huge wooden drums, and containers of floodlights; white vans advertising local foods and copious supplies of fine wines and organic juices; costume suppliers and fancy-dress outfitters bringing in their ranges; boxed trailers with sides that lifted to reveal stalls selling sweets, old-fashioned toffees and popcorn; fireworks companies – the biggest and the *best* fireworks companies; two large vans, the size of Home Removal lorries, transporting the New London Philharmonia Orchestra; Range Rovers from three national newspapers; a smart BMW with 'BBC' emblazoned on its doors.

And then there were the rumours. Of celebrities – from talk-shows, pop groups and Premiership footballers (and perhaps even more importantly, their wives). Of events; a fly-past by the Red Arrows; goody-bags (for a random few) to rival the Oscars; a raffle of outrageous prizes, including one's own desert island.

The hype and expectation was reaching fever-pitch by the time that Saturday afternoon – a wonderfully perfect, actually hot, July afternoon – was drawing to a close. The preparations were over. The evening was about to unfold; an evening that everyone at Malplaquet – everyone, of whatever size or age – would remember for the rest of their lives.

The light of the late-afternoon sun was just beginning to dim slightly as the Thompson car with its four occupants drove through Malplaquet's pair of impressive wrought-iron gates. In time-honoured fashion, Mr Thompson slowly braked just before the old hump-backed Oxford Bridge, and feasted his eyes on the low stretch of water, the rising avenue of mature trees beyond, and the two imposing domed pavilions at the top of the slope.

'Well, I've said it before, and I'll say it again,' he announced. 'It's just like *another* world, it really is.'

Before anybody could groan or complain, the car behind emitted a sharp blast on its horn, making them all jump.

'Hmph,' grunted Mr Thompson, 'some people just don't appreciate the finer points of landscape gardens. Thank goodness Mr Biddle knows how to bring the best out of this place.' He edged the car slowly forward, enjoying the views.

As they crossed over, Jamie looked at the bridge's urns with their stone faces, one of which Vicky had once claimed to have heard speak. At this precise moment, they were completely lifeless, as dead and immobile as they were generally thought to be. It occurred to him that it was odd to be disappointed that there were no signs of life in their grim and detached stares. Not only did he feel pessimistic, he now felt rather stupid as well.

Malplaquet, as Mrs Thompson rightly observed, had 'never seen anything like this before'. It wasn't just the incredibly long queues of cars waiting their turn to be directed to the Overflow Car Parks, nor even the huge numbers of visitors in their eighteenth-century dress, so that everywhere you looked were velvet frock-coats, tied neck-chiefs, three-cornered hats, and beautiful and extravagantly hooped dresses of red and blue with lace infills and trimmings. It was rather the absence of Malplaquet's usual qualities; the absence of silence, of space to breathe and wonder, of time to delight in its vistas and colours. Everything was now hustle and bustle; raucous shouts, piped music, yards of black cabling around trees and along pathways, scaffolding and stages, signs and barriers.

Malplaquet had been taken over, completely and utterly overwhelmed.

'It reminds me,' offered Mrs Thompson, 'of that Music and Fireworks evening we came to last summer. Do you remember, Jamie, the one you wanted for your birthday treat?'

Jamie briefly thought of correcting her mistake – it hadn't been *his* choice – but he just nodded; his mind was already pre-occupied with the memory of precisely that evening as well. It was when, for him at least, it had all begun. The footprints in the badgers' set. The two voices talking about Nigriff and the new 'Assistant Guide.' The bell ringing. And Granny telling him to see her the next morning because it was 'time you knew.' The thought of her jolted him back to the present.

'I need to go and see her,' he suddenly blurted out.

'Who?' said his Mum, hoping it was a friend his own age. 'What's her name?'

'Granny,' said Charlie. 'Bet you.'

'Granny,' said Jamie.

'I win,' said Charlie. 'Too easy.'

'And *you* can shut up,' said Jamie.

'That's enough, you two,' said their Father. 'You're here to enjoy yourselves, not to start bickering. Why do you want to see her anyway, Jamie? I asked her if she wanted to come, but she said there were too many people. So she was staying at home.'

'I don't think that's the real reason,' said Jamie. 'She's not been feeling herself recently, didn't want to go far. Sorry – I think I should see her.'

His parents looked at each other. They knew from experience that there was no point in *insisting* that a boy of nearly fourteen should keep them company; he'd just sulk and spoil the occasion. And it was thoughtful of him to be so *concerned*, a worthy quality that Mrs Thompson called his 'feminine side' (which Charlie reckoned had taken over Jamie's whole body). And their younger son was already making eye-contact with a group of school-friends (mostly girls. . . .). Which meant they'd have some time to themselves.

'Okay,' said Mr Thompson, after a brief raising of eyebrows with his wife. 'You know where our seats are for the music, don't you? Stand 4, Row G, 11-14. And make sure your phone's on.'

Jamie nodded appreciatively, gave them a wave as he turned on his heels, and dashed off through the gardens to Granny's cottage, weaving in and out of the crowds of historic figures as he ran. He had no idea what was going to happen, nor what he could possibly do, but he knew he had to see her.

And he was hoping to see Nigriff as well.

Jedekiah Biddle stood at the top of the South Front steps of Malplaquet House, taking in the scene before him. It was now mostly in shadow as the low sun sank behind the mansion. The usual grassy stripes of the lawns were hidden under a vast collection of sideshows, amusements and rides for the masses. They included Dodgems, an enormous Ferris-wheel, laser clay-pigeon shooting, stalls selling baked potatoes and pancakes, roundabout rides for the tinies, a couple of skittle alleys lined by straw bales, and a set of circular trampolines. The noise and commotion were fantastic.

Especially pleasing was the loud blare of music. Biddle had wanted some strident Rock music, but he had been over-ruled by the

Regional Manager. '*Classical*,' she had said on the phone. 'This is not one of those awful pop concerts. We don't want to scare people away.' Biddle gave a wry smile as he felt the heavy rhythmic thump from the huge speakers sited either side of the natural tree-lined arena; Tchaikovsky, Beethoven and Berlioz could have an equally dramatic effect as Rock music on sensitive or small ears.

Looking down on the thousands of people swarming around below him, he felt very much like the Lord of all he Surveyed, and knew that the next few hours would bring about his greatest triumph. The restoration of his ancestor's treasure to its rightful ownership. Justice served. The foundations laid of his future fame. It was hard for Biddle to resist a self-satisfied grin – so he gave in, and he smiled with such a frightful grimace that a young boy, walking past and happening to glance sideways, hurried down the steps two at a time.

The evening naturally depended on all going to plan, but he was confident that he had organised to the last detail all the events and activities. All the possible eventualities that any person could think of had been thoroughly covered.

He took in a long deep breath, glad of the fresh air after the stuffy and tedious gathering in the Music Room. Nibbling fussy canapés, and making polite but dreary small-talk with the key players of the National Trust, had bored him rigid. The only amusement had been the ludicrously extravagant 'eighteenth-century' costumes on show, hired to portray their occupant's influence and status. This had resulted in a clutch of princesses, three generals, four crowned heads of Europe and two popes – who until now had spent the evening criticising the historical accuracy of their competitor's garb – and deposing each other in passionate outbursts of theologically imprecise name-calling. As for Biddle himself, it had been gratifying to receive so many compliments about the authenticity of his own attire, but he had hated all the comments (of which there had been several) about Captain Biddle being 'presumably a pirate?' And as he fingered some of the lines and scars on his face, he wondered why they had begun to itch so much. Maybe it was the recent stale and dry air indoors. It didn't matter particularly.

A hand was placed firmly on his shoulder from behind. It was the Trust's Director-General in her curvaceous and eye-catching

Marie-Antoinette outfit, smelling strongly of alcohol.

'Ahoy, my noble Captain. Can I . . . come alongside?'

'If you insist, Director-General,' replied Jedekiah coldly.

'Call me . . . Magdalena. . . . My friends call me 'Mad'. . . .' She giggled. Jedekiah sighed. He didn't want to hang around with a drunk, even his boss. He wouldn't need his job after tonight anyway.

'If you insist – Mad.'

'Oh, I do, I really, *really* do.' She leaned forward, and Jedekiah stepped back. 'We should, er . . . talk,' he said.

'Anyshing in mind?' she said sweetly, looking coy (and unstable).

'It's the . . . um . . . ha-ha,' he said. 'The party putting the last stone in place.'

Her eyes were now looking in different directions, not focussing. 'A party? Lasht one shtoned? Whoshe place?'

Jedekiah shook his head. 'No, no – the *ha-ha*.'

She fixed him with a disapproving stare. 'Don't larff,' she said, 'snot funny.' Then she gulped and let out a loud belch. 'Wind's up,' she uttered. 'Sea's a bit ruff. . . . Goin' down. . . .' And, troubled by the rolling deck, she stumbled indoors.

Jedekiah turned away and stared towards the far bank of the Octagon Lake, still picking up the last of the evening's sunshine. On the grassy slope between the two classical temples that framed the view, stood a single white fabric tent, a splaying cube of roughly three metres with a shallow pointed roof. It was guarded by two of Biddle's security team, wearing their thermal-imaging headgear.

Biddle knew that inside the tent was a large wooden crate, protected by straw bales. In the late afternoon, and in total privacy, he had let down the front of the box to reveal the face.

The face who would watch over and guarantee the success of his plan that night.

The one who would ensure that Jedekiah Biddle's dreams were fulfilled, the one who was absolutely central to his purposes.

John Biddle.

Captain John Biddle, who had returned. Returned to the place where he had been so cruelly duped centuries before.

Returned to reclaim his property.

14. Opening the Grounds

Standing on the South Front steps, Jedekiah smiled. He loved the neatness and tidiness of his plan. He loved the fact that he could honour his ancestor in this way, that the man could even be present for the occasion. And he loved the fact that when his plans had succeeded, his own fame would exceed that of any Biddle.

He stared towards the ha-ha beyond the Octagon Lake, noting the sun glinting off the helmeted heads of four security guards strung out in the ditch. As far as the public and the Trust were concerned, the job of the full complement of twenty around the perimeter was to keep out intruders. Their *real* job, of course, was to accompany the tiny evacuees as they left later on for somewhere much safer. For their new homes. For their new *permanent* homes.

The four guards, stationed behind the wall joining the two lakeside temples, had been the most capable of the Napoleonic troops he hired a few months ago – or, to put it another way, had been the least *incapable* of them. . . . So they were now watching over another figure that was central to his purposes. Biddle knew that it would be placed mid-way on the stone parapet. It was a tiny person, no more than six inches high.

A tiny person who was indeed standing there, facing Malplaquet House and its gardens.

Nigriff, feeling more alone and desolate than he had ever done in his life.

Nigriff, who wanted more than anything to see and to speak with his friends, but who also knew that it would be best if he never saw them again. He had already, via the faithful Yenech, bid them farewell.

It was *essential* that they were all able to depart – and quickly. He would play *his* part, and do it well. His mind was made up.

It took Jamie far longer than he had expected to reach the Octagon Lake. This was partly due to the crowds (avoiding voluminous dresses required serious body-swerves when running at speed), but also because of the variety of tempting entertainments en route. A hog-roast had been *really* difficult to ignore, and even though he hadn't stopped, it had slowed him down for some mouth-watering seconds. The New London Philharmonia with their frantic *William Tell* overture was equally compelling, but at least the rapid tempo had helped his pace. So he wasn't in the best of moods when finally he rounded the lake and tried to hurtle past a small white marquee. It was situated close to the water's edge, in prime position for looking across the water to the South Front and all its activity.

'Oi kid, clear off!'

A security guard, dressed all in black, wearing a helmet with large goggles, and brandishing a polished dark stick, suddenly stepped out in front of him.

Jamie didn't take kindly to being told where to go in *his* garden. Well, perhaps not his *exactly*, but Jamie felt he had more claim to it than this thug. Trying to get his breath back, he looked him straight in the face (or, to be accurate, in the lenses). 'Why should I? I've got every right to be here.'

'Not *tonight* you haven't,' came the fierce reply.

Jamie thought quickly. 'Because of this tent?'

'None of your business. Get a move on – quick!'

Jamie could have continued the 'conversation;' Biddle clearly had something valuable in the tent, but he himself had more important matters to worry about. Still out of breath, he dragged himself up the grassy slope and onto the pathway and noticed, standing in the ha-ha itself, a row of four more sets of similar headgear. These helmets were all turned to something in the middle of the parapet. Jamie followed their gaze. It was an upright tiny person, standing isolated and motionless.

Jamie immediately halted, and for a few seconds just stood there, watching one of the greatest friends he had ever known. Nigriff gave a courteous nod in a quiet greeting, and raised his right arm in a slow wave. Jamie responded in kind, acutely conscious of the unspoken and powerful friendship between the two of them. He felt a lump in his throat, and swallowed.

Jamie took a couple of steps towards him, but saw the guards stiffen, and knew they were about to stop him. He gave Nigriff a discreet 'thumbs up,' hoping it would be taken to mean, 'Hi, it's great to see you again, don't worry, we'll think of something, it'll be alright in the end.' This was a lot for a simple hand gesture to convey, especially when most of the message looked improbable.

Nigriff gave a second slow nod of the head, so Jamie felt that the message had got through.

There was nothing to do for the moment but to walk round the corner to Granny's. Jamie was relieved that he'd seen the little man still alive, still safe. But there was a sadness in his step that he hoped the dear old lady had an answer for. Just before the Bell Gate, he noticed her buggy parked on the path, which was unusual. She always kept it in her yard.

The guard who had moved Jamie on was talking into the microphone arm curled across his face. 'Yes, sir, everything's good down here. . . . No, no-one at all, sir, apart from the kid. . . . By himself. . . . We moved him on. . . . The cottage, I think. . . . Yes, sir, all sorted, it went on the buggy an hour ago. . . . No-one saw us. . . . After one minute. . . . There'll be nothing left, sir, a total accident. . . . Thank you, sir, goodbye.' He felt pleased. It was undeniably tedious, just guarding a tent of straw bales, but he now had the approval of his boss, which would mean a hefty bonus after the successful explosion.

'Sorry, Granny, but I can't *believe* you haven't been to see him,' said Jamie in exasperation. 'He's standing there, only yards away, and you're in here, ignoring him?'

'I'm *not* ignoring him,' she replied. 'I can't think of *anything* else.'

'It's no good *thinking* of him,' said Jamie. 'We need to *do* something, make some plans.'

'I've *got* plans – well, one anyway. I've got the buggy ready.'

'The buggy? What for?' He hoped it wasn't their getaway car.

'I've taken the inhibitor off the engine,' she said proudly. 'I reckon it'll do 30 now.'

So it *was* the getaway car. Jamie could hardly speak. 'It won't be easy.'

'I know,' she said. 'We've got to overpower the guards, then. . . .'

'. . . zoom down the M1 with an open buggy crammed full of Lilliputians?' said Jamie. 'Maybe we can make the Channel Tunnel – or better, Heathrow.' He paused. 'I'm sorry, but it's *not* the answer.' He sat down and put his head in his hands.

'I know you're right,' she said softly. 'It's a stupid idea, but what else can we do?'

Jamie looked up. 'There is *something*,' he said purposefully. 'We can talk to Nigriff. If they'll let us. Come on, let's go.'

The line of five National Trust buggies drew to a halt at the designated position on the north-west boundary of the gardens. There was polite but unenthusiastic applause from the waiting members of the workforce, gathered in a semi-circle, who had done a sterling job to finish the ha-ha so quickly. In front lay the equipment for the topping-out ceremony. Above the final gap in the parapet stood a metal tripod, from which was slung an oblong of dressed stone, gently swaying only centimetres above its intended resting-place. Standing on a nearby rack was a very expensive spade, its D-shaped handle and shaft carved from a single piece of mahogany and the head and blade made of solid silver. On this was inscribed, in beautifully flowing letters, '*Used by the Director-General to complete the Ha-Ha and thus the Restoration of Malplaquet*'. Next to it was a perfect cone of cement (authentically 18th century in mix and preparation) and a bottle of champagne (authentically French).

The scene was set for the symbolic moment of the whole evening.

The great and good (and slightly arthritic) of the Trust eased out of their buggies, and shuffled slowly into due position of importance. Ralph leaned across to Vicky, quietly snorting in disapproval of the occasion so far. 'Good thing *we* didn't take this long, Miss. It'll take thirty minutes to lay one stone. Just look at them.'

Vicky smiled. It was hard not to laugh at the random collection of historic personages that were re-attaching their sashes, adjusting their wigs – or just trying to stay on their feet, like the Director-General, who was clearly in a foul mood. Perhaps the bump on her forehead was the cause.

'Pushed overboard!' she hissed at the amused wall-builders as she staggered past, leaning on an embarrassed young assistant. 'It was him! That *pirate*!' She nodded at the Property Manager, standing to one side and talking furtively into his phone.

'The boy and the old woman. . . ? Yes, yes, give them two minutes only. . . . and in the field, *outside* the garden. . . . Stay with them, they might try something. . . . No, *don't* phone me again, you know your orders.' He snapped the phone shut.

'Remember, *two* minutes.' The guard, clad in black and the unusual headgear, escorted Granny and Jamie from her gate straight into a field adjoining Malplaquet. After a few paces they turned to their right to face the gardens and stopped.

Before them lay the old stone wall of the ha-ha, rising out of a gentle ditch, and along this stretch it was much less than their own height. Beyond it, and framed by the two lake pavilions, were the various entertainments and crowds spread out over the South Front. At intervals against this wall stood three more guards, carrying short thick sticks like old-fashioned truncheons and looking menacing.

Jamie and Granny looked at Nigriff with relief. He returned their gaze. The two began to walk slowly forwards, not for a second taking their eyes off their friend.

'No further!' The guard's sharp command halted them two metres away from the wall. Not thinking, Granny held out her arm as if to try to touch Nigriff, but withdrew it quickly as the guard yelled, '*No* touching!' and smacked his club against the top stones. This startled the three friends, but got them talking.

'It's good to see you,' said Jamie. Granny gave a murmur of

agreement; she was finding it difficult to speak.

'Those are *my* feelings exactly, young sir,' replied Nigriff, as courteous as ever. 'Our companionship has been of great comfort to me recently.'

'How are you?' asked Granny gently, trying hard to keep her emotions under control.

'In the circumstances, Madam, I am in remarkably good shape. I can only attribute that to my many months of dedicated and arduous training with the Thompson Quad Squad.' Nigriff had a glint in his eye as he said this, a touch of humour that much reassured Jamie and Granny. It was so good to see and hear him, especially when he was making a joke at his own expense. He seemed very calm.

And oddly, this made it more difficult to have a conversation with him. There was much that Granny and Jamie (as the pair discussed it later) wanted to say to Nigriff; to try to change his mind, to persuade him to take the people back to Biddle's house, even with its undeniable captivity. At least they'd be alive – and, once there, they might be able to escape anyway. It had happened before in their history.

Anything had to be better than saying goodbye to Nigriff.

It was he who spoke next. 'My good friend, General Thorclan; is he well?'

Granny nodded. 'I'm not exactly sure where he is. I saw him earlier. He said he'd be seeing people this evening. With Yenech and Melanak.' (She wanted to say they were probably in the North East, but was conscious of the guard's presence).

Nigriff thought for a moment. 'They are fine people, all of them,' he said. Then, also aware of the guard, said, 'I would like to think that they are preparing people for their departure.' Then his tone changed, and he spoke wistfully and more quietly as he looked down. 'To see them once more would be undeniably cheering.' Hearing Granny give a little gasp, he lifted his head and looked at her with resolution and much fondness. 'We all have a role to play, Madam. And our paths may be unexpected and not understood. But they will be for the best.'

Granny, her voice beginning to tremble, said, 'But Nigriff, you. . . .' She was interrupted by their escort. 'Ten seconds!' he snapped brusquely.

Nigriff spoke again. 'There will be a *signal*,' he said firmly.

'A signal?' said Jamie.

'A firework,' explained Nigriff. 'To indicate that the last stone is in position. That the wall has been completed.'

Granny and Jamie were both puzzled. 'Why should that matter?'

'Time!' instructed the guard, pushing them back with his stick. Nigriff spoke again, but his words were drowned out by the guard's – 'Keep walking!'

Jamie shouted back, ignoring the stick thrust against his chest. 'Nigriff, *what* about the wall?'

He saw Nigriff shouting, his hands cupped round his mouth, two or three words perhaps, but they were impossible to hear. Jamie looked across at Granny, who seemed deep in thought. They retreated a few metres and sat down, waiting for the guard to return to his position.

Granny leaned across. 'He *is* up to something,' she said quietly, undeniable relief in her voice. 'I'm *sure* of it. That last thing he said.'

'But we couldn't hear it!'

'When you get to my age, Jamie, and your ears aren't what they were, you learn to lip-read.' She smiled. 'I think it was in code again.'

'So what did he say?'

'Three words,' she said. 'I think it was, *Front-eared seal.*'

Jamie thought this was ridiculous. 'What does *that* mean?'

'It'll be his crosswords,' she said. 'Yenech might know, if he was here. But something's going to happen.'

The Director-General of the National Trust didn't notice her Property Manager return to the group after his phone-call. She wasn't looking well, one hand flat across her brow and the other firmly clasped around the handle of the spade that stood beside her.

'Mr Biddle doesn't look happy,' said Vicky.

'Nor his female friend,' said Ralph. 'And she's not used a spade before.'

Magdalena was now trying to direct the unwilling tool towards the cement, waving it around, and finally lunging forwards and collapsing. She could now inspect the mortar much more closely, as she was lying right next to it. . . . People rushed to her aid, and the assistant loudly blamed 'a divot and those funny shoes.'

Hauled upright, Magdalena's second attempt was more successful, largely through the support of a general and the prayers of a pope. She took two steps to the edge of the ha-ha with a spadeful of cement, and carefully allowed it, with unexpected dignity and attention, to slide off into the ditch where it landed on the ground with a dull 'plomp.'

'It's going to be a long night,' muttered Ralph. 'I reckon the Roman army will finish the job off. Or finish *her* off. Don't mind which really.'

Vicky smiled. 'Looks like they're okay now,' she said.

Indeed they were. A Ruritanian prince and the Financial Controller (worried about the waste of resources) had come to her aid, and they had dumped a sufficient quantity of the mix into the allotted space on the wall. Magdalena only had to gently pull on the chains and lower the stone into position. Leaning again on the spade, she yanked hard, and was surprised as everyone else to see the stone steadily rise.

Ralph wildly applauded and, deciding to really enjoy himself, stuck his fingers in his mouth to give an appreciative whistle. Vicky poked him in the ribs and whispered, 'Behave!' although she was trying hard to stifle a laugh.

The mechanism was checked and the process began again. This time it *was* actually sinking, when Magdalena suddenly stopped pulling. She let go of the chains, picked up the champagne, held it aloft, and merrily called out, 'I name this ship. . . .' The long-suffering assistant grabbed her arm – which unfortunately loosened Magdalena's grip on the bottle. It fell, hit the ground sharply, bounced once, disappeared over the edge – and landed safely in a fresh pile of cement.

'That was *your* fault!' shouted Magdalena to the poor girl. Then she noticed Biddle. 'No, it wasn't – it was *yours*! *You* sank the ship!' Biddle stared back. Ralph *and* Vicky clapped wildly.

The stone was eventually placed in position. It was hard to tell by precisely *whom*, but it certainly wasn't by the Director-General, who was now attempting a speech. 'I declare this wall *open*,' she declared. 'And *closed*.' She then sat down heavily on the grass, stretched out, announced, 'The end,' and shut her eyes.

Right on cue (remarkably so, everyone thought, given the preceding chaos) a rocket whizzed into the darkening sky and exploded in an impressive burst of red and white stars. Its loud report made the ground under their feet shudder, rippling away from them beyond the trees and into the rest of the gardens.

Some distance away, and alerted by the rocket signal, the orchestra introduced the next musical item (a trumpet solo) with a dramatic brass fanfare and a roll of drums. The noise was tremendous, and the reverberations from their instruments could be felt by all the nearby spectators – and even, on the north-western boundary, by the special group gathered round a sleeping 18th-century French queen.

The idea of an earthquake occurred to some people, although nobody seemed concerned. Nevertheless, there was movement of some sort below them. The ground was literally trembling.

And it didn't seem to be stopping.

Even a minute after the fanfare had ended and the trumpet soloist had begun his drawn-out plaintive notes, the gentle quivering under their feet continued. Jedekiah was as bemused as anybody, but knew that he had to appear to be in control.

'Ladies and Gentlemen, this is what happens when you hire the biggest and best speakers – they make their presence felt! There's obviously a technical problem – someone crossing their woofers and tweeters I suspect.' He gave a forced laugh to convey a sense of order and amusement that convinced nobody, least of all himself.

'Summat's going on,' said Ralph to Vicky. 'I've never felt anything like this in all my life.' Although even as he spoke, he felt the rippling decreasing in strength.

'I thought it might be *Biddle's* work,' replied Vicky, 'but he's as clueless as we are.' She then turned in his direction. 'Hello, what's he up to now?'

Jedekiah was on his hands and knees, crawling towards the edge, his face close to the ground, like a dog sniffing out a scent. He had heard something, like a sharp crack or a splitting of wood, possibly below them. Passing a peaceful Marie-Antoinette (happily asleep with the gentle lull of the grass), he knelt on the newly laid parapet stone and peered over. What he saw made his mouth drop wide-open. He knelt there transfixed, staring at the base of the ditch.

Intrigued, others immediately ran over to join him, and soon an astonished line of guests atop the wall was gazing down. No-one had ever seen anything like it.

In a wonderful contrast to the waning light, there below was what looked like a gleaming puddle, expanding in the grassy dip as if a pipe had burst. However, it wasn't the rate of growth that was so extraordinary (fast though it was), but its precise nature. Although apparently a fluid, with small ripples, it had a transparency and clarity that suggested glass, but a lightness more akin to a vapour, or a molten substance. It was also shimmering with a beautiful and soft blue light, luminous and tranquil, glowing with the iridescence of opal and pearl. It took one's breath away.

Spellbound, the onlookers were content just to watch its magnificent and stately progress, as it spread easily along the hollow in both directions, its light casting turquoise and ultramarine shadows on the stone and in the air above. Already nearly half a metre deep, it had caught up the bottle of champagne in its flow. This was bobbling along the base of the wall, clinking along the way. Most remarkable of all, however, it was noticeable that the azure currents were not bending any of the submerged grasses, merely flowing over the top of them like an ethereal mist.

'The colour's beautiful,' whispered Vicky, not wanting to disturb the sight nor the moment. 'Like a peacock's feather.'

'Or a kingfisher,' added Ralph. 'Amazing.'

'Expensive,' muttered the Financial Controller, remembering where she was and what she was meant to be doing. She called to Biddle. 'You said there was going to be a firework, and lasers - a 'small display.' What's all this then?'

Jedekiah got to his feet to defend himself. He hated the accusatory tone, and the fact that he didn't have a clue what was going on. 'It's the Light Show,' he said. 'I did tell you about it. And I'll pay for it.' And so saying, he knelt back down, for the surface of the shimmering 'water' was now within reach. He cautiously placed his hand under its incredibly placid surface and was shocked at the result.

15. The Garden Kingdom

An amazingly strong current grabbed Jedekiah's hand, yanking it sideways and threatening to pull him in. Biddle swiftly snatched it out, alarmed and confused. What *was* this stuff? He looked along the wall to his far right, expecting to see it banking up against the dead-end, where the ha-ha was halted by the higher and flat expanse of the North Front.

But it wasn't. This gaseous watercourse was shooting across the edges of the first XI cricket pitch, a piercing blue ribbon heading straight for the next stretch of wall, the continuation of the north-east boundary. And then, even as Jedekiah Biddle looked down to the source, it was no longer a mere stream, forming a simple moat. It was stirring up eddies and surges from within, with splashes and even crests of waves smacking against the stone walls, throwing up luminous bluish and white flecks against the darkening sky.

He leapt to his feet, ignoring the excited chatter of the others around him. He no longer cared if he appeared worried or anxious; whatever this thing was, it was a threat to his plans, and he had to act fast. He began to run towards the mansion and the South Front.

'Come on,' said Vicky, getting to her feet, 'we've got to follow him.'

'Okay,' said Ralph, standing up as smartly as his age (and stiff knees) would allow him. 'You're right.' He began to follow her, already a few metres behind. 'Lovely stuff, that. And I thought I knew about *everything* here. Lovely stuff.'

'I can't believe Jamie's missing out on all this fun,' said Mr Thompson to his wife as they sat in the midst of the crowds on the grandstand. 'That last trumpet piece was outstanding – quite wistful and poignant. Made me feel quite emotional; I could feel the hairs on the back of my head stand on end.'

'What, *both* of them?' she teased, smiling at him. He just grinned back at her little joke; they were enjoying themselves so much, it was impossible to be anything but good-natured. 'You're right, it *is* a pity,' she added, 'but I suppose Jamie has never *really* been into wistful and poignant trumpet solos.'

The two of them sat there, happily nestled up against each other, absorbing the relaxed atmosphere and views. The evening twilight had settled down now, and the lights positioned around the grounds were making more of an obvious impact. Subtle glows under bushes were providing soft green hues, specimen trees were picked out as silhouettes against the night sky, and the temples looked stunning, their golden stonework a wonderful contrast to the dark backdrop. There was even a gorgeous bluish haze just visible above the roof-line of the mansion, in the direction of the earlier sunset, which was catching people's attention. The warm air and gentle breeze enfolded the couple in their carefree and serene state.

'I've always said this place was magical,' said Mr Thompson, 'always *known* it. I've just never *felt* it before. I could die a happy man right now.'

'If you don't mind,' said his wife, 'I'd prefer it if you didn't *just* yet. Not before the next piece.' She looked down at her programme. 'I've been looking forward to it for days. I know it'll make me cry.' She rummaged in her bag for her handkerchief in joyful anticipation.

Mr Thompson took the booklet off her. 'Oh, yes, 'Au Fond du Temple Saint,' the duet from 'The Pearl Fishers' by Bizet. It's . . . er . . . very famous. What's it about again?'

'It means, *At the back of the holy temple*,' translated his wife, conscious of one or two people who were shuffling at their ongoing conversation. She lowered her voice. 'It's divine. About two old friends, fishermen in Ceylon, who are recalling a beautiful woman, a priestess, whom they saw in a temple. They both fell in love with her at the time, like rivals, but in this duet they promise that *nothing* will now stop them from being true friends.'

'The warmth of friendship,' offered her husband.

'That's lovely,' she said, holding his hand more tightly. 'Where did you get that from?'

'Actually, it's one of Jamie's phrases. He does come out with them sometimes.'

'Well, perhaps there's hope yet,' she replied. 'Oh, my word, that's *wonderful*.'

People nearby had quietly gasped at the sight as well. Across the grassy hollow, to the west of the main lawn, a wide circle of floodlights on the ground had lit up the Rotunda. Beneath its dome, in the centre of the ring of columns, stood the full-size gilt statue of Venus, gleaming and beautiful. From within the dome, moving spots of light circled around her body, the changing shadows suggesting movement and life within. A rising mist began to swathe the whole temple.

The first chords were heard, and the two vocalists playing the roles of the friends, Zurga and Nadir, slowly strode on from either side and stood before the vision of beauty in respectful adoration. They turned slowly to face the audience and began to recall the precious moment when they had first seen her, their rich baritone and tenor voices filling the night air and soaring with the accompanying violins.

They described how 'Une femme apparaît!' *(A woman appears!)* and 'La foule prosternée *(The prostrate crowd)* La regarde, etonnée' *(looks at her amazed)*, praising her as 'Ô vision! ô rêve!' *(What a vision! What a dream!)*. The combination of words, music and setting were simply overwhelming; Mrs Thompson was already dabbing at her eyes at the end of the first line. But if the truth be told, it was impossible for anyone with any feeling not to be drawn into the mystery and the beauty.

And that was the reason why nobody there heard the sound of

running water, a growing stream rapidly making its way down either side of the encircling ha-ha.

Nobody that is, apart from the Property Manager, barging his way through the entranced crowds, desperately trying to reach the Octagon Lake.

Trying to keep up, and only a few seconds behind, was his son, John, who had just caught sight of his father after wandering round by himself for most of the evening.

Only a few metres behind him was Vicky.

And after her came Ralph. Perhaps not *strictly* behind her, but he would be following the same path a minute or so later. Only one thought was on his mind; 'I'm too old for this kind of lark.'

'I don't know what to do,' said Jamie, still seated in the field next to Granny. 'There's not another Lilliputian anywhere – which means they're either in hiding or trying to escape. And there's no sign of Thorclan or the rest. We should be looking for them, trying to help, but I'm *not* leaving Nigriff all alone here.'

Granny agreed. 'There's no way I'm going anywhere either. I belong *here* – by my home, and with my friends.'

'If they're planning an escape,' mused Jamie, 'they'll be in the north-east, hopefully.'

Granny was deep in thought. 'Maybe,' she said. 'And maybe it *is* for the best.' She paused. 'I just wish I knew what this stuff about the 'seal' is. Biddle will obviously take it out on Nigriff if the people don't turn up. But it's over my dead body.' She glared at the four guards in front of them. Although it was now almost dark, fortunately the spotlights on the twin lake pavilions provided some ambient light. Nigriff stood erect and resolute, as he had been for almost two hours now.

The sound of the Pearl Fishers Duet broke through the air. Granny swallowed hard, and turned to Jamie. 'It's one of my favourites,' she said sadly. 'I can't believe I'm listening to it and feeling so miserable. Thank goodness I'm with friends.' She slipped her arm through Jamie's. He was suddenly all too aware of the frailty and the age of this remarkable woman.

They both looked yet again at Nigriff as the opening bars of the music floated across the gardens. If one could ignore the guards, it was an extraordinarily peaceful scene. Nigriff himself seemed at ease, perhaps confident that his countrymen could hurry away from Malplaquet unhindered.

Granny and Jamie talked about the timing later, but it was precisely when Nadir sang 'au fond du temple saint,' that they noticed a slight movement in that *very* place – at 'the back of the temple' to their left. It was emerging from the shadows. A person, timing its appearance to absolute perfection to match the words. Except that it wasn't 'Une *femme* apparaît,' it was a man. A soldier, dressed in full military uniform, with his complete set of medals and honours (including Plop, Scab, Glob).

Thorclan.

Marching proudly and steadily onwards to centre stage.

Nigriff hadn't noticed his entry, but the guards certainly had. Standing in the shallow ditch, they watched him walk confidently past them at their head-height. Years of army discipline and honour were evident in this display of loyalty and commitment. Step by step he marched onwards.

'They'll get *him* as well,' objected Granny, and began to shout. 'No! Run! Run while you can!' She got up and rushed forwards, only to be stopped by a guard.

Nigriff had assumed that she was yelling at him, but seeing the direction of her gaze, had looked sideways. A friend – his *best* friend – was coming to stand alongside him, coming to join him in captivity.

Thorclan kept up his steady and unwavering pace, his eyes firmly fixed ahead. The watching guards, on bonuses for the quantity and quality of Lilliputians, gave each other a 'thumbs-up.' Even if the worst happened and they caught no others, this one had to be worth more than average. Especially if quantity was worked out by weight.

Thorclan's timing to the music remained impressive, testimony to hours of attempts by Granny to civilise him with her gramophone records. He knew this piece well, and adjusted his pace accordingly. So at the very moment when Zurga was passionately urging his companion, 'Non, que rien ne nous sépare!' *(No, let nothing part us!)*, the old general arrived at Nigriff's side. He saluted, took Nigriff's arm and enclosed his

hand in a firm grip. The formalities over, he then stood at his
side, hands still joined. Nothing and no-one would ever come
between them.

There was clearly something in the air at that moment, for
Granny and Jamie held on to each other even more firmly.

Jamie's parents were still cosying up to each other, swept along
by the mood of the occasion.

An Assistant was offering a hand to a drowsy Director-General,
helping her to her feet.

And from the opposite temple, the one behind Granny's
cottage, out walked another couple, from the wings as it were,
arm in arm. Two more inseparable friends.

Yenech and Melanak.

The security team were even more delighted, turning to each
other and grinning. Their prize money had just doubled again.
This was all *too* easy. They could just wait there and collect the
catch. It was turning out just as Biddle had predicted.

'They're good people,' Granny lamented, watching the small
group on the parapet, '*such* good people. Coming to be with
Nigriff like this. But my heart weeps. We can't do anything for
these four – nothing at all.'

'Granny, you're wrong,' said Jamie. He was looking to either
side – and he'd spotted something else. 'Look – it's not just the
four of them. There's more. *Dozens.*'

It was true. In ones and twos, other Lilliputians were appearing
from the twin temples, walking into the light. People they knew
only too well. People who had done so much in the past few
months. Yassek. Hyroc. Wesel. Gniptip. Professor Malowit.
Hamnob. They kept on coming, heading directly (sometimes at a
run) for the central figure to shake his hand (or even to give him a
hug), before taking their place at the ends of the growing line. All
of them, now firmly looking beyond the boundary wall towards
the astonished old lady and her young friend, were conspicuously
ignoring the celebrations and glee of the men in front. Jamie heard
one yelling across to his mates, 'Like shooting fish in a barrel!'

Granny sighed. 'They should be at the north-east,' she said.
'Now they're not going anywhere apart from Chackmore Manor.

The best of them.'

'And there's the *worst* of them,' said Jamie, squinting in the gloom and pointing beyond the lake to the floodlit spectators on the South Front. An adult male was picking his way through them, his long coat, flowing wig and aggressive manner making identification easy, even at a distance.

'The beast,' commented Granny. 'Come to collect his treasure. A pirate, just like the other. In fact, *worse* than him.' She then realised that Jamie wasn't listening, but was craning his head to stare along the ha-ha in either direction. 'Jamie, what's the matter?'

He didn't immediately reply, but then said, 'I dunno. It's like a sort of *roar*, but quieter.' He thought again. 'Or maybe splashing. Like water?'

There was no denying it, and soon Granny heard it for herself. From either side of the garden came the astonishing sound of a stream in full flood, a stream bursting on boulders and hurtling round corners, a torrent that was powering its way over whatever lay in its path.

And it wasn't just the noise that caught their attention. On three sides of Malplaquet's garden a luminous and bluish haze was now hovering above its outer limits, perhaps akin to the Northern Lights but obviously never before seen in England. Expanding slowly but purposefully onwards, it seemed intent on circling the gardens, enclosing all within in its mystical, and strangely comforting, embrace.

The entertainments had temporarily stopped, the musicians laying down their instruments. Everyone was standing still, gazing at this wonderful phenomenon.

The tiny people in a line, perhaps more than two hundred of them, now stretching from one temple to the other.

Granny and Jamie.

The audience in the grandstands.

The Great and the Good (and the Hungover) of the National Trust.

Biddle's security team in the ditch.

Jedekiah Biddle himself, and his son not far behind him.

Slightly further back, Vicky. And some distance beyond her,

doing well for his age, a panting Ralph.

Everyone was wondering two things. Firstly, what *was* this extraordinary 'Light and Sound' show, and secondly, what was going to happen when these twin torrents met, probably near the pavilions just beyond the Octagon Lake?

They soon had their answer to the second question, and the men strung out along the southern boundary were in the best position for it.

Or rather, they were in the *worst* position.

They were in the sloping ditch of the ha-ha.

The converging walls of 'water', racing onwards to an inevitable collision, came round the final corners with the speed of an express train.

It was an awesome sight.

It wasn't just the stunning and shimmering blue colour of the substance, nor its fluid but gaseous nature as it rushed forwards.

Nor was it just the noise, the crash of waves and the thump of its surges against the side walls.

It was also the fact that all this power, all this relentless energy was having hardly any impact on the land itself. The rolling tide swept past and through patches of weeds and grasses with less effect than a gentle breeze; leaves lying on the grassy slopes stayed exactly where they were, lifting only slightly. Dandelion heads, despite being engulfed and overwhelmed by this sudden flood, bent slowly and released a mere handful of seeds.

But Biddle's men, positioned around the perimeter, had been having a very *different* experience.

Initially transfixed by this ethereal onslaught, the guards had been picked up like dolls and rolled and tumbled onwards. Thus, by the time the opposing tides met in front of an astonished Jamie and his friends, the flood was a writhing mix of gasping and struggling men in soggy outfits, their helmets and goggles torn from their heads, and their clubs being tossed around on the choppy waters. The Lilliputians raised their linked hands and cheered, and even gave a bow in unison, as if being thanked for a good show in a theatre.

For a few minutes, this maelstrom swirled before them, then it slowly calmed, and the spectacle appeared to be over. This was obviously worrying. The men would be free. However, the two torrents clearly had their own ideas. They had met, jumped about in excitement – and were now going to have some more fun.

Some of the men, relieved at the decreasing force of the water, were starting to clamber out of its depths onto the bank. But not for long. The substance greedily tugged at them again, and they were all flung away down to the south-western corner. Here a large waterfall formed above and around the cascade, hurling yelling bodies and smashed helmets in a sensational flume into the shallow Copper Bottom Lake.

Once the men had regained their footing and waded to safety (out of the usual dark and cold stuff), most ran off across the fields to their homes or the nearest pub. However, a few brave (or avaricious) souls retraced their steps beside the torrent to the lakeside temples and the joyful Lilliputians; they weren't giving up such a prize without a fight. Nevertheless, even as they dipped just the end of their sopping boots in the current, it snatched them up, swept them away, and swiftly deposited them once more below the cascade.

The record number of attempts was four by one man, but after an overhanging tree had grabbed his walking-stick from his cold hands as he tumbled past, he was never seen again.

Granny and Jamie, standing back from these encircling and powerful waters, had been apprehensive, even fearful, about these events. But as they watched Biddle's henchmen being thrown around and defeated, their concern changed to sheer delight. They began applauding, and linked arms to dance round and round in a little jig, which was soon copied by a few pairs of little people.

'I've *no* idea what that stuff is,' Granny said excitedly, 'but it's brilliant!'

Jamie was looking at it. 'It's the *colour*,' he said. 'Deep blue, and like it's alive. I *know* I've seen it before.' He furrowed his brows, and suddenly his eyes opened wide. 'That's it!' He turned to Granny, tugging at her arm. 'Do you remember, in the Alcove, that trip?'

'*Remember?*' she queried. 'I can't forget it. Sitting on a bench and flying around the sky? I'm surprised we weren't. . . .'

'Yes, I know,' said Jamie. 'But we saw Malplaquet, and it became Lilliput, with those fantastic colours, with the fields and the houses. That's what *this* is! It's the island. Right here! The garden's *turning* into Lilliput. . . !'

This conclusion was easy to believe. The stone walls of the ha-ha were like cliffs, with sparkling waters breaking against them. And on these cliff-tops stood a line of the island's inhabitants, looking out over the sea, a line spreading out along the coast as hundreds of Lilliputians emerged from their dwellings. Many crept to the edge peering over, children held from behind by their parents. Their garden home, for so long merely a parkland in the countryside, was now to all intents and purposes becoming their own country.

It made complete sense to Granny. 'This is *it*, Jamie,' she breathed solemnly. '*This* is the New Empire. The Garden Kingdom. And they can stay *here*, in their real home. Safe. Thank goodness they didn't try to escape.' She was about to give him a celebratory hug, but saw his serious look.

'How did we forget *them*?' Jamie muttered, staring at the two guards by the tent. 'And *him*,' he added, more glumly. 'How on earth did we forget him?' Jamie was looking at Biddle, getting ever nearer, and he'd realised to his utter and profound dismay that a most appalling thing had just happened.

The encircling sea, so dread-full and awe-inspiring, was *not* the Lilliputians' salvation. It was the opposite. Their downfall. For there was no way out – and their enemies were within.

They were trapped, caught within their own homeland.

Just as their ancestors had once been.

16. Power and Glory

Biddle was still trying to get past the swarms of spectators who filled every available space between the mansion and the Octagon Lake. Rapid progress was impossible. His plan to swamp the place with visitors had succeeded far too well. . . . He hated the people who recognised him as the creator of this spectacle, wanting to shake his hand, even talk to him. His long-nurtured dislike of ordinary mortals was surfacing in irritable comments, spat out in any direction; 'Yes, yes, it *is* great, but no, I can't stop. . . . I'm in a hurry, get out of my way. . . . No, I can't sign that, don't be ridiculous.'

Disgruntled and angry individuals were soon accosting an embarrassed Director-General about the 'appalling and rude behaviour of *your* Property Manager.' She wasn't amused, and knew something had to be done.

Across the lake by the tent, one guard, watching their frustrated and impeded boss, turned to the other. 'We've gotta help him,' he said 'He's in a *real* hurry. . . .'

'There's that buggy over there,' he replied, nodding towards one parked up by the Bell Gate. 'We could give him a lift.'

In *theory* it was a good idea to pick up Jedekiah and save him walking the last couple of hundred metres. In theory it was even a *kind* idea.

In *practic*e, it was neither good nor kind – it was disastrous. For them anyway.

'Granny, that guard's got your buggy!' shouted Jamie.

She was resigned to it being used. 'We couldn't stop him, Jamie. We'll never get past this water anyway.'

The car-thief was pressing the button to start the engine. Hearing its gentle purr, he slammed his foot down hard on the accelerator, knowing that these truculent vehicles needed every encouragement (and some rough treatment) to persuade them to move.

But this one didn't. Granny's tinkering and the removal of the inhibitor had transformed it, and the engine, freed at last from years of restraint and timidity, growled and roared into life. The buggy felt as if it was in pole position for an F1 race. It had been born for this moment.

Its rear wheels spun violently, churning the ground into wide grooves, whilst the front ones leapt into the air like a prancing horse raring to go. Then they crashed down and the buggy surged forward, bouncing across the path and onto the grass with such force that the driver was thrown back in his seat, letting go of the steering wheel. . . .

When he regained his composure (and the steering), he was amazed to discover that his vehicle had gone from 0-50mph in 2.1 seconds, and it was only five metres away from colliding with an object.

A tent. A square white tent by a lake.

A lake that his friend, very scared, was diving into.

This seemed wise, so the 'driver' leapt out of the buggy to do the same, splashing in just as the buggy hit the tent.

It thumped into the canvas structure and its bales of hay, and came to a sudden halt perched on top of the mess. The impact made the crowds turn in its direction, straining in the gloom to see what was happening. This became easier as some flames began to quickly lick around the unusual structure; a National Trust buggy, swathed in white cloth, proudly resting on a mound of straw.

'Very neat,' said Mr Thompson approvingly. 'Skilful driving to get that up there.'

'But *why* are they setting fire to it?' asked Mrs Thompson.

Her husband knew the answer. 'It's like a Viking burial – you know, somebody famous getting buried with their boat.'

'So who's died then?'

'Nobody's *died* – but I bet this buggy has seen years of active service and it's getting a proper send-off. Brilliant idea – Biddle's probably. And isn't that *him* down there, dancing round it? Bit close to the flames though.'

The Director-General was also looking at the character in the long coat, and was being advised by her Regional Manager. 'He *has* to be stopped, Magdalena. It's one thing after another. He *looks* appalling. He's upset the visitors. He's blown apart the Trust's budget. . . .'

A huge 'boom' from the midst of the bonfire erupted in a shower of flames, and a mushroom-cloud of white smoke billowed into the night sky.

'And *now*,' he added in disbelief, 'he's blown apart the Trust's buggy.'

That wilful damage was the final insult. 'Get *our* security people down there,' Magdalena ordered, clear-minded and decisive for the first time in hours. 'And the St. John's Ambulance.'

Jedekiah Biddle was lying semi-conscious near the pyre, his hands across his eyes. The straw was crackling furiously, the intense heat destroying the splinters of wood at its centre. The skeletal and barely-recognisable remains of Granny's buggy were silhouetted against the soaring flames and the sparks rushing up into the darkness.

Near Biddle lay the pair of goggles that he had flung off; the pair of goggles that had so efficiently transmitted the image of the searing heat of the fire and explosion. Parts of his face had suffered deep gashes.

Vicky arrived just after John, who was standing back from his father, not knowing what to do. The young boy had never seen him in such a state of weakness. Vicky tried to put a comforting arm around his shoulders and pull him away from the danger, but he squirmed aside and flung it off with real contempt. 'It's my *Dad*,' he said. '*He* needs looking after, not me.' She looked around; the St John's Ambulance staff were arriving with their kit and a stretcher.

'Excuse us, miss, let's get him away. It might go off again.'

Bending low, and trying to shield themselves from the heat, a team of three men and a woman quickly checked that he could be moved, placed the stretcher by his side and gingerly dragged him onto it. As they carried him away, one of his arms slipped away from his face, revealing his facial injuries – especially the darkened and gummy eye-sockets. Vicky gasped. John stared but said nothing.

They watched as the medical staff, working at a safe distance, strapped him securely on the stretcher. Ralph had just appeared, breathing heavily. He murmured to Vicky, 'Good to pin him down – that way he can't move.' She nodded in agreement.

John spotted the pair of goggles on the grass. Intrigued, he put the headgear on, and saw lots of yellow-green human shapes. He swung round to look out over the fields.

'*I'll* have those,' said Vicky, yanking the helmet off his head. 'They're dangerous – injured your father, I reckon.' She pulled at the wires and twisted the eyepieces away from their mountings. 'And I think your Dad needs you.' John looked at her quizzically, and wandered off towards him.

The stretcher party made their way back up the South Front, the crowds parting to allow them through. 'Poor kid,' said Vicky. 'Never had a chance with a Dad like him.'

'You're right,' said Ralph. 'I met the lad once or twice. Seemed a nice boy.'

'Come on,' urged Vicky, 'time to see Nigriff.' They moved away up the slope as a fire-crew with extinguishers sprayed foam over the blaze behind them.

Reaching the top, they were astonished by the sight of hundreds – indeed *thousands* – of tiny people strung out right along the boundary wall. And many more were streaming out from nearby bushes and the undergrowth towards the edge, squeezing in amongst others, peering at the wondrous blue waters below. 'Well, I never,' muttered Ralph, whistling under his breath. 'It's not just Nigriff. Everyone's here; the whole lot.'

'Including Granny and Jamie,' added Vicky, waving across to them.

The greeting was returned. Granny and Jamie were standing at the water's edge, trying to have a conversation with Nigriff across the three-metre moat. He turned round and was delighted to see the two other friends – as were Thorclan, Yenech and Melanak.

'I cannot say how relieved I am to greet you, Madam Vicky, and also you, the good gardener Ralph.' He bowed low.

'Not as pleased as we are to see you, Nigriff,' said Vicky. She kissed her right index finger, bent down, and touched the side of his face. Nigriff blushed. Thorclan cheered. Yenech and Melanak looked at each other and smiled.

'Madam Vicky, you are *too* kind, but your favours are nevertheless most welcome. Especially to one who is so undeserving.'

'Not true,' said Ralph. 'You're a *hero*. An absolute *hero*.' He clapped in appreciation. The Lilliputians took this up, and applause rippled out in both directions, like a line of dominos falling over.

Nigriff accepted this adulation as humbly as he could, and held up his hands for quiet. In the background they could hear the music and entertainments starting up again after the disruptions. 'It has been a *momentous* evening,' he said, 'which I am honoured to have played a small part in.'

Jamie shouted across. 'Nigriff, what was all that stuff you told Yenech about the North East? That you wanted us to leave there?'

Jamie's questions were echoed by many Lilliputians. They were delighted that they now appeared to be safe, but these points had to be answered.

'I *will* explain everything,' said Nigriff, looking at all in turn. 'But some other matters also need to be dealt with.' He spoke directly to Granny. 'Madam, first allow me to express my condolences on the loss of your transport. I also feel its loss. We have had many hours of contented travel in that previously splendid vehicle.' To his right Thorclan murmured, 'Hear, hear!'

Granny appreciated the sensitive gesture. 'Thank you, Nigriff, most thoughtful of you. To be honest, it would have failed its MOT anyway, and knocking out Biddle in its final moment of glory is fine. No, I can say goodbye to *that* old thing, but. . . .' She paused and took a breath. 'It's saying goodbye to *people* that I find hard – but thank goodness that I don't have to, now that everything's sorted.'

There was no response from Nigriff, no reassurance that a

farewell was not needed. This puzzled Jamie, even made him feel nervous, and it obviously had the same effect on Granny, for she carried on speaking to hide the awkward silence.

'And, Nigriff, what did you mean about that *seal*?'

He now looked bemused, so Jamie joined in. 'That's right, Nigriff. One with its ears at the front. . . . A *front-eared* one, you said.'

Jamie was surprised and delighted by Nigriff's response, as the little archivist threw his head back and laughed loudly, a laugh that relieved depths of anxiety, a laugh that provoked a chain-reaction down the line as the story was explained. Soon the only ones *not* laughing were Granny, Jamie, Vicky and Ralph, but they *were* smiling, enjoying seeing these tiny people so happy and carefree.

Nigriff finally stopped, and adopted his more serious (and more common) look. He signalled for silence. 'Are you sure,' he said solemnly, 'that it wasn't a *back-eyed walrus*?'

This frankly bizarre question set off another burst of hilarity along the cliff-top, with Lilliputians wiping their eyes in merriment, or even rolling around on the grass and clutching their sides in helpless mirth (and in a few cases almost falling into the water).

Jamie tried to be sensible. 'No,' he said, 'it wasn't a back-eyed walrus, you *definitely* said a front-eared seal, but I've no idea what it looks like.'

This only made matters worse. Some people – especially Yenech – were in danger of losing all self-control and were having difficulties breathing. But Thorclan and Nigriff decided that enough was enough. The latter held up his hands for quiet.

'What it *looks like*, Master Jamie – and other esteemed friends – is *this*.' He held out his arms in front, and opened them wide. 'It's the *frontier*. Not *front ear*. One word, not two. And it's now *sealed*; the last stone is in place. The land is complete. It's perfect.'

Granny whispered to herself, 'Of course. How could I have missed it? *Frontiers sealed*. The prophecy. Pope was right.'

'The Garden Kingdom,' added Ralph. 'Well, I never.'

'The New Empire,' said Vicky. 'It's happened.'

'Restoration,' said Jamie, 'of the old Empire.'

'And Destruction,' added Thorclan, 'of our enemies. The way it should be.'

Jamie was thinking. 'Hang on, Nigriff, you always said that Destruction meant that our enemies would get stronger.'

'And indeed they did,' replied Nigriff. 'That interpretation has been proved correct. Of that I was always *certain*. But I deemed it wise not to tell you my hope – not certainty, *hope* – that the sealing of the frontier, the completion of the wall, would bring about the demise of Biddle. And *he* brought about his *own* downfall, precisely by the very means that he intended would destroy us.'

'And again I say, just the way it should be,' said Thorclan. 'My word, this has been an absolutely *splendid* campaign. It's going to need at least three chapters in my autobiography.'

'So you see,' continued Nigriff, 'Restoration and Destruction have indeed gone hand in hand, the one proceeding from the other.'

'And the North East?' asked Jamie. 'Exactly why did you tell people to go there?'

'If I had been completely *wrong*,' said Nigriff, ignoring the raised eyebrows at this unusual confession, 'then it would indeed have been possible for everyone to escape via that route. However, if my hopes proved to be correct, then the sealed frontier would perhaps not only have made it extremely difficult to depart, but also I had faith that my friends and kinsfolk would not desert another Lilliputian in his hour of need. That they would provide a second ring around Malplaquet, a bond of loyalty that nothing would ever destroy.'

As people contemplated Nigriff's words, they all – humans and Lilliputians – felt proud of themselves, but also admiration for Nigriff. As always, for his intelligence and insight, but also now for his trust in them. For his trust in their friendship. It was remarkable and thrilling.

Granny interrupted their thoughts. 'Nigriff, you are, as ever, a *genius*. And a *great* man. But now that it's *over*,' she said, 'can we please go home?'

A searing flash of light in the sky above made everyone look up.

'Not yet,' said Ralph, 'we're not going anywhere before the Laser Display.' They all turned to face the mansion, now floodlit along its entire length. From behind the roof-balustrade branched out three multi-fingered streams of bright green light, radiating like the leaves of a vast tropical plant, filling the sky above the crowds. A grey-green mist, forming thin clouds, hovered and swam between these lines, and as they began to swing from left to right and back again, crossing over each other, words of uncoiled ropes appeared in their pathways. First, *The Buildings*, followed soon by *of Malplaquet*, then by *and its*, and lastly by *Gardins*, hastily replaced by *Gardens*.

Some spectators weren't impressed by this faltering start. Mr Thompson rubbed the back of his neck, already stiff from staring upwards. 'It's *clever*,' he said, 'but I've seen better.'

'That's neat,' said Mrs Thompson, watching the outline of a classical building appear above, as if drawn in fluorescent green cabling. 'That's the Queen's Temple, isn't it?'

'I don't think so,' he replied. 'It's hard to tell. Might be one of the Lake Pavilions. No, I've got it, it's the main portico just behind us.'

'And that's definitely the statue of George I on horseback,' enthused his wife. 'And look, they're making its front legs go up and down, like it's walking. That's very clever.' This was suddenly interrupted by a loud bang that echoed across the gardens, and all three lasers switched off. There was a collective groan of disappointment.

'Probably overloaded,' stated Mr Thompson, congratulating himself on his intuitive knowledge of laser equipment. 'The staff couldn't handle the technical difficulties of that last image.' He glanced at his wife, expecting a look of admiration for his expertise.

He didn't expect her face to have an odd greenish tint to it, slightly luminous and almost deathly. He looked at other people: theirs looked the same. It was in the air itself, some strange trick of the light, as if the lasers were working again and weren't just slicing through the sky but were colouring the whole atmosphere. Mr Thompson was just wondering if this was part of the show, when he looked across the South Front lawns . . . and saw the first of them.

In the far distance, slowly and silently rising behind the Corinthian Arch, and casting the widespread eerie and murky glow, was the most enormous and majestic figure of an angel, shimmering with the coldness and brilliance of fresh-cut emerald. Its strong wings were folded at its sides, and its hands were clasped together over a fearful sword pointing downwards. Piercing and unblinking eyes stared straight ahead from its sombre face. It was impossible to tell its size or precise location – such things seemed irrelevant – but it seemed hundreds of feet in height, and dominated the view.

He felt a tug on his arm. His wife, trembling slightly, was pointing to the west. He followed her gaze, and saw another figure, almost identical in looks and manner but slightly smaller, rising beyond the trees. Instinctively they turned round and saw a third appearing in the opposite direction. And from the soft green light that was growing stronger above the mansion, it was obvious that a fourth angel was now present on the northern side of Malplaquet.

All was absolute silence and stillness. These four figures were now hovering above and around the gardens, guarding the perimeter, indicating nothing of their intentions apart from their necessary presence. One could sense the apprehension of the spectators, unsure of what they were seeing and experiencing. Had the Trust had conjured up these images? Some people were finding it chilling; others were scathing. 'If this is one of Biddle's tricks,' whispered the Financial Controller to the Regional Manager, 'it's not that clever. And it won't be cheap.'

'Bit creepy, if you ask me' he replied. 'Makes me feel uncomfortable.'

'Biddle won't be comfortable either,' said the Director-General. 'This is his last night here.'

And then the reason for the angels' appearance became clear. Dozens of other figures gradually came into view.

From their vantage point, looking back towards the mansion, all those people gathered on the boundary beyond the Octagon had a perfect view of the procession as it swelled upwards over the roof-line. Still shimmering with a green light, the figures and creatures began to fill the sky from the north.

At the front, seated on a horse throbbing with life and energy,

came George I, proud and regal, waving to his astonished subjects
below. Immediately behind him paced four lions, obedient but
equally noble and majestic. 'There's the two from the South
Front,' said Jamie, 'the ones I saw at Hawkwell Field.'

Granny looked more closely. 'And the two from the North,'
she added. 'Perhaps they're friends.'

Behind them marched the imposing figure of the Roman
general from the top of the Cobham monument. He was holding
the reins for a pair of horses pulling a chariot, in which stood a
calm and graceful woman. Jamie saw Thorclan nudge Yenech,
pointing up at her approvingly. Melanak pulled Yenech closer
to her.

As before, the Roman Army followed behind, but not in their
usual serried and disciplined ranks, marching to a mission. They
were jostling and laughing with each other; it was more like a
carnival, for the campaign was now over and they were about
to rejoin their families and friends. As they passed overhead, a
tiny general below stood stiffly to attention, saluting these fine
troops. Other members of the Grecian Army joyfully waved their
greetings to fellow soldiers.

They were followed by a vast cavalcade of figures, most of
which Jamie recognised: the Saxon Deities, erect and awesome
in their ancient authority; four notable Greeks, in animated
conversation; Queen Caroline, kind-faced and gracious; four small
lions (possibly from the main gates, thought Jamie) rolling over
and over, teasing and pawing at each other like newly released
kittens; Britannia seated incongruously on a camel, with four of
her attendants from the pediment on the Grecian Temple; a group
of bronzed muscular figures from the South Portico, enjoying
themselves with plenty of good food and bad wine; the pebbled
lion and horse from the Alcove, speckled like boiled sweets,
trotting side by side.

Then came squatter figures, like small trolls, with piercing
eyes and rough hairy faces. Ralph leaned across to Vicky. 'The
faces from the Oxford Bridge,' he said. 'Didn't you have a chat
with them once?' 'It wasn't exactly a chat,' she replied. 'It was
all a bit scary. . . .'

A procession of animals was led by the playful and scampering monkey with its mirror, reflecting light in all directions, and then by the steady and beady-eyed tortoise, a lioness, the mosaic golden owl from inside the dome of the Gothic Temple, and four winged creatures with the head of an eagle and the body of a lion. 'On the lodges by Buckingham,' explained Granny. 'I'm surprised they were allowed in. Wouldn't like to tangle with them.'

And finally, at the rear of this collection and keeping them all in order, came the lumbering and snapping figure of the crocodile.

This magnificent and awesome cavalcade passed overhead in a continuous stream, heading out towards the final temple, the Corinthian Arch, still presided over by the awe-inspiring angel. But just before reaching it, they all wheeled round, breaking up their procession, moving more swiftly, at a run or a canter, even leaping with unrestrained joy and delight. For a few moments, the vast dome of the sky above Malplaquet was now full of these jubilant creatures, merrily whirling and rejoicing, enjoying the strength and life in their limbs. Then they gradually swung lower and lower to their usual stone resting-places in Malplaquet, settling down but forever to be wonderfully free and alive.

And as the last ones disappeared from view, the four angelic figures sank beneath their respective horizons with sublime grace and authority, and all was once again hushed and at rest.

'That was *awesome*,' said Jamie, turning to the others. 'Pity it's over.'

'Don't speak too soon,' said Granny, who had been keeping her eye on the gryphons returning south to their lodges. 'Look.'

Finale

Jamie looked back to the silhouette of the arch, conscious of a strange alteration of mood, like a sense of welcome. From its very centre, as if from a door, was now issuing a growing flood of white light, a light that was intense yet not painful, a light with the sheen of silver and the purity of mercury. It was flowing forwards like a life-giving breath, pure air and spirit, inviting and entrancing.

As it spread out and enveloped the countryside in its glorious mantle, vague shapes drifted forth, grew in size, and became recognisable. It was a wonderful and fine city, a veritable feast and confection of turrets and towers, columns and archways, traceried windows and sweeping bridges, ancient stones and fine chimneys, doorways and battlements, delicate balconies and grand staircases. All dancing with the colours of polished metal and ivory, burnished bronze or shining pearl.

'It's the *temples*,' whispered Jamie to Granny, both transfixed by the beauty of the glorious scene, watching the dazzling monuments expand to fill the sky above.

Nigriff, his eyes sparkling and alive with joy, was similarly overcome. 'I have at last set eyes on it,' he said quietly and with awe. 'This is none other than Mildendo. Our capital. Our dwellings. Our homes.'

This vision of majestic and radiant buildings, piled high like a medieval hilltop town, was full of beauty and grace. It shimmered and flowed, its scenes shifting and changing to form new paths and squares, vistas down alleyways, broad walks by shining rivers. It invited each person to enter and enjoy, to roam its streets, to breathe its air.

Below, the crowds were amazed by this stunning display; it was simply beyond belief. 'How on earth do they do *that*?' asked Mr Thompson, ready to admit his ignorance about lasers. His wife said nothing, feeling peaceful beyond words.

'What on earth is this?' asked the Director-General, her question met by blank faces. 'Well, whatever it is, *we'll* take the credit.' She paused, remembering the schedule. 'Someone make sure the choir and the orchestra are ready.'

The Regional Manager leaned over. 'We can set off a few fireworks. I rigged up some earlier. Should add to the occasion.'

She nodded in relief. The end was nearly in sight. It had been quite an evening.

Around the *entire* perimeter of the gardens, a line of tiny people were standing on the boundary wall, the ha-ha. For so long it had been in a ruinous state, but it was now fully restored and complete, whole and perfect. Side by side, these people were together at last, united in their hope and desire. Above them ebbed and flowed glorious buildings, some resplendent and majestic, others more homely and comforting. Their city, their land, awaited. They knew that their time had come.

And Granny and Jamie knew it.

Nigriff and his nearest friends stepped back, breaking the line and creating a space for approach, and he beckoned the old lady and her companion to join them. Granny, full of mixed emotions, responded with frustration. 'Nigriff, you *know* we can't get across. It's that river thing – the water.'

'You are not the *enemies*, but the *friends* of Lilliput,' declared Nigriff. 'You will come to no harm. Please; come closer.'

Granny and Jamie accepted his word. Holding hands, they stepped into the shallows, feeling immediate delight as the blue wrapped around their ankles, soothing their tired feet, cooling and warming at the same time. They waded further in, soon up to their waists in the welcoming waters. It felt as if it was actually washing *through* them, restoring life and energy and hope.

Then there was suddenly a swelling, a gentle lifting of the current, which picked up the two of them up in its embrace and seated them gently up on the grassy shore as the wave withdrew.

'Nigriff, that stuff is *so* neat,' uttered Jamie. 'I'd swim in it for hours if I could.' He held out a finger towards the little man.

'Master Jamie,' said Nigriff, grasping it warmly with both hands, 'that is also *our* fondest wish. And that is why. . . .'

'. . .you're leaving,' said Granny swiftly. 'But I don't want you to.'

Her words cut through the air. Vicky bit her lip and rested her head on Ralph's shoulder. Jamie was stunned by Granny's bluntness, realising that he was about to lose some of the best friends he had ever made.

Thorclan, Yenech and Melanak felt their hearts leaping as they thought of leaving this world with its dangers and difficulties – but they also knew it had been a place of joys and beauty, of loyalty and care.

Nigriff thought of his ancestors, of his dear homeland. He thought of Gellisleb, the one who had been kidnapped and had lived at Malplaquet. The one who had made sure that it could, in some way, still be Lilliput. But Nigriff also thought of Granny, now looking pale, and older than he had ever noticed before.

She was speaking again. 'I *know* it's for the best,' she said. 'But when you get to my age . . . saying goodbye . . . so many friends.' Words began to fail her. 'And . . . and . . . here has been your *home*. *Our* home.'

Nigriff held out his hand, palm upwards. In response, she held out her own in similar fashion, trembling slightly, and placed it on the ground next to him. Nigriff stepped on to it, and looked tenderly up at her.

'Madam Maria,' he said, 'you have never spoken more truly. You have blessed us beyond imagining. For the people of Lilliput, you turned their place of captivity into a place of safety, of security. You indeed made Malplaquet *a* home. But . . .' and here he paused, aware of the impact of his words. 'But it could never be our *real* home.'

Granny couldn't reply, but simply sat there, surrounded by so many friends, listening to the waters of Lilliput washing against the cliffs, wrapped in the light of the city above, and knowing full well in her heart that Nigriff was right.

But it didn't make it any easier.

'Master Jamie,' continued Nigriff, turning to him, 'you also will figure large in the annals of Lilliput. As befits your role, you have shown courage, and loyalty, and integrity. You have shown wisdom beyond your years. And I personally will never forget you; it is perhaps my greatest honour to call *you* a friend.'

It was Jamie's turn to be lost for words. He noticed Thorclan and many others nodding in agreement, and heard himself saying, 'Thanks, Nigriff, but I didn't do much really.'

The little man turned to Vicky and Ralph and performed an elegant bow. Vicky was rubbing her eyes, but managed a slight wave back. Ralph touched his forehead. 'You go careful now, Mr Nigriff. You go careful.'

Nigriff stepped off Granny's hand, and signalled to his countrymen to re-form the line on the cliff-top. Then he put one hand to his lips, kissed it, and held it out towards her. On either side, all of his countrymen copied this simple but heartfelt gesture, a united salute to her love for them. It was all Granny could do to kiss her own index finger and move it slowly towards Nigriff. She placed it against his right cheek and held it there, not wanting to move it away.

Far behind them, the orchestra began to play the first bars of their last offering. It was a choral piece, 'Lux Aeterna.'

'Everlasting Light,' said Nigriff gently, stepping slowly away from Granny's touch. 'Our new home.'

The four adults suddenly saw that the blue waters in the ditch were fading, but that along the wall the light was increasing in intensity, and becoming so bright that they were having to shield their eyes from its growing brilliance.

Granny's mournful cry cut through the night air. 'I can't see you, Nigriff! I can't see you anymore!'

His words rang back immediately, in strong and confident tones, at once both reassuring and mystifying. '*Light* in darkness. Look *up. Light* in darkness.'

The four friends did indeed look up, towards the glorious city, now shot through by streaks of pure light, as the first rockets of the fireworks on the boundaries of Malplaquet pierced its magnificent dwellings and streets.

Even after all the previous excitements – the blue light, the blowing-up of the buggy, the lasers with their animals, the wondrous city – it was the Firework Finale that stayed in people's minds for years. Perhaps for ever.

All along the perimeter jets of white fountains soared upwards as the choral harmony began, a purity of sound that led into the first words,

'Lux aeterna luceat eis, Domine'
(Let eternal light shine upon them, O Lord)

As these voices rose and fell, so did these white plumes, in perfect time, ripples of light in waves, rolling along the wall, gathering thousand upon thousand of elated figures in its mighty swell, thrusting them ever upwards, a radiant sea surging even higher and further, peaks and troughs in the harmonies matching the tide's rise and fall. Soaring trebles lifted the shining flares higher into the night sky, the slower tempos of the deep basses giving the strength from below. The ebb and flow of the voices and the light was like being carried out to sea, swept along on a tide of joy and yearning, floating and being drawn into the very essence of peace itself.

Then came the gradual increase, the heightening of will and desire, as a slow and lilting calm worked up towards its climax, the crescendo of the full choir expressing a joint prayer of praise and hope:

'Requiem aeternam dona eis, Domine,
Et lux perpetua luceat eis.'
(Eternal rest grant them, O Lord,
and let perpetual light shine upon them)

The final burst and shafts of brilliant white light reached up to the very heavens, above and beyond the radiant city on high, in this celebration of pure song, the last notes hanging in the air and resting on the hearts and minds of those present.

And as all those on the ground stared up for the last time at the wonder above, they saw that its streets and houses were now thronged with people, leaning out of windows, waving handkerchiefs, greeting each other, moving from door to door in celebration, the final fireworks exploding above its roofs and towers.

Then it began to slowly shift and decrease, to alter in its shape, to become more familiar – to become in fact the whole gathered collection of Malplaquet's temples, poised and gleaming in the night-air, slowly disappearing into the gathering darkness.

Rather wonderfully, the sparks from the last rockets weren't falling and fading but were still floating in the air above, finding their place in the firmament, moving with purpose into their positions.

Applause was ringing around the gardens, people whistling, cheering, totally overwhelmed by the whole marvellous experience and Laser Light Show, without any idea about how it had been created or what it all meant.

Although a few of them knew.

Four, to be precise. Who were standing by the southern boundary of the garden, looking up and pointing at the sparkling patterns in the sky.

'That's Papilio, the butterfly,' said Vicky.

'And I reckon that's Pisces, the fish,' said Ralph. 'Looking a bit like a Vazedir, to be honest.'

'That's Flos, the flower,' said Granny, very thoughtful and reflective. 'At least I'm not on a floating bench.' She shook her head in wonder. 'The night-sky of Lilliput. Who'd have thought it?'

Jamie had spotted one that was familiar. 'The mermaid,' he said. 'Just like in the prophecy – *the sea-people great appear*. Brilliant.'

There was so much to think about, to talk about, but there was also so little that could be said. They were all briefly lost in their thoughts and emotions. 'They're safe,' said Granny eventually. 'And that's all that matters.'

'So we've done it?' said Ralph.

'Reckon so,' said Vicky. 'Pretty good, eh?'

Jamie's phone rang. It was his parents. 'Hi, yes, I'm fine. . . . Superb, we had a really good view. . . . Yes, I loved that city bit as well. . . . No, I was with some friends s. . . most of them have gone now.' Granny nudged him and whispered something in his ear. Jamie nodded and returned to his conversation. 'Granny says can Dad come round tomorrow morning, she's got something for hims. . . ? Okay, see you in a bit, by the steps, yes, bye.'

He snapped the phone shut, and was immediately struck by the ordinary and familiar sounds across the lake on the South Front lawns, the noises of people gathering up their items and children, starting to wend their way home. He looked at his three friends quietly chatting, gently reassuring each other with touches on arms.

Jamie understood that this garden would never be the same again – but he also knew that somehow, maybe within but also beyond it, lay another place and another people.

And he would never forget them.

When Jamie and his father pulled up in the car the next morning, there was no sign of life in the cottage at all, which rather unsettled him until he saw the note pinned to her door; '*Gone to the Alcove. Back soon*'.

'She won't be,' said Jamie. 'She'll be ages. Come on.'

The two of them passed through the Bell Gate and set off along the path, Mr Thompson resuming the conversation they'd been having in the car. For a Sunday morning, he was unusually animated.

'I don't know why I've not seen it before – well, not *seen*, but not *noticed*.'

'Noticed?' said Jamie nonchalantly. His mind was elsewhere, wondering what sort of a state Granny was this morning. Last night had been difficult for her; it was obviously wonderful in that her friends were now safe, but also deeply sad because they were gone.

'That's right,' said Mr Thompson. 'Oh, I've always *known* that Malplaquet was designed to be a reminder of another world, an *ideal* world. I've probably mentioned it to you once or twice.'

'Yeah, once or twice,' agreed Jamie.

'Like I said, I've always *known* it,' he continued, 'but last night I *felt* it. The music – and that blue light – and those images – and the fireworks. Made the garden *feel* different. Does that sound odd?'

'No, not really. I kind of know what you mean.' Jamie smiled to himself.

'And here we are – and there she is,' said his Dad. 'Morning, Granny.'

She was seated on the bench inside the shelter of the Pebble Alcove. She looked up at their approach and welcome; their arrival had clearly disturbed her from her thoughts. Jamie noticed there was a sadness in her eyes, but he was relieved to hear the life in her voice.

'Goodness me, I'm sorry, I was miles away. Memories, you know.'

'Memories?' queried Mr Thompson.

'Old friends,' said Granny. 'This place reminds me of them. Makes sure I don't forget them.'

'I see,' said Mr Thompson, not having a clue what she was on about.

'You wanted to see my Dad,' said Jamie, giving her a useful prompt.

'I did indeed,' she said, then paused before saying, 'Would you like to take a seat?'

Jamie and his father sat down on either side of her. It made Jamie think of last summer, when he had first taken a good look at the mermaid. When all this had first begun. He looked up at the figure picked out in pebbles, and then his eyes wandered around all the other shapes and constellations, until he suddenly realised that he was only half-listening to what Granny was saying to his father.

'. . . It's been in my family for years, so I know it's genuine. I think you'll find it very interesting. You were talking about it last summer.'

Mr Thompson looked at her in puzzlement as she reached into a deep pocket on the front of her dress. She pulled out a folded piece of paper. A very old piece of paper. Tied with a red ribbon.

She handed it to him.

He carefully untied the knot, unfolded the document, and began to read the old handwriting, which was faded but still legible in its flowing script. His hands started to tremble slightly.

Granny explained. 'The signature at the bottom says 'A Pope.' That is *Alexander*, not any old pope. That confuses some people.'

Mr Thompson was in a mild state of shock. 'This is the *Fifth Essay* of Pope's! Y*ou* had it, all this time? The one that people have been trying to find for ages . . . for decades . . . centuries. *You* had it? This priceless document?'

'Well, yes, I suppose I did,' she replied, much to Jamie's amusement. 'But I wasn't sure *exactly* what it was last summer. But now I know. And I thought other people would like to know about it.'

Mr Thompson was reading out the first few verses.

'*A child no more, the Man appears,*

*He comes of Age, the Hope of Yea*rs'.

'What's it about again?' said Jamie, as innocently as he could.

'This is written in praise of a great man, Jamie, a very great man. A leader of his people. Some one who would defend his country – and bring about a great Empire.'

'He sounds remarkable,' said Granny. 'A truly remarkable person.'

'He was indeed,' said Mr Thompson. 'Will we ever see his like again?'

Granny turned to Jamie, looked at him and smiled.

'Oh, one would hope so,' she said. 'One would indeed hope so.

The Previous volumes in the Malplaquet Trilogy
by Andrew Dalton
illustrated by Jonny Boatfield

The Temples of Malplaquet

Jamie has just turned thirteen, when a normal family trip to
Malplaquet and its mysterious temples reveals some very strange
goings-on. . . . Tiny footprints lead to the discovery of curious
little people living in the gardens. These Lilliputians have been
there for hundreds of years, moving from one home to another, till
the ancient prophecy is fulfilled and their four separate provinces
are reunited.

But is Jamie really the 'Guide' and 'Fount of Wisdom,' or will
he and his friends do more harm than good? Meet intriguing and
vividly painted characters along the journey, such as Nigriff, the
six-inch high Senior Imperial Archivist, Horatius Gratton, the
frustrated owner of an incompetent flat-coated Retriever called
Hobbes, and General Thorclan, leader of the Grecian army.

The Lost People of Malplaquet

In this second book the mystery deepens and darkens as we
learn more about the Lilliputians in the strange gardens at
Malplaquet. Their enemy, Jedekiah Biddle, takes over a nearby
manor house, and his son starts at the school – in the same class
as Jamie. Nigriff helps Jamie and Granny to discover more of
the garden's secrets, especially its links with Lilliput itself, and
Vicky doesn't trust one of her Volunteer team. The tiny people
try to 'gain the capital,' as the Prophecy states, General Thorclan
is as commanding as ever, and Yenech finds a new female
friend. . . . But the dangers are increasing; Jamie's brother,
Charlie, is spending far too much time with young John Biddle
– and Biddle himself also organises a huge Napoleonic Battle at
Malplaquet as a threat to the little people. But he hasn't reckoned
on the statues getting involved. . . .

Printed in the United States
153039LV00002B/125/P

9 780718 830939